MICHAEL McLAVERTY
THE CHOICE

Also by Michael McLaverty from Poolbeg

The Three Brothers

Lost Fields

Call My Brother Back

The Brightening Day

Truth in the Night

In This Thy Day

Collected Short Stories

*In Quiet Places: The Uncollected Stories,
Letters and Critical Prose of Michael McLaverty*
edited by Sophia Hillan King

MICHAEL McLAVERTY
THE CHOICE

POOLBEG

First published 1958 by
Jonathan Cape, London
This paperback edition published 1991 by
Poolbeg Press Ltd
Knocksedan House,
Swords Co Dublin Ireland

The financial assistance of the Arts Council of Northern
Ireland is gratefully acknowledged.

ISBN 1 85371 110 1

Cover design by Steven Hope
Cover transparency courtesy of the Ulster Museum
Belfast
Printed by The Guernsey Press Ltd Vale Guernsey
Channel Islands

To
FRANK AND IDA HANNA

One realizes that human relationships are the tragic necessity of human life; that they can never be wholly satisfactory, that every ego is half the time greedily seeking them and half the time pulling away from them.

WILLA CATHER

CHAPTER

I

Two hours ago he had handed up his theological exam papers and here he was in the compartment of an almost empty train, hurrying home to see his mother, who was ill. There was no cause for alarm his superior had told him when giving him permission to leave the seminary a few days ahead of the other students. He had packed his suitcase quickly and hurried down the drive. But in his unexpected haste from the college he had forgotten to take two slips of azaleas he had planted on a sunny day in late February. He had nursed them carefully, watched them leap into leaf, intending to take them home to his mother and plant them in the garden at the back of the house. He only hoped now that none of the other students would spot them and take them away as a living relic of the old college. If the slips were still there when he'd return in September he could dig them up and post them to her. Yes, that's what he'd do; and after all it would be a better time of the year to transplant than now. The decision quelled his annoyance, and taking out his breviary he endeavoured to read. But the jigging and jolting of the train strained his eyes and he closed the book, spread out a newspaper on the opposite seat and lay back with his legs stretched out.

The train rattled emptily through the countryside. Men were busy making hay in the fields and cattle were hugging the cool shade of the hedges. He glanced at his watch. In thirty minutes, if the train were up to time, he'd see the grey spire of the church above the trees, and at the railway station he'd step into the booking-office and give his father a surprise. Nobody expected him home for another three days.

He put his hands between his knees and rubbed them together controlling the nervous joy that tingled through his swaying body. Lovely to get home — home for three long months, and then back again for the final year and, please God, his ordination and then Nigeria. His mother? — God would surely spare her till his ordination. Her last letters contained no words of complaint, only words of encouragement. You'll never be far away, she wrote, for a spiritual land brings you close to us, carries you with greater speed than the fastest thought, and what seems long in years is really short to those in love with work, absorbed in their vocation.

He closed his eyes and reined in the oncoming joy of seeing her. Sunlight settled in the carriage and spread a red glow upon his closed eyes. He yawned, stretched his arms and touched his suitcase that rested in the rack above him. He twitched the hanging label and sent it spinning round on its string. Outside, the white engine-smoke gapped the telegraph wires and broke like sheep across the fields. He got up and leaned out of the window. The wind tossed his hair, and as he gulped its coolness deep down into his lungs he yearned to be outside dabbling his feet in the old canal that paralleled the track. Strange that on a warm day like this no children were bathing in it.

If he were in the college some of the lads would now be setting off for a dip. Oh, he mustn't forget to tell his mother about last Sunday's aquatic performance. It was last Sunday — wasn't it? Journeys, even short ones like this, seem to cart away a load of time.

He smiled as he recalled last Sunday's expedition. His colleagues in black, towels under their arms, marched gravely down the college drive but once outside the open gate they sped across the fields with unclerical speed, wrenching off their collars as they smelt the sea. Big Peter Mooney was always first in, diving in off the concrete pier, churning the water white and spouting out spray like a fountain. Peter enjoyed it, especially if he could catch some unfortunate non-bather and pitch him in, clothes and all.

'But I got one over him, Mother,' he'd tell her. 'I don't know how the devil I thought of it. But when I was pulling on my togs I noticed Peter's clothes in a neat pile near the shore. His name was in red thread on the inside of his collar. And what did I do but pull on his clothes over my own togs, put on his hat, and saunter innocently down to the pier-head. I gazed at the lads bobbing about in the water or jumping in off our old rowboat moored near the steps.'

'What's it like, lads?' I shouted.

'Lovely — come on in, Christy. It might be the last swim we'll have till September.'

'Not today, girls, I don't feel like it. B-rrr, it's too cold.' And at the same time I noticed Peter had disappeared below the water and I knew the next breath he'd take would be at the pier-steps behind me. I knew, too, that in a minute or two I'd be hurled off the pier without an option. The lads were swimming below me, chatting away to me, to give Peter time.

'Come on, Christy,' they were yelling. 'You're a funk.'

'Not today, girls, not today' — and I flicked a pebble at them. Then a shadow cooled me, and there was Peter gripping me in his wet arms and the lads encouraging him: 'Throw him in — Roman collar and all. In with the coward! Baptism by total immersion.'

'I've good clothes on, Peter. Pax, pax! A reprieve,' I said, pretending to struggle.

'The judge and jury condemn you to the depths of the sea. In he goes! Help, Cassius, or he'll sink!'

And in I went. I swam around to steep the clothes decently and I whispered to the lads what I had done. They laughed, and Peter jumped and landed deliberately on top of the black hat floating on the waves. No one told him what was afoot and when he came out, last, and was searching everywhere for his clothes they pointed to a sodden heap on the pier-head.

'Three cheers for Christy Magee!' they all shouted as they saw him wringing out his clothes like dish-cloths. And that evening it was laughable to see his trousers spread out on his window-sill on the top storey and the drips from each leg dark as lightning-conductors on the grey wall of the college.

Mother will enjoy that, he said to himself; it'll lift her heart.

At that moment the train whistled as it approached a road-arch near the town. He dusted his sleeves, combed his hair, and lifted down his suitcase. The train was slowing down, passing the shelving bank with the name of the station Rockcross printed by his father in early geraniums. He saw his sister Mag's house near the line and above on the hill his sister Julia's and her children's washing fluttering on the clothes-line. Poor Julia, two children to mind and an unreliable husband to worry about. Both Mother and Father warned her against Richard Colton but she went on with her marriage like a true Magee.

The train reached the end of the platform where a bed of velvety wallflowers against white palings glowed in the sun. He stepped out of the compartment and was surprised to see his father waiting for him.

'How is Mother?' he said, hurrying forward with his case.

'Not too bad, Christy.' He took the suitcase from him. 'She had a fairly restful night. Father Superior wired to say you were on your way. It was good of him to let you off.' He lifted an empty cigarette packet from the platform and threw it into a wire basket on their way out of the station.

'You needn't come any farther, Father.'

'It's all right, Christy. I'm taking a few days off.'

'Then she's really bad?'

'She is.'

'So it's not what you told me in all your letters?'

'We didn't want to distress you before your exams. It was

your mother's wish that you mustn't be upset. I wrote Father Superior and he advised me what to do.

'Mother will fight her way out of this, please God,' Christy said and looked at the palm of his right hand and shut it tightly. 'Mother was never afraid.'

'A time comes to us all, Christy, when the body breaks the strongest spirit.' He walked slowly, trying to slacken his son's stride. They were silent and were aware of the smell of leather as they passed the saddler's shop with its yellow fishing rods against the open door. Men touched their caps as if he were already ordained. But no one stopped to speak to him. If only they had gripped his hand and greeted him in their old way he would have taken hope, but in their distance and reserve he sensed everything his father hadn't yet revealed.

They crossed the main street where three dogs were playing in the middle of the road and a few boys trundling hoops. His father put down the suitcase and wiped his brow.

'It's very close, Christy. Too warm for this time of the year. You've great weight in that case.'

'Books are heavy, Father,' and he lifted the case from the pavement.

'Christy, son, your poor mother is far through. We think she has only a short time to live.'

And bit by bit he told everything his letters had concealed: her operation in the hospital and her sad homecoming. 'The hospital could do no more for her and we took her home. She thinks she'll get better. She doesn't know how ill she is. Her sickness is a hopeless one, Christy. I have to tell you. She has a malignant ulcer.'

Their pace had involuntarily slowed down. He saw the tears in his son's eyes and he halted at a little bridge over a stream strewn with dry-topped stones.

A willy-wagtail hopped from stone to stone, its tail jerking like a mechanical toy. 'Do you remember when you were small you used to pelt the willy-wagtails because you

13

heard they carried the thorns to make Our Saviour's crown?'

Christy didn't seem to be listening to him. He poked a piece of moss from the stones of the bridge and crumpled it in his fingers.

'If she had died, Father, and I hadn't seen her or spoken to her!'

'Your mother said that God in His own way would do what was right for you and for her. I'd have told you everything in a letter but she made me promise not to. If you didn't sit for your exam it would have held you up for a whole year and postponed your ordination — that was her main worry.'

Christy nodded. His father lifted the suitcase and they went on up the hill towards their house at the edge of the town. Children who were usually skipping or playing hop-scotch at the gable-end were nowhere to be seen, and there was no sign of life about the house except that the front door was open, the cat curled up on the mat, and the sun shining on the mirror and the barometer in the hall.

Inside was his youngest sister Alice and she welcomed him in a whisper and Christy's voice instantly dropped to the same key. He was about to ascend the stairs when Alice touched his sleeve: 'She's not upstairs. We put up a bed for her in the parlour. She doesn't know you're coming today. We didn't want to tell her in case something would have held you up at the last moment. Wait, Christy, I think she's sleeping. If she's awake I'll tell her you're here.'

She tiptoed towards the parlour, pushed the door open gently, and tiptoed back again with a finger on her lip: 'She's sleeping quietly. You may peep in, but don't waken her. She gets very little sleep these days.'

Christy peered round the door and saw her lying back on the pillows. The blind was drawn against the sun and in the diffused light her face was the colour of death and her hair so grey that it made her look years older than fifty. Her thin hands were lying limp on the pink eiderdown, and in the silence he couldn't hear her breathing or even distinguish a rise and fall in the bed-clothes. The room was as quiet as death and cooled by the smell of methylated spirits.

'You'll see a great change in her, Christy?' his father said when he came back into the kitchen living-room.

'She's wasted away to a shadow.'

'No wonder. She hasn't eaten solid food for days on end. Just milk food and sips of cold water to cool her lips.'

'She hasn't lost consciousness?'

'Thank God, no. Her mind's as clear as the church bell. When she wakens she'll talk the piece out with you. She even wants to knit, though the poor thing has hardly enough strength to ply the needles. But she was always like that — always wanting to fill the idle minute.'

Alice was laying the table, placing the cups noiselessly on the saucers, and rushing to lift the kettle when it hissed on the range.

'And how long does she usually sleep?'

'Sometimes an hour, and sometimes only a few minutes.'

They were just seated at the table when Alice heard a faint call from the room and ran to attend her.

'You couldn't guess who's here, Mother? Christy!' they heard her exclaim. 'Father Superior allowed him home a few days before the other students.... No, he's only arrived this very minute.... Your brush and comb and your pink bed-jacket.... You're as proud as Lucifer.... No, I'll not let him in till I have you decked out in all your finery and furbelows.... Had you a nice sleep? ... That's great. I never saw you looking better.'

Christy was standing near the door waiting for Alice to call him. Alice raised the blind and the sun slanted on a vase of pink roses on top of the low bookshelves near the window. She'll not be fit to read much now, he thought, and will never add another book to her shelves.

'Now you're fit to be seen by the ladies from the demesne or the shawlies from the lane. That rhymes, Mother, doesn't it? Ah, the nuns made a great mistake when they didn't ask me to specialize in English for my Senior.'

Alice swept towards the door and though she saw Christy on the threshold she called out in a loud voice: 'Christy, you can come in now.' And after a pause Christy entered and his mother stretched out her arms to him.

He sat on the bed beside her, and as she scrutinized his face she shook her head sadly: 'You're pale, Christy. But sure you had a strenuous year, and what else can we expect.'

'Nothing to equal yours, Mother. And to think I've only just heard of your operation.'

'You mustn't blame anyone for that. It was my command, even it'd be the last I'd ever give.'

'Nonsense, Mother. There's great times ahead for us all.'

She smiled thinly: 'The great times will be in the next world for me if I'm lucky. St Anthony will have to use his influence on my behalf.'

He smoothed the fleshless hand that lay loosely in his own.

'Never fear, Mother. You'll be up and around in a short while and the two of us will skip off on a holiday to Dublin before the college reopens.'

'And how are you yourself, Christy?'

'Never felt better, thanks be to the good God. And you'll be all right soon — wait till you see.'

She asked him to close the door, and when he was again seated she rested a hand on top of his.

'I'll tell you the truth, son. In a short while I'll be gone from you all and I'll not be here to see you ordained. But I know you'll always remember me in your daily Mass, and that consoles me. Some things look hard in this life but if we accept them without murmuring, good will come of them — if not for the sufferer at least for you, your good father and your three sisters. They think I don't know that my end is near. I do, Christy, and it gives me time to prepare though it's hard when you're sick to pray in the way you desire. One can leave that too late.'

The door was knocked and the father brought in two glasses of wine on a tray.

'You'll take a sip, Mary?'

'I will, Tom. I'll drink Christy's health even if it's the last thing I do this lovely day.'

Tom propped her on the pillows, and handing her the glass of wine he tiptoed from the room and closed the door.

'A good husband, Christy, and a good father to you all.'

He raised his glass and touched hers: 'Here's to your good health and may we live to enjoy many more.'

She drank a little and motioned to him to take the glass and leave it on the tray.

'It's hard for me to tell you this. But I must tell you, son. Tell you all. The other evening after Father O'Brien heard my confession I forced him to tell me the truth about my illness. I told him I wasn't afraid to die since God had allowed me to see you all reared: Julia and Mag married, Alice a pleasant girl of eighteen years, and you Christy on the threshold of ordination. Many's a mother isn't as fortunate as that. Your father doesn't know that I know that my death is near. And I forbid you to tell him. That sounds like another order but we'll call it a wish. He's a good man, Christy, and when I die I leave him in your care. You'll advise him best what to do. You're all grown up and he's still a fine, strong man. I don't want him to be alone and it's my wish that he marries again. A lone man is no good to himself nor to anyone else.'

'But if he doesn't want to marry again, I'm not to force your wish on him.'

'No, no, I'm not issuing an order. If the time ever comes, you know what my wish was and you'll tell him accordingly. In a year, if God wills, you'll be ordained and sent to Nigeria. I want you always to be worthy of your calling. Go, even when you are a priest, to confession often. Be hard on yourself in that respect and that will keep you right. Continue your studies, let the pursuit of knowledge be high

17

up in your vocation. And as for Alice, the kindest of them all, you'll pray she'll make a better match than poor Mag and Julia. You'll advise her.'

'I'll advise her. But young girls are headstrong in that respect.'

'You said that like an old parish priest,' and she smiled and closed her eyes. 'Try to hold them together in this little town. It's small and gossip-hungry but there are worse places. And write often from Nigeria. The world has grown smaller and a letter once a week or so will not break your fingers.... Hand me that glass and I'll finish it to please your father.... Get something to eat and come back again. Take a good meal for I'm sure you're starving. Leave the door open for I like to hear the tiny movements about the house.'

She smiled to him as he went out and lay back contentedly against the pillows. God was good to her. If she died now she'd die happily for she had told him all she had longed to say. And to think he arrived three days before his time! If only she could die three days before her time, that, too, would be good. A long illness can kill more than the patient. Alice was worn out dancing attendance on her. And poor Julia, and Mag and their Aunt Brigid had all done their share.

No, there's nothing as wearying as a long illness. Time is shuttered up and no one is free. And it's strange how you clutch at life, observing each moving thing — things you failed to notice when you were well. The church spire, for instance, that you could see through the side window, and the starlings, or was it pigeons, scattering from it when the bell tolled out the Angelus. She had never noticed that before in all her life. And yesterday, the fair day in the town, the cattle moved past in the early morning and brushed and bumped against the gable and left their hairs, she was sure, on the rough bits of the plaster. But of late one missed the children. They no longer play ball at the gable.

They often peeped in at her through the window and on seeing her propped against the pillows they'd stare for a moment, go away, and return with others. She didn't mind them. In fact she was glad to see them and smile at them, though she felt now there was something in her smile that frightened them and held their curiosity. A pity they didn't come back now. Their mothers must have scolded them. But their absence convinced her, long before she extracted the truth from Father O'Brien, that she was seriously ill. Cancer! They feared to use the word amongst themselves and dared not breathe it to her.

She didn't want to die, but that wasn't the same thing as being afraid to die. For Tom's sake she wanted to live: to hold the family together, to see Christy ordained, and Alice happily married. But you can't have all you desire in this life: we were born to rise and fall, to enjoy and sorrow — the eternal see-saw of life. If only in these last days she had strength to read or to knit or to pray it would have made the days pass quickly. But on a sick-bed with the body weak and the spirit dulled, prayer did not come easy: she could feel but not will. The time for real prayer was gone, and all she could do was to wish into being the words her lips could not form or the images her flitting mind could not hold. Father O'Brien told her to offer up her sufferings with the sufferings of Christ. But when her body was racked with pain her consciousness seemed to break away, and it was only in recollection that she could offer up what should, she felt, have been done there and then.

To please Tom she often forced herself to eat solid food, but the subsequent retchings disturbed and distressed everyone, and of late they forced nothing on her. She was wasting away — there was no doubt about that. The ring on her finger, at one time so firmly embedded in her flesh, could now slip off easily and they often found it on the floor or lying in the crevices of the bed-sheet. After that it was no use trying to deceive her with the customary greeting: 'You're looking well today.' And then they had shifted the button on the neck of her nightgown so that she wouldn't notice how thin her neck had shrunk — that deceived no one. She saw too many illnesses in her day to believe her own was any different. But she wouldn't complain. Sure it pleased them to deceive her in this way, and it increased their pleasure when she affected belief in their forced deception. But it was a pity they all treated her as a child that couldn't put two and two together. Did they think when you were ill you'd lost your reason and had slipped back to babyhood?

'She's just got away a short time before us all' — they'd soon be repeating that age-old saying among themselves. When she herself was young she thought it meaningless, but now she realized the truth in it: the headlong rush and dash of time. Yesterday the children were young and the clothes-line in the garden fluttered white with nappies. And in a few years the clothes on the line lengthened as the children grew, and then gaps came in it as they married and scattered. Please God, it'll never happen that there'll be a lone man's shirt hanging from that line and maybe a ragged dish-cloth drying shamefacedly beside it. No, no, that can't happen to poor Tom.

She recalled her first meeting with him. It all began in a simple way. She was teaching in the boarding school and had to catch an early train in the morning. Tom was always on the platform outside the booking-office and always opened the carriage door for her as she came forward. And in the afternoon when the train came in and she was leaning out to open the door he stepped forward smilingly, opened it for her, took her hand, and helped her to descend. That was the beginning. At Christmas he took to sending her a card and she in turn sent him one. They had many happy days together, and when they were married they had their children; holidays at the shore, and always the cheap rail-tickets from the company if she thought of doing a day's shopping in Dublin or Belfast. In a short while she had left all that behind and in a short while she, too, would be only a memory among the many memories of her children.

She sighed and listened to the tinkle of cups coming from the kitchen. She raised herself on the pillows and saw the sun shining on the field of corn outside, a field separated from their own garden by three parallel rows of bullwire. She loved that field. It refreshed her to look out upon it, to see the swallows dart across it, or on wet days to see the lobes of rain hanging from each ear of corn. She had seen the field being ploughed, had seen the horses stretch their necks over the wire and pluck at the grass on the inside of the fence. She had seen, too, the seed scattered, had seen it grow, and shoot into life. And to think she'd never see it harvested, and the stooks in rows and the crows on top of them in the dewy September mornings.

Many things she'd never see again. There was the thrushes' nest in the holly bush and the glossy leaves splashed white where the nest had hidden from the rains of May. That was a lively time, from the building of the nest in the early mornings till weeks later when the parent birds flew out with bits of eggshell in their bills. And then the morning the young were pushed out from the nest and how they lamented all day in the long grass or balanced uneasily without their tails on the wire of the fence before being tumbled off by the wind. And the parent birds lost their glossy coats, and had grown thinner as they reared their family with such intense anxiety. And poor Alice had to keep the cat in during those days. No wonder she said one evening: 'Mother, the poor cat hasn't a dog's life in this establishment.' That was Alice all over, always bright. Even when she wasn't the size of a chair she was always dressing up and scampering into the field to gather poppies and compare their hairy stems with the fair hairs on her own arms. And it was there Christy used to fly a kite on the windy days of March. And on Sundays the men from the lane used to twig goldfinches with bird-lime on the hedges. The police fined a few of them and she was blamed for sending an anonymous letter to the barracks. She never did that, but they blamed her and didn't speak to her or Tom for years. Ah, well, that was past. They would attend her funeral and maybe on the way back they'd say: 'She's gone to her rest now, the old informer, and the birds, as they did for St Francis, will sing her requiem.'

She smiled and thought of Christy's attempt to keep uncharitable talk out of the house. He had brought home one evening a cardboard missionary box and placed it on the sideboard and said: 'When you find you have been lacerating the neighbours just drop a few pence into that as penance.' And then the evening he came in and found us all sitting very quiet and glum and he clapped his hands together and dropped a half-crown in the box: 'Come on the lot of us and we'll have a good half-crown's worth tonight! This house is dying for a good bit of ridicule. Come on: where will we begin? Will we take the shopkeepers first or the schoolteachers or the clergy or the lazy stationmaster that's my father's boss? We'll toss for it....'

She sighed, gave a faint smile, and heard the chairs being pushed in to the table. Alice entered, and noticing that she looked better than she'd done for weeks she concluded that it was Christy's visit that was the cause of it.

'Did Christy take a good meal?'

'He did, Mother. He ate as much as a Cavan football team.'

'I'm glad. All his studying wouldn't be much use to him if he lost his health.'

'I heard you,' Christy said, coming into the room. 'I heard you, my old pagan. If we put our health first nothing would ever be done.'

'But you must be prudent.'

'Prudence can excuse a weight of laziness.' He sat on a small chair so that she could see him without having to turn her head.

'Tell me, Christy, have any students been turned back or, should I say, have any poor fellows been turned out?'

Listening to her bantering talk it was hard for him to

22

believe she'd only a short time to live and for a moment he wondered if the doctors could be wrong or if a miracle were taking place in a body that bore so many signs of rapid dissolution. Her eyes, the only living things in her wax-like face, stared him to attention.

'No,' he said, 'no students in my year have turned from the road,' and before she could ponder the equivocal answer to her question he began to tell her of last Sunday's bathing expedition. He told it slowly and when he had finished she said: 'You're an article! I hope the poor fella hasn't got his death of cold.'

'Is it Peter Mooney to get his death! He's as strong as a County Meath bullock.'

'Go on, Christy, tell me more.'

He told her of a trick they played in the last theological lecture of the term. They rigged up a gramophone behind the dais and midway through the lecture they pulled a string and there burst forth above the lecturer's voice 'O, Rose Marie I love you'.

She smiled and shook her head: 'And here we all were, Christy, thinking you did nothing all day long but study books.'

'A woman's imagination is even worse than her dreams.'

He noticed her eyes slowly closing and he continued talking, letting his voice trail to a whisper, lulling her into the sleep he wished for her. And at last when there was no movement from her he rose slowly and walked backwards to the open door and slipped away.

'She's asleep,' he said to his father and passed into the scullery to help Alice with the dishes.

'Please, Christy,' she protested as he took the drying cloth, 'I can do them in two ticks. It'd be better for you and Father to go for a walk. If you don't go now you'll not get out at all, for Mag and Julia and Aunt Brigid will be in on top of us before we know where we are.'

'Couldn't you and Father go and I'll hold the fort?'

'I'm used to handling poor Mother and I'd rather not leave her now. Some other day I'll let you stay. Go on, Christy, I know how Father hates hanging around the house all day.'

'We'll go. But I must say you're a great little boss. You'd make a great Reverend Mother if you were in a convent.'

'Me! I hope I'll be the mother of six children.'

Mag and Julia were in the house when Christy and the father arrived back from their walk, and both of them reproached Christy for not calling round to see them. Indeed, they'd heard of his arrival from the neighbours, no less. The summer was long, he told them, and they'd both be sick of his calls before his return to the college in September.

They noticed he was paler in spite of his walk in that warm summer air. And he in turn noticed that they were strained and nervous in his presence. Married life had aged both of them: Julia in rearing her children, and Mag worrying, he supposed, because she hadn't any to rear. Her time would come in spite of her delicate husband but worrying over it wouldn't help.

They drank cups of tea in the sick-room, talking to Christy about the college and occasionally glancing at their mother to tell her how well she was looking. And when they were finished and the cups cleared away the father suggested they should say the rosary and let Alice go to bed for she was on her feet since early morning.

Julia kept watching her father the whole evening, and as he felt her anxious eyes upon him he sensed she wanted to say something that was for himself alone; and after the rosary had been said he went outside to the garden and sat on a seat under a flowering laburnum tree where he often smoked his pipe of an evening.

The heat of the day oozed out from the tool-shed at his back and there was a heavy smell of roses thickening the air. He lit his pipe, and in a few minutes he wasn't surprised to see Julia coming out to the garden and calling to him.

'Are you going home already?' he said, concealing his awareness of her agitation, and rising to his feet.

'No, Father, not yet. I wanted to ask you something — something important.' She put her hand on his sleeve and made him sit down again.

'I'm terribly worried,' she began nervously.

'It'd be better if God called her soon and not let her suffer any longer,' he said, and immediately felt his face burn with shame, aware that that wasn't her real worry.

She opened her handbag, drew out her handkerchief and blew her nose.

'That's only one of my worries, Father. I've others. Poor Richard's in trouble again.'

He relit his pipe and a moth flew round the lighted match. She pressed his arm and sat close to him like a child for protection.

'Could you lend me money, Father, to tide us over this spot of trouble? It's not for myself I'm asking it. I'm thinking of Christy, of our good name, and of my two innocent children. I don't want Richard to be dragged into court and his name plastered in all the newspapers. He'd have to shut his office this time and there'd be nothing for us but the open road.'

A light was switched on in Alice's room and it shone down to the garden and lighted up the yellow gold of the laburnum blossom. The father drew the pipe from his lips and smoke streamed from the stem.

'But, Julia girl, I'm tired handing you out money. You'd think to hear you talking I'd a mint of money. And look at the expense ahead,' he explained, thinking of the funeral.

'But I'll pay you back every penny of it. I will indeed. It's only a loan I'm asking for. There'll be my share from my mother's insurance.'

He was suddenly angered by that remark, ashamed of her lack of reticence, and realized that her life with Richard Colton had swept away all the traces of dignified rearing her

26

mother had given her. This evening she had abased herself and he would humiliate her further.

'What insurance do you mean?' he asked.

'Mother's life insurance. Isn't there two thousand with profits due at her death?'

He unscrewed the shank of his pipe and looked away from her to the darkness of the hedge. So Richard and herself, he thought, have already discussed the outcome of Mary's death and what it would mean to them in money. And to think that this was a daughter of his!

'You'll lend me three hundred, Father, won't you? It'll be paid back as soon as we're over this hurdle,' she continued with tearful urgency.

'Money, money!' and he beat the palm of his hand with the bowl of his pipe. 'Yourself and Dick would let all the money in the country flow through your hands like a sieve.'

'S-sh-sh, Father, Alice might hear us' — and she glanced up at the lighted window with its drawn blind.

'It'd be a good job if someone heard you. And I may tell you here and now that I'm not in a position to do anything for you. As a wedding present I bought you and Mag the houses you're living in. And a year ago I lifted your precious husband out of debt and now he's deep in it again.'

'It's drink and cards has him the way he is. And you know, Father, how good he is. He's the most generous of men when …'

'When he's spending his clients' money,' he added hastily.

She opened her handbag again, daubed her eyes, and besought him for the sake of poor Mother not to quarrel with her.

'It's drink that's ruined him,' she said, 'and it's not a fault, it's a disease.'

'I've known men who drank but who retained their honesty. I suppose you'll tell me dishonesty is a disease, and when you've done that you'll be telling me the ten commandments are a disease. Dick should learn one lesson: pay his debts first and enjoy himself afterwards.'

'Please, Father, please …'

'Only for what's happening to your poor mother I'd give you a piece of my mind,' he said with unconscious irony. 'I would indeed. As God's my judge I don't know what's come over you since you got married. You think of nothing but money. I wish to the good God I'd nothing only the clothes on my back and a change of shirt. I got four thousand pounds from the sale of my brother's farm in Monabeg. God be good to him, he didn't realize the legacy of trouble he was bequeathing when he left me that. But you and Mag have got a good bite out of it. There's still a little left but it's for Alice and Christy. You'd want to swallow up their share! But I swear you'll not get it!'

'Ah, Father, don't be vexed with me. It'll be paid back out of Mother's insurance.'

'So you've your poor mother buried before her time.' He shook his head. 'I'm ashamed of you. There's a hard drop in you wherever it came from. You usedn't to be like this. Since you linked your life with Richard Colton he has changed you. But you were headstrong in your love for him and wouldn't listen to advice.'

She sobbed, resting her head on the back of the seat.

'I'll not forget this evening in a hurry. Christy at home, poor Mother on her death bed, and you cut me as coldly as a judge.' She threw her arms wide and wrung out her words: 'Do you not see the difficulty I am in? Surely you know I wouldn't ask you at such a time if it weren't necessary for us all — for our good name.'

He lowered his voice: 'A time will come, Julia, when you'll have to let justice take its proper course. A few months in jail for embezzling would sober Mr Richard Colton, Auctioneer and Valuer and …' He hesitated, and to his own mind murmured: 'Estate agent and embezzler.' He shook his head and strove to shake away that thought from his mind.

The light was switched off in Alice's room and the patch of garden around them became suddenly dark.

Julia jumped to her feet: 'I'll not stay here listening to you abusing my husband. I'll go to the bank in the morning and ask for a loan by handing over the title deeds of the house — your wedding present that you cast up so frequently. I'll not be beholden to you any longer. And remember this: for better or for worse I married Richard and I'll stick by him always. We are expecting our third child in another seven months or so.'

'I'm glad to hear that though I dislike the way you announce it.'

She turned from him, but he called her back. 'Sit down, Julia,' he said slowly. 'I'll write you a cheque. But it'll be the last I'll ever be able to write for you. The little that remains I'll sign over to Alice and Christy. There's great comfort in having nothing but one's good name. When the drawers are empty there'll be nothing to take and nothing to give.'

'I'll pay you back from …'

'In God's name don't mention that again.'

'You needn't worry about Christy,' she said, realizing she had succeeded. 'Christy will have little call for money in the African Mission fields.'

'Your mind, Julia, takes long strides. Christy's not ordained yet. You'll have him out in the Nigerian bush before his time, and you'll have your mother … No, I'll not say it.' He rose to his feet and told her to stay where she was. He went into the house and left the door open. The light from it stretched out to the garden and lighted up the holly bush and the white splashings on the leaves where the thrush had nested. The white spots caught her eye and looking at them she thought it was a child's daisy-chain, and then suddenly she thought of her childhood and how when she was young she and Mag used to creep through a hole in the hedge and play in the field beyond in the long summer days, while their mother sat on a plaid rug with Alice, the baby, beside her. She sighed at the remembrance of it all, gave an involuntary shudder though the night was warm, and again took out her handkerchief.

In a few minutes her father came from the house and closed the door behind him. He hesitated for a moment till his eyes grew accustomed to the dark, then he stooped below the clothes-line and went across to her and handed her a cheque.

'Don't fold it yet, the ink's not dry.'

She took it without thanking him, and as he stumbled away from her in the direction of the door his brow grazed the clothes-line and he stopped, held it up for her, and told her to stoop. With his hand on the door-latch he turned to where she was in the darkness beside him and asked if Mag knew about this.

'I don't think so,' she said.

'She either does or she doesn't. Yes or no?'

'I told her about Dick's trouble. Surely I can confide in my own twin-sister.'

'So she knows you were to ask me for money?'

'I mentioned that I might ask you.'

'And did she side with you?'

'She didn't say a word against it. Of course she can get everything from you without asking.'

'Julia, that's untrue. I never, to my conscious knowledge, favoured her more than you. You are all equal in my affection.'

'You can't deny that lately she has been more favoured.'

'Do you mean the three weeks' holiday I paid for them at Blackrock when her husband was off sick? You wouldn't begrudge a sick man a holiday.'

'You offered it to her without her having to ask' — and she stretched out her hand to the latch. His own touched hers and he tried to press it as a sign of forgiveness. She brushed it aside. The latch clicked and as she went in ahead of him he called softly: 'Julia, girl, come back,' but she ignored him and went inside to the sick-room. He came in behind her and stood at the foot of the bed and watched Mag pulling on her gloves and lifting her handbag from the floor.

'And how do you think she is, Mag?' he asked, his voice shaking.

'She's splendid, Father. It's a long time since I heard her talk so well or look so well.'

'I hope, Mary, you haven't taken too much out of yourself.'

She smiled up at him and then looked at Christy, and then at Mag and Julia. 'You've all been very good to me, more than I deserve. I don't want any of you to stay up with me tonight. I feel strong and calm and I'm at peace. Get a long sleep, Christy, for I'm sure you're fagged out after your journey.... Poor Richard's very good to take charge of the children and let you out so often, Julia.'

'Richard doesn't mind one bit, Mother.'

'You've two good children, Julia, and you must bring them up to see me on Sunday if God spares me.'

'Come on, Julia, for I have the key of the house and Joe will be out from his choir practice long ago,' Mag said. 'Good night, Mother ... good night.'

'Good night, Mag and Julia, and God bless you.'

Christy volunteered to go a bit of the road with them and as they waited in the hall till he got his coat they all agreed they never heard Mother talk with such clarity. And where she got the energy from they just didn't know. Only last week you may say she was at death's door. Could it be that a miracle was taking place or that the doctors' diagnosis was wrong?

'It's her great spirit that's keeping her alive,' the father said. 'She's eating nothing. Even the sight of food distresses her. When Father O'Brien was giving her Holy Communion this morning he told me she wouldn't last much longer.'

'Oh, if only she would eat,' Mag said, 'there might be some hope.'

31

'It's a blessing that Christy is home,' Julia said, tightening the fingers of her gloves.

Christy came forward pulling on a light coat and joined them at the door.

'I'll not be long, Father. I'll only go as far as the convent and turn back.'

'You needn't hurry. I'll be staying up tonight. I do hope Aunt Brigid won't toddle along. Your mother has had a busy enough day.... Good night, Julia and Mag, and safe home.'

THEY had scarcely gone from the house when Aunt Brigid, holding her Pekinese on a new leather leash, pushed the open door with her foot and called out: 'Is there anyone there?'

'I'm here, Brigid, I'm here.'

'Is the cat in or out?'

'She's out on her nocturnals so you may lead in Sergeant without fear of assault and battery.'

The Pekinese, breathing as if about to choke, and his pink tongue hanging out, was led in forcibly on the new leash. Brigid unhooked the leash when she was seated in front of the range and he immediately hopped up on her lap and gazed around, first at the four corners of the room, then at the darkness underneath the sofa, and then at the smoke-rings from Tom's pipe that were rising and disappearing against the electric lamp.

'You didn't meet the girls and Christy?'

'No, I came the long way. Sergeant's getting too fat this last while back and I wanted to give him a bit of exercise. I heard Christy's home.'

'He'll be in before you go away.' When he looked across at the ugly face of the dog on her lap he told her to put him down or he'd have her coat covered with hairs.

'I gave him a good brushing before taking him out,' she said with slight annoyance and patted the dog's head. 'And how is poor Mary today?'

'She's in good form but very tired. There's no one in with her at present. Poor Alice is worn out and I sent her to bed.'

'I'd have been up sooner only I'd a few things to tidy up before closing the shop,' she said, thinking that his innocent remark about Alice contained an accusation of her own lack of attention to her dying sister. 'Indeed, I suppose, I haven't done enough for Mary in all her trouble.'

'There's little one can do under the circumstances, and you have done all you can,' he said gratefully. 'An incurable illness is a cross for us all, but it lies heaviest on the poor patient.'

She smoothed the dog's head: 'I'll be the last of the flock when poor Mary goes.'

He looked steadily at her as she bowed her head. Her black hair hadn't a strand of grey, and her plump face made her younger than her forty-odd years. She had an easy life of it compared with Mary, and her confectionery shop which she kept as neat as herself never afforded her much worry. But there was a kindness in her that was never showy or false.

'If she's not sleeping, Tom, I'll stay with her for a few minutes. You know I'd sit up with her if Sergeant had the good sense to sleep. But he knows the place is strange and that's what set him barking the last time I tried it.'

'Don't worry about that, Brigid. There's enough of us here to take turns, and now that Christy's home he'll be able and glad to relieve us.'

'You were very good to take her out of the hospital. She'd have hated to die there and away from the children.'

'It was Alice who managed that. It was she who volunteered to nurse her at home.'

She clipped the lead on Sergeant and led him into the room, and in a few minutes he heard her voice warming up. He glanced at the clock. It was half-eleven. He'd give her to twelve, not a minute more. If she wanted a chat and a long sit why didn't she come when Mag and Julia were here instead of leaving everything to the last minute. Surely to goodness she'll notice how tired Mary is and not in the mood for tittle-tattle.

The kettle bubbled over on the fire and he jumped to his feet and lifted it off, the spilt water hissing and turning grey on the range. Pushed to the side was a small saucepan with cornflour. At the stroke of twelve he'd put some of it in a bowl and bring it to Mary. That would be a hint to Brigid to roll up her score for the night.

He sat down on the sofa again. He heard his wife give her dry cough. Then there was silence for a few minutes and then Brigid's voice changing into high gear. He'd not give her to twelve — he'd cut ten minutes off it. Had she no sense in her head than to sit there gabbling at this time of night? Wouldn't you think she'd be talked dry after attending her customers all day?

He got up suddenly and put some of the cornflour in a bowl. He warmed a little milk to go with it and carried it inside.

'I've her settled down for the night, Tom,' Brigid said.

'This is her little nightcap. Sit up, Mary, and take a spoonful or two. It's been simmering ever since Alice went to bed.'

She sat up, and more to please him than to satisfy her desire for it she held the warm bowl in her hands while he fed her with the spoon and Brigid dried her lips.

'We'll leave you now, Mary, and let you sleep in God's good name.'

'Yes, Mary, sleep,' Brigid said. 'It's a lovely quiet night. There's not a breath of wind. Not a stir in the grass nor in the sky.' The dog yawned and swept the rug with his tail. 'Good night, Mary dear.'

At the hall door they halted while she told him of the great improvement she had seen in her since yesterday. Tom nodded, and looked up at the clear sky.

'You'll have a lovely walk home and you'll probably meet Christy on your way. Sergeant, by the cut of him, will not be averse to a little nourishing sleep.'

'Yes, indeed. But he never oversleeps, except when he's off

35

colour. He never fails to waken me in time for Mass in the mornings.'

He stifled a yawn: 'A pity you didn't give him a good Christian name instead of a barrack-room name like Sergeant.'

'It was the late Sergeant's wife that gave him to me and I couldn't show my appreciation better than by calling him Sergeant.'

'After his father, so to speak.' He shifted from one foot to the other and moved towards the gable-end of the house where the moon cast a sharp triangle on the road.

'He's a dear. He could almost tell you what you're thinking.'

'It's as well, maybe, that he can't do that.' As he stooped to fix the heel of his slipper the cat whirled round the corner, spat and tore at Sergeant with her claws, the dog yelping and entangling himself in his leash.

Brigid lifted him up, pressed him under her arm, and as she consoled him, the cat stood by with every hair raised.

'That's an atrocious cat, you have! Bad scrant to it!' She struck the cat with the leash.

'She's an unmannerly cat and I'll speak to her with the tongs when I go in.' He moved away from the house and expounded to her with affected interest on the strange behaviour of cats: cats that led lives of complete independence, cats that were unbiddable to ordinary domestic manners, and cats that had as much kindness in them as wintry weasels.

He had inveigled her as far as the bridge and there he bade her good night. He sighed audibly and as he hurried up the hill he could hear the little bell ringing on Sergeant's collar as he escorted her home.

Later when Christy had come back and gone to bed the father got ready for the long night's vigil. Mary called to him and asked him to turn her on her right side for she felt she could sleep better that way. He put his arms around her, and with one slow but gentle movement he turned her as she had

36

wished, and as he did so the thinness and lightness of her body struck him with real sorrow, sorrow for the fading and withering of her flesh, sorrow for the absence of relief and comfort no one could give her. In the presence of others he could never exhibit his love for his wife but now that they were alone he stroked her head, the thin hair dry to the touch as withered grass. He kissed her on the cheek, and as he made the sign of the cross on her forehead she raised her emaciated hand and stroked his. Neither of them could speak, but each at that moment felt the unhealable break that was coming into their lives. He lay down beside her on the eiderdown, not knowing what to say or what to do. All he desired for her was a sound deep sleep, a sleep free from one stroke of pain.

As if sensing what was in his mind she said: 'God was good in sending Christy home to me so soon. I feel great peace coming over me, great peace. Take out the little oil-lamp and let up the blind to the moonlight. I love to see it for I can mark the hours by its position in the room. I have my beads and I want for nothing. Good night, Tom, and God bless and comfort you always. I'll sleep now and you needn't disturb me.'

He stole out of the room, switched off the harsh light in the kitchen, placed the quiet oil-lamp on the sideboard, and sat on the sofa. The glow from the range shone on the rug, on the red tiles, and on the cat that was purring contentedly in the stillness. The house had at last settled down and the pad of Christy's feet on the floor above had ceased.

It had been a long day, a day of constant going and coming. He would have liked to read but if he switched on the light its reflection would reach her through the open doors and she'd surely call him and order him to go to bed. And if he closed his door it was possible he mightn't hear her if she happened to call out during the night. He sat quite still.

Ashes fell in the grate and he started. No, he mustn't doze. He must keep awake. He slipped out to the front door and lit his pipe. There was no sound anywhere. There was not a light in any of the neighbouring houses, nothing only the bright sky, the blue shining slates and a speck of glass star-like on the road. Then from the other side of the town he heard the rumble of the goods train, and in his mind's eye saw the moon shine on the tarpaulin-covered wagons and on the terrified eyes of the cattle that were jostled about in the crowded carriages. He heard the train whistle, and, then its echo sharp and clear running over the hill at the back of the house. The rumble dwindled as the train entered a tunnel on the line, and a few minutes later it expanded again and with it there merged the metallic rattle of the couplings. That sound was in his ears all his life and, he supposed, it would still remain with him long after he had retired from the service. But he had a good fourteen years to go till that closure, and God knows what would happen between then and now. He had always yearned for a change of station, for somehow this town never appealed to him, and even after the children came he still longed for a change but Mary always opposed him. She was dead-set against leaving; it was her home-town and she didn't wish to uproot herself from it and from Brigid. And then again they must always think of their children and their children's future — that must be their first consideration.

Six years ago he could have got a stationmaster's job farther down the line but Mary entreated him not to apply for it. It would be disastrous for Mag and Julia and they on the threshold of marriage. Disastrous! He took the pipe from his mouth as he recalled Mary's words. Disastrous! Mary was right, but not in the way she had foreseen. Both Mag and Julia had already crossed that threshold, and the inside was not the happy anchorage that they had anticipated.

Poor Julia — tonight he had seen a little more of what married life had done for her. And God alone knew how it would all end for her. Then there was Mag: she never made open complaint about anything but still everyone knew she was praying for a child to brighten the loneliness of her home. Her husband wasn't a bad chap though he had little or no health to speak of. He was as pale as that moon in the sky, and no wonder. That drapery store he works in has an unwholesome smell about it. The place never seems to have God's daylight shining into it, and in the winter the smell of the gas heater would give a statue a headache! For all the wages he's earning he should clear out of it for the good of his health and try and get some open-air job. A job as a traveller would do.

A curlew cried overhead, and he raised his eyes but could discern no wing-movement in that star-strewn sky. He turned inside and listened at the sick-room door. The room was lit up by the moon and it seemed to magnify the silence and the sleep within. He tiptoed away and once more took up his stand at the door leading to the street. He sighed, thinking about their life together and what she had meant to him and to the children. God would judge her as a wife and a mother. As a wife he couldn't have asked for better: their love for one another had grown with the years — they had always prayed for that, prayed that their love would never grow cold.

And as a mother she was an example to everyone. If she had a fault it was one of excess devotion to her children. She lived for them. Indeed he often thought she did too much for them. She was certainly more attached to them than he ever was or ever could be. He failed in that respect and the cause for his failure lay, he thought, in some unknown region of the past, some occurrence in his life that drove him into a lonely, unaccountable detachment.

He should have forced himself to interfere a little more in his children's undertakings and if he had done that Julia might now be free from her worries with Richard Colton. He never cared for that fellow at any time and he should never have concealed his dislike of him from Julia. That florid face of Richard's and that swaggering manner always repelled him, and since his marriage to Julia neither face nor manner had undergone a deep-sea change.

He'd never forget Richard's approach to him last year to borrow money, never forget the accent and the language: 'My embarrassment is only of a temporary nature, I'd wish you to understand. I have an excellent and dutiful wife in your daughter Julia. I have two healthy children and I am happy to state that the consensus of opinion holds that the eldest child is the spitting image of his grandpa. I am, you realize, in charge of a large vessel with puny steering equipment. Granted I have grounded a few times, which is not unexpected in the rocky waters of this town, but the tide will turn soon and Captain Colton and his crew will reach a safe and secure haven!'

How under God was Julia duped by that cargo of wind! Tonight, he supposed, the same captain had handed over the steering to Julia. Well, they can steer wherever they like, for it was certainly the last time he'd throw them a life-line. Captain Colton, like Robinson Crusoe, can wade ashore in his bare feet or go in goatskin trousers for all he'd care! Better for Julia she had married a signalman or a good honest-sweated engine-driver instead of that gadabout with his auction bills staring at you from every gate-post or tree-trunk about the countryside. 'And that reminds me,' he said aloud to himself, 'he hasn't yet paid for the hiring of the advertisement at the station. I suppose he'll leave Grandpa to settle that little affair.'

Thinking of him he felt a sourness creep into his soul. Julia was a fine girl before she married the likes of him. And now she was changed for the worse. To think that tonight she could speak to him in the way she did! No, no, he musn't think about her now, musn't harden his heart against her. Surely she'll think over what she said to him and realize her mistake. But she should have taken his hand when he touched hers as it reached for the door-latch. It was that affront that hurt him more than anything else.

He knocked out his pipe, came inside, and closed the door. There was still no movement from the room nor any sound from upstairs. The whole house was asleep. He stretched himself on the sofa and put a cushion under his head. He was wide awake and to keep that way he thought again of the past and of the poor hand he had taken in the rearing of his children. Only once did he ever make a major decision in their rearing and see it through. That was when he insisted that Julia should postpone her wedding for a year and wait for Mag. It was a customary thing to do, he had said, to have twins married on the one day. It wasn't for economic reasons he had made that suggestion though Richard, with his usual swaggering humour, held that it was. No one knew the reason for the postponement except himself, and he even managed to keep it from Mary. Somewhere he had heard or read that among twin girls one was usually infertile — which one he never knew — and not wishing to destroy Mag's chance of marriage he begged that Julia's wedding should be postponed for a year. It was a strange request. But with Mag childless after six years there might be something in the theory. These old theories didn't grow on the bushes, they were the outcome of years of reflection. A pity it wasn't Julia was the barren one. And if, as she says, another child is on the way it looks as if she has taken Mag's share of motherhood.

When the clock struck three he got up, lifted the ring off the range and quietly dropped in a few pieces of coal. The cat stretched itself, shook one front paw and then the other, and walked towards the front door. He let it out. The air was cold now, the grey light grey as the road, grey as the houses, greyer than wheaten bread. The dawn was not far off. The stars had faded, and from the backs of the houses cocks were crowing. He walked to the gable-end and saw a primrose light brimming on top of the hill. From among the dark leaves of a tree a blackbird was giving out a few sleepy notes and in a short while the other birds would be wakening one by one. It would be another day of heat and sunshine, another day of heaviness upon the heart, of whisperings throughout the house. And it would begin as usual with Alice going to early Mass, and him preparing the breakfast and having boiling water ready in case the doctor would arrive early to give Mary an injection to ease her pain. And God help her she seldom complained of pain and even made slight of it to the doctor.

He shrugged his shoulders and slipped back to the house. He'd take a nip of whiskey, and if Mary stirred he'd bring her a little sip of wine. He stooped and opened the door of the sideboard, and without making one clink of noise drew forth two glasses, a bottle of whiskey and one of wine. He manœuvred the tight cork from the whiskey bottle and as he did so it squeaked like new leather. He halted and listened. No one stirred and shaking the cork from side to side with trembling fingers it at last gave way with a sudden pop. Once again he listened, and then as he leant forward to lift a glass the bottle slipped from his fingers and smashed like a flash of lightning on the tiled floor. He stood still and felt his face swell and burn in the rapid pace from his heart. The rising fumes from the spilt whiskey made him cough and as he choked back the coughs his eyes watered freely. He moved away from the splinters of glass and sat on the sofa, listening, expecting his wife to call out or Christy descend the stairs. But there was no sound from any place, nothing but the terrible throb of his blood like the throb of a far-away train. Wiping the sweat from his forehead and covering his mouth and nose with a handkerchief he got down on his knees and picked up the pieces of glass, one by one, and put them in the coal-scuttle at the side of the range. He wiped up the spirit with old newspapers, and as they would do for lighting a fire in the garden he stowed them in a box in the scullery.

All desire for a drink left him and he went into the sick-room. The light had grown stronger and he stood for a minute gazing down at the stilled restfulness of his wife. She was lying on her right side, in the same position as he had left her. But there was something strange about her that startled him. He inclined his head to listen to her breathing, but he could hear nothing only the pound of his own pulse. 'Mary!' he said in a whisper. 'Mary!' and he put his hand gently on her forehead and realized she was dead. He ran for Christy, and in a minute Christy was out of bed, and Alice awake. Both rushed downstairs.

'God have mercy on her soul! I knew she wouldn't last long,' Christy said, rising from his knees. 'But I didn't think the end was so near and she in such good heart yesterday. She's at rest now, and she knows more than we know.'

'If God had only spared her till you were ordained, Christy,' Alice said, drying her eyes. 'That was her dearest wish.'

'God wills these things and we must accept them humbly and without reproach.'

'She is nearer to God now than any of us and she'll be praying for us all,' the father said and moved to the window. The sun was striking through the holly tree, shining on the yellow straw of the nest, and on the strings of spiders' webs in the unweeded garden. All the birds were singing now but he didn't hear them. His underlip quivered and he pressed his teeth against it to control himself. He turned and without looking at them he asked them to go and tell the others.

And when Christy and Alice had dressed and gone from the house he knelt alone by his wife's bedside and opened up his heart in prayer for her soul and in thanksgiving that she was allowed to live until their children were reared. He turned her gently from her side and she lay with her rosary beads clasped in her hands as if prepared for her death-bed. He pulled down the blinds on all the windows of the house, and out of custom, which he saw no reason for, he stopped all the clocks in the house.

Julia and Mag were the first to arrive and he went into the room with them, and after they had said a prayer at the bed-side Julia asked at what time she had died.

43

'I couldn't truly say, Julia. All night long I thought she was sleeping and I didn't wish to disturb her by continually going in and out of the room.'

'Oh, I wish I'd stayed, just to be with her before the end. Surely she wanted something, a drink of water or a spoonful of brandy, or she may have wanted to say some last word to us.'

'What Father did was right,' Mag said. 'It's what any of us would have done. None of us would have wanted to disturb her when she was at rest. And Mother always hated people fussing around her.'

'But I'm sure she knew death was near at hand and she'd have wanted someone to comfort and strengthen her.'

'The last thing she asked for were her beads and to be turned on her right side. And it was in that position she slept away and didn't move,' the father said.

'And were you in the house all the time?' Julia asked.

'I stood smoking at the front door for a while.'

'Maybe she called out and you didn't hear her.'

He shook his head: 'There wasn't a sound the whole night either in the house or outside it.'

'Oh, why didn't some of us stay with her when we knew Alice was in bed! I couldn't very well stay and leave the two children.' She looked at Mag. 'I'll never forgive myself for not staying. To think that poor Mother died without the blessed candle in her hand or a priest by her side.'

'Father O'Brien attended her in the morning,' Mag said.

'But, but, half a day or more elapsed since his visit.'

'She died in peace and her soul is with God — I'm sure of that,' the father said. 'For some reason she wanted no one to sit up with her. I slipped to the room door often so that she wouldn't hear me. You know how definite she was about her own wishes, and I thought I was pleasing her by pretending I was gone to bed.'

'Maybe that's why she didn't call out, thinking that no one would hear her. On this occasion, Father, you shouldn't have listened to her or heeded her. After all she was a very sick

44

woman,' Julia said and burst into tears. Mag put an arm on her shoulder and led her from the room. 'Oh, if only one of us had stayed!'

'Don't say that again for goodness' sake,' Mag said. 'Did you not see how cut Father was when you said it? It's like a criticism of him. Control yourself, here come two of the neighbours.'

The two neighbours shook hands with Julia and Mag and asked to be allowed to prepare the room.

'Don't mourn too bitterly for your poor mother for she was a living saint,' they said. 'She was good and kind and never said a bad word about anyone. She lived for others as well as for her own children. It's easy for a good woman to die. She can face her Maker with a shining soul, a soul dressed in its wedding garment of Grace.'

The two neighbours hung up their coats and rolled up their sleeves, and as they prepared the silent room they paused to exclaim to one another: 'You'd know to look at her lying there that she died in peace. There's a smile on her face.'

'And why wouldn't she smile and she with a son going for the priesthood.'

'Aye, and a husband that never wasted his life in a pub. A man that can take a drink like a gentleman. A man that has the railway station as neat and clean as a Christmas present.'

'And that lazy stationmaster Wilson gets the credit for all Tom Magee's work. A right oul pagan is the same stationmaster. Never goes to any church. Wouldn't you like to see him go off on a Sunday with his Bible under his arm like many a decent Protestant. He believes in nothing, the oul rascal.'

'It's a blessing of God we never had a railway accident with a man like that in charge. When he retires Tom Magee will step into his place.'

'And a good job too. He'll have the third class carriages dickied up till you think you're travelling first class.'

45

'What'll I do with these roses in the vase? They need fresh water.'

'When one of the girls comes in get her to cut some fresh ones. The garden out there is suffocating with the smell of them. A few less would let the perfume escape over the hedge, if you know what I mean.'

'I wish my man would plunge a spade in that patch of ours. Many a time I told him to ask Tom Magee for a few garden-ing hints, or a few slips that would grow. And do you know what he told me? He thanked God on his two bended knees he wasn't a Magee. He preferred a wild rose or a primrose to any highfalutin thing Magee would grow, and he pre-ferred a good smoke in a pub than a smoke under a laburnum tree.'

'There's a great differs in men. Tom Magee's a fine strappin' young man yet. I wouldn't be at all surprised if ...'

'Nor would I. I'd say he was younger than my own man. And mind you I wouldn't put it past my own man to marry again if I were under the sod.'

'I don't think Tom Magee's that sort of a man.'

'They're all that sort when it comes to the bit.'

'There'd be opposition from some quarters. Some say he has money past him. That'd be an additional attraction. And then again it would strengthen the opposition.'

'He has Alice to think of.'

'Alice's a fine little piece and a young girl like her would leave him in the lurch at the first chance of a ring on her finger.'

'If she'd any sense in her head she'd stay with her father.'

'Her sisters didn't do very well for themselves in spite of their fine rearing. What Julia saw in that husband of hers will always be a mystery to me.'

'And poor Mag's by the look of him could do with a few raw eggs every day. The poor fellow looks as if a whiff of wind would carry him over the hedge and into the next world.'

46

The door was knocked and Alice came in carrying a thin cardboard box containing the burial shroud. She handed it to the women and they took it without a word. And when she was gone from them and the door closed they stared at the box in silence.

One broke the string of the box and sighed. 'You can't take much finery with you into the grave.'

'Aye, that's true. That pauper's dress is all that any of us can take and it's easily carried.'

4

ONE Sunday a few weeks after the funeral Christy watched his father setting out for his usual Sunday afternoon walk, and noticing a lonely look about him he put on his hat and overtook him.

'I thought I'd take the good of the air and come with you, Father,' he said. 'I suppose you'll be calling on Julia and Mag on your way back?'

'I don't know. I'm just going as far as the lake to watch the lads fishing. Somehow it refreshes me.'

They walked through the town, his father with his hands behind his back, and Christy trying to make conversation by describing the bit of sea-fishing he often did of a Sunday from the rocks near the college. His father didn't seem to be listening to him and they continued their walk in silence. Since the funeral Christy noticed these sudden silences, and at night as he stood at the window before getting into bed, he often saw the glow of his father's pipe as he sat alone under the laburnum tree. There would be scarcely a movement from him then, just the flare of an occasional match and the tobacco smoke drifting in the moonlight among the branches. That familiar scene saddened him and he prayed that his father would soon drag himself out of this dejection of spirit, and that he'd hear him singing, as of old, in the mornings or whistling to himself as he laboured in the garden. Not a hand had he laid on the garden since the funeral, and only for himself and Alice the weeds would have reached the back door and destroyed the vegetables. No doubt about it Father would have to pull himself together otherwise Alice might walk out on him some fine day and leave him to fend for himself. It was too much to expect a girl of eighteen to stifle her bright ways for the sake of an ageing man.

They reached the lakeside and sat on a green bench under an oak tree. The air was cool there, the leaves bright green and veined against the sun, the ground riddled and spotted with light. Small boys were fishing for roach at the water's edge and a bigger boy was casting a spoon-bait for pike. There was a warm smell from the water, an unfresh smell of crushed twigs. Water-lily leaves lay like green trowels on the water and a dragon-fly sparkled above them like a suspended firework. The boys' voices echoed across the lake.

The spoon-bait plopped into the water and Christy's father shouted to the lad who was fishing: 'You'll never catch a pike there, lad. They're all hiding out of that hot sun. Go down to that cool stretch near the reeds and you might strike one.' The lad thanked him and moved to where a peninsula of reeds cast a paling of shadow on the water.

'Do you remember the first day you brought me here to fish?' Christy said. 'I'd just made my First Communion and you bought me a varnished yellow rod in two sections. To this day I can recall the taste of that varnish and the two scarlet bands on it like the red on a goldfinch.'

'I remember that day well. But it wasn't because of the fish you caught with the new rod that I remember it. It was because of something you said. It was a simple thing, but somehow this day brings it back to me.'

'I can't remember anything I said,' Christy smiled, rejoicing that their moods were merging. 'I remember the hook caught in the collar of my sailor-suit and you had to cut the piece out with your scissors. Is that what you're thinking of?'

'No, Christy, I'd forgotten that bit of it. It was of another thing I was thinking. You were staring up at the blue sky. There were puffs of cloud in it no bigger than your fist and you shouted: "Look, Father, the sky's receiving its First Holy Communion!" When I told that to your mother, God rest her, she thought it a strange remark for a child to make, and from that day she prayed you'd get a vocation for the priesthood.'

'Poor Mother! I trust in God I'll always be worthy of her prayers.'

His father paused and concealed a sigh. 'It's a hard life — the priest's life — though it might look easy on the surface and easy to a young man like you. But it's a lonely life. When you work on a railway and see priests coming and going you sense the loneliness in it. But when you chose the African mission fields you multiplied the loneliness.'

'One doesn't need to go to a foreign country to experience loneliness. Now that Mother's gone you yourself will have to fight against it.'

'A man who is content in his own mind will never fall foul of it. I mean it will not destroy him, drive him to drink. To be content with little is to be content with all.'

It disconcerted him to hear his father talk like this and he yearned to make a joke of it but the tone of his father's voice held him back.

A boy landed a roach and they saw it gasp and spread its red fins as the hook was wrenched from its mouth.

'And are you content, Father, as you are now?'

'No, Christy, I must confess I'm not. Times I miss your mother so much, I do not wish to live.'

'When a man hates life and wishes to die he's giving way to despair,' Christy said. 'He's wishing to throw away the gift of life God gave him. You'll have to fight against that, Father, and the best way is by getting back to your work in the garden, your fishing, and your day's shooting.'

The father shook his head: 'I have other plans and I may as well tell you what they are. I intend to apply for a change soon: a stationmaster's job in some quiet place that the railway company will select for me when one falls vacant. I'll make special mention of my home-place Monabeg. It's small and there'd be no great rush for it.'

'But I thought you'd automatically become stationmaster

here when old Wilson retires. Surely he hasn't more than a couple of years to go?'

'That's one reason why I want to apply for a change soon. I don't want to be offered Wilson's job. I would refuse it and that refusal might be the end of all offers made to me by the company. You know I never really cared for this place and it was for your mother's sake and later for Julia's and Mag's that I stayed here so long.'

He joined his hands and gazed at the water. The lad's spoon-bait plopped into it and the rings of water widened out, shook the water-lilies, and lipped against the bank.

'The more I think of it, Father, the more I am convinced you should stay here. Monabeg would be a step down for you. You'd have less pay.'

'I wouldn't need high pay now that my family is reared and my needs fewer.'

'But your dignity as a workman and your years of service demand that you be decently compensated.'

'The dignity that I want is not of the outside. I want the dignity that comes from a contented mind, from working in a place I think I'd love.'

'But then you'd be away from Julia and Mag and not be here to advise them in all their little affairs. Many a man would be glad to be near his married daughters. It'd be an unnatural thing to leave them if you can avoid it.'

'Have I not done enough for them, Christy? I sent them to boarding schools and I'd have sent them to the university if any of them had shown the least interest in that direction. What more could a man do or be expected to do for them? In a dozen years or so I'll have reached my retirement. Surely it wouldn't be selfish of me to live out those years in a place of my own choosing?'

'When a man has a family it seems to me he's no longer a chooser. He brought them into the world and he must not leave them to the world.'

'Do my daughters' husbands not take my place?'

'Julia's husband, to say the least, is not as steady as the rock of Peter. I saw him drink more than was good for him after the funeral.'

'You can't expect me to be a father to him?'

'You're his father-in-law — you must consider that.'

'I've considered everything, Christy. When I go away it'll teach them all to stand on their own feet and make their own way in the world. I'm not going to be a hand-me-down crutch for any of them to lean on. A change would do me good, I feel that.'

'You should think more on it. Look ahead to a time when you may be left alone in the world.'

'Many a man lives alone and never regrets it. And many a man is less alone when he is alone.'

'Men like that never knew the comforts of a home with a wife in it. It'll be a different tale with you.'

'No, Christy, we're all too afraid of change and that's why nothing is ever done. Moss grows on the standing stone. I'll have no regrets leaving here.'

'There are regrets buried deep in every man's heart that he knows nothing of. Loneliness will coax them from their hiding places. It'll be too late then to turn back,' Christy said. 'Have you thought about Alice in this matter?'

'She has no interests here that I know of and a change would do her good.'

'Listen, Father,' Christy pleaded, 'don't do anything rash. Wait for a year before applying for a transfer. You're upset over Mother's death and you're acting without thinking.'

His father explained that he had pondered it day and night and that he mustn't delay any longer. He pointed out that the railway authorities would take into consideration the death of his wife and recommend a change. He turned to his son and entreated him not to turn him back from the plan he had set his heart on.

'I'll only ask you this, Father. You'll not send in your request before I return to college. That's not much to ask.'

'Five or six weeks — that's all. I'll wait till then but I may tell you you'll see no change in my attitude.'

Another roach was landed and placed alongside others that were covered with cool leaves. The lad with the spoon-bait had caught nothing and with an impatient swipe of his rod he sent the silver bait flashing to the point of the reeds. He began to troll and suddenly the line tautened, and the rod bent and dabbed the water with great rapidity. There was a shout from the younger boys and they flung down their rods and gathered round the bigger lad.

'I can't hold him! I can't hold him! He'll break the rod on me,' the lad shouted as his line fizzed through the water. Christy's father jumped to his feet and seized the rod. He held it steadily in his strong wrists, playing the fish away from the reeds, reeling in or letting out a yard or two as he moved along the bank. The fish plunged deeply, the tip of the rod pierced the surface of the water, and the line whizzed out from the screeching reel. The fish turned suddenly and the taut line cut the water like a cheese-wire. The rod was given two quick jerks and the fish surfaced, leapt into the air, and disappeared again in a deep whorl of water, a whorl that sent waves lapping against the banks.

'Oh, he's a bruiser!' the boys yelled, and men and women out for a walk heard the shouts and drew near.

'Don't give him a slack inch! Hold him steady. Keep the bugger from the reeds!' some of the men advised.

He didn't seem to hear them. He kept his eye fixed on the line, gauging the direction the fish was taking. It headed up into a loop of the lake and he followed after it along the bank, lessening the strain on the line. Men and boys stumbled after him almost pushing him into the lake. Once he slipped, the line went loose and an 'Ah!' rose from the crowd. But as he quickly reeled in he found the fish still there, solid and heavy as a sunken log. The fish suddenly turned from the shallow water and darted in the direction of the reeds again. He held steadily against it, and once more it leapt from the water,

53

exhausting and choking itself with too much air. He reeled in, and as he felt the fight go from the fish he handed the rod to the lad who owned it.

'Now, lad, you finish him and do yourself proud.'

'He's too big for me, sir.'

'Go on, boy, there's not much fight in him. You hooked him well and now you must land him. Reel him in to the side and I'll help you to gaff him.' A man thrust a walking stick into his hand and as the fish slid in on its side towards the bank he gaffed it through the gills with the handle of the stick. A cheer went up as the enormous pike lay choking on the bank, its spiky fins raised like a fan. People pressed close and then stepped back, repulsed by what they saw. On its under jaw, swollen like a balloon they saw a huge pink growth, wrinkled and layered like fungus, and embedded in it was the glittering spoon-bait streaked with blood.

'Cancer!' somebody said and spat out.

'Pitch him in again! There's a smell from him. Phew!'

'Keep away from him, boys. You'll be smit. Don't lay a finger on him.'

'It's been an expensive walk for me,' said the man who owned the walking stick, and he tossed his stick into the lake and wiped his hands on the grass. The boys too flung their dead roach into the water, and watched them bob against the floating stick.

'Come away from it, Father,' Christy said.

'I'd like to take the hook from its mouth if the lad wants it. I'm not afraid of it.' He gazed at the sharp teeth, the frog-like mouth of the fish, and the bloated fungus under its jaws.

'I don't want the line, sir,' the lad said, cutting it off at the reel-head. The fins of the fish folded and then rose again as it thrashed the ground with its tail.

'A pity, a thousand pities, you can't carry him home in triumph. Ah, lad, you'd have something to talk about for the rest of your days.'

Boys were levering branches under the fish to push it into

the water but men pulled them away and told them not to pollute the lake with it.

'Away for a spade some of you and we'll bury it in good healthy clay,' someone said.

Flies gathered round the fish and on the grass where blood lay. Boys beat them off with branches until someone arrived with a spade.

'A pity, Christy, it has to end the way we'll all end. A pity for the lad's sake it didn't end with his photo in the paper and his great pike strung up beside him. That would have been a fine ending to his day's fishing.'

'He'll catch many another before he's much older.'

'But he'll remember this ugly one all his days. Strange how ugly things stick in the memory. Beautiful things we're more apt to forget.'

'You needn't let it root in your memory or worry any more about it,' Christy said, deeply aware now that a man so sensitive and so fatherly as his father would never be at peace if he ever lived away from his own family. He doesn't know his own nature. He'll have to be coaxed away from this foolish idea of leaving. They'll have to get together and save him from himself.

On their way from the lakeside Christy asked him to come round to Julia's for a while but he refused. He'd some things to see about at the station. But he might call round afterwards for an hour or so.

The station was deserted when he arrived there, the blinds drawn against the sun in the stationmaster's house. The stocks in the flower-beds that had their fill of sun all day were now shadowed by a brick wall and as he turned the hose on them spots of water fell on the warm wall and quickly dried out again. He now sprayed the ivy growing round a lamp standard and turned the hose on the dusty panes where it rattled like hailstones. The fine spray of water cooled and sweetened the air and he sat on a seat in the sun and lit his pipe, glad to be alone for a while.

The shining railway lines curved away in the distance and their wooden sleepers gave out a smell of tar. A goldfinch sang in the telegraph wires and its song was sweet and loud because of the surrounding quiet. That Sunday-quiet of the lines, the hum in the telegraph wires, and the pebbles at the ends of the platforms were the unchanging pattern of every station, he mused, and when the time would come for him to go away to a new station the only change he'd experience would be the change to a new set of people — and that he'd welcome, or welcome a thousand times if it were to Monabeg he was sent. There was nothing in this town to detain him, nothing that he'd miss, nothing that he'd regret. Alice was his only problem and that would not be a big one. There was no young man, as far as he was aware, that she had any interest in. Anyway she was only just eighteen.

When he had finished his pipe he set off through the deserted Sunday main street, past Richard Colton's office where the blue sun-bleached blind was askew at one corner, and the window ledge littered with dead flies and wasps. The brass letter-box was verdigrised, and the foot-scraper cluttered with straw and dusty scraps of paper. Laziness and neglect were written all over it. The very look of the place, he thought, would repel any respectable client. And since Julia married him the place had got steadily worse. Poor Julia who set out to reform him and straighten his tie! If only she had listened to advice!

On reaching home he saw her empty pram outside the open door. There was no one in the kitchen or in the parlour, but glancing outside he saw Richard in the garden, lying full length on the seat under the laburnum. His feet were crossed, a handkerchief covered his face from the sun, and his hands lay limp across his stomach.

'The captain taking his Sunday rest,' he said to himself and was surprised at that moment to see Richard sit up, rub his face with the handkerchief, and yawn.

'You'd think he knew I was talking about him,' he reflected and went into the garden.

'Ah, is that yourself,' Richard said, yawning. 'I'm enjoying your garden. Julia and Alice took the kids up the hill for a stroll and I tumbled down here to rest the old bones.'

'You didn't meet Christy. We were at the lake together and he left to call on you.'

'When he finds the port empty he'll steer round to Mag's. He hasn't many more weeks ashore now before he returns for his final cruise.'

'I trust in God nothing will come between him or us before he finishes.'

'Ah, man, nothing of a tornadial nature will happen. Next year his barque will sail into harbour with a full cargo of clerics.'

Tom looked fixedly at him and Richard sensing a rebuff dropped his jocular air and proceeded to praise the garden and the roses, exhorting him to exhibit the roses and not be leaving all the prizes to McGready of Portadown.

'At the moment I could get a prize for the weeds,' Tom said, not taken in by his flattery.

'If you started a nursery you could make it pay.' He gave a laugh and patted him on the shoulder. 'I'll soon have a nursery of another description. Julia, I suppose, told you she'll soon be in full sail again.'

'Yes, she mentioned she was expecting early next year. She'll have her hands full then.' He plucked off a few seeds from the laburnum and crumpled them between his fingers.

'By the way,' Richard exclaimed, as if the thought had just occurred to him, 'I met that slippery Bob Quinn coming from Mass this morning and I told him to give your wife's estate his full personal attention and not put it on the long finger.'

'And who asked you to do that?' Tom replied, his face reddening.

'I did it to oblige you. Some of these foxy lawyers can keep

57

a bit of business on a long hawser if you don't jib them up about it.'

'In any dealings I've had with Bob Quinn I've always found him satisfactory. I'm sorry you spoke to him of my affairs. And coming from Mass was no time to raise it. As far as I'm concerned there's no hurry on that little matter of Mary's estate. I'll call on him in the morning and tell him so.'

Richard drew deeply at a cigarette. Never before had Tom crossed words with him or asserted his opinion, and for the moment this sudden and strange retort puzzled him. He blew out the smoke loudly and flicked the ash from the cigarette on to the grass.

'It was on Julia's account that I spoke to Quinn. Unknown to me she approached you for a little loan and she's anxious to settle it with all possible speed. As you are aware we'd hate to live on charity.'

'I'm fully aware of that,' he answered with dry irony. 'But that doesn't give you the right to speak to any of my friends about my affairs.'

'Ah, here they come,' Richard said, relieved to hear the sound of Julia's voice hushing the crying child. Both went out of the garden to meet them.

Little Dick holding on to Alice's hand suddenly broke away from her and ran to his granda who immediately lifted him up in his arms. Julia was in black, and her black shoes and stockings showed traces of dust. She was in a hurry to get home and wouldn't wait for tea when her father asked her. Marie, the baby, was cross because of the heat of the sun; she was past her sleep and it was better to push on home at once and not delay any longer. She strapped the baby in the pram and taking little Dick from his granda's arms she placed him at the foot of the pram.

'Wait till I get them a few biscuits,' her father said and hurried into the house. When he came out again he saw that Richard and Julia and her two children had set off.

'They're in a great hurry today,' he said to Alice, who was standing on the road gazing after them.

'Everybody's cross today,' she said. 'And Julia complained to me when we were out that you haven't put your foot inside her door since Mother died.'

'A visit to Julia is a strain on me. She's ready to fly at me at the first opportunity. If I said the grass was green she'd probably say it was grey.'

'Her nerves are in a bad state. Even she does quarrel now and again, she misses you when you don't call. And what makes matters worse you visit Mag's, and that annoys Julia when she hears of it.'

They went into the kitchen and Alice prised off her shoes to enjoy the feel of the cold tiles under her feet.

'You'll call oftener with her — won't you, Father?' she entreated. 'It strikes me Julia needs you more than any of us. When I saw the cheap clothes her children were wearing my heart went out to her. I don't think Richard was a great catch after all. He's not half good enough for her. Oh, I'll not say what I think' — and she suddenly burst out crying.

'What's wrong, Alice pet?' he said, stroking her head, and sitting beside her on the sofa.

'Everything seems to be going wrong with Julia. It isn't that she complained about anything except about your lack of visits. But I feel all the time there's something deep on her mind.'

'Did she tell you she's …'

'She did, God help her. She's not getting much rest. Now that Mother's gone we must help one another all we can. And we must stick together. In a short while Christy will be going back to college.'

He paused, looking at the imprint of her feet on the tiles. 'A time may come, Alice, when someone may ask you to marry. I hope you'll pray for God's guidance in that direction and that you'll not let any loyalty to me stand in your way. I want you to know that you're not bound to me, hand and foot. If the worst came to the worst I could always manage with an old blade of a housekeeper.'

She raised her head and there were tears still in her eyes. 'Father,' she said, in an earnest voice, 'would you yourself not marry again?'

'Alice, child, what are you saying!' He turned away from her. 'What put that thought in your head!'

'I'm sorry, Father, for saying the like of that. God forgive me.' She stretched out her hand and touched his sleeve. 'I didn't know what I was saying. I said it without thinking. Everything has upset me today.'

'You're a good girl, Alice. You're the only one that's like your mother, God rest her.'

'You'll not hold what I said against me.'

'I said you were like your mother. I never held anything against her.'

With tears in her eyes she threw her arms round him and kissed him.

THE day Christy was returning to college his three sisters, his father and Aunt Brigid were gathered on the platform to see him off. Aunt Brigid, like her nieces, was dressed in black, but she hadn't Sergeant with her because the noise of the engine always drove him into a barking frenzy. To hide their sadness they were all talking with forced gaiety, and as the steam from the engine hissed loudly they had almost to shout to one another to be heard. Christy leaned out of the carriage window and tightly held his father's hand. With tear-filled eyes his sisters were smiling up at him, and Aunt Brigid, her cheeks red with excitement, was twisting a handkerchief in her hands and giving nervous little laughs.

'At Christmas, please God, I'll be back,' Christy said as the steam ceased hissing and the train lurched forward. His father continued to hold his hand and walked along the platform beside the crawling train.

'Don't apply for a change,' Christy pleaded. 'Wait till Christmas. That's my last wish for you.'

'It might be too late then. Pray that I do the right thing.'

'I'll do that, Father. But take my advice and wait. No melancholy and no brooding. Don't neglect the garden, the fishing rod, and the old gun. Goodbye and God bless.' The carriage had reached the end of the platform and he released his grip from his father's hand and continued to lean out of the window and shake his handkerchief.

The father stood waving till the train was out of sight, disturbed leaves and bits of paper settling between the rails. The arm of the signal lifted stiffly to the horizontal, and as he walked back along the platform the train whistled as it approached the road-arch at the edge of the town.

His three daughters and Aunt Brigid, grouped in the centre of the platform below the clock, waited for him. They dried their eyes and put away their handkerchiefs.

'Christy's had a sad homecoming and now a sad leaving,' Mag said when the father joined them.

'It won't be long spinning round to Christmas,' he answered.

'But it will only be to go away again — and then to Nigeria,' Julia put in. 'Oh, a pity he didn't go for the home missions. Surely he could leave his community and remain at home in his own country.'

'Christy has a sense of honour. He chose the African mission fields and it's there, please God, he'll do his life's work. It's not for us to say where he should go or where he shouldn't. He chose highly and we must sacrifice our wishes to his. A missioner is at rest and content in any country.'

'Our home is gradually breaking up. First Mother and then Christy,' Alice said and burst out crying.

The stationmaster passing into the booking-office touched his cap, smiled, and the father appealed to Alice to control herself. Aunt Brigid linked her arm protectively.

'Now, now, Alice,' the father said, 'if Christy didn't leave us you'd cry worse. We must be satisfied with things as they are.... I'll have to go now for I've a stack of work to do before the goods train lumbers along.' Pressing Mag's hand he whispered to her to go up to the house with Alice for a while. He glanced at the station clock, told Alice he'd be home about six, and then suddenly left them to join a porter who was sitting impatiently on the shaft of a piled-up truck.

Going out from the station Mag and Alice walked ahead, and Julia deliberately slackened her pace till the others were out of earshot and turning to Aunt Brigid she implored her to visit Father often as she was the only one that could cheer him up and keep him from fretting about Christy.

62

'It's nice of you to say that, Julia.'

'But it's true, Aunt Brigid, it's true' — and having reached Aunt Brigid's shop door she parted from her and overtook Mag and Alice, and all the way up the hill to the house she kept remarking how good Aunt Brigid was and how well black suited her and made her look like Mother.

Entering the house the three sisters sat in the kitchen. It was quiet and cool and nothing stirred in it but the whimper of the kettle at the side of the range. Julia sighed, took off her gloves, and placed one on top of the other. She opened her handbag and tapped her powder-puff below her eyes. 'Poor Christy's gone! The beginning of the end of another departure. And then there's Father! He's changed in his ways. He wasn't listening to any of us at the station and was glad to get rid of us.'

'Did you not see,' Mag explained, 'he had his work to attend to and our tears embarrassed him.'

'I feel there's something on his mind. Christy often remarked of late that Father might apply for a change.'

'It's sorrow that's on his mind, and that'll wear off in time,' Mag said. 'Every man talks about a change after some heartbreak.... From now on, Alice, you'll have to be more than good to him. He has no one but you.'

Alice began to cry again and Julia asked her what on earth she was crying for now.

'I don't know. It's about Mother and Christy and Father and myself. It's about everything and I can't help it.'

'So you're crying for yourself — is that it?' Julia said coldly.

'Maybe I am. I nursed poor Mother and I failed my senior certificate and now there's nothing worthwhile for me except I matriculate and go to the university. And I can't very well do that and leave Father. I'll be a housekeeper all my life.'

There was a long pause. Then Julia suggested she could ask Aunt Brigid to take her into the shop.

'And be a shop-girl!' Alice flared up, but seeing that that

63

retort might have hurt Mag she added quickly: 'Your husband works in a drapery store but nobody would dream of calling him a shop-boy. Your Joe is a draper's assistant. He has a responsible position while I'd be nothing only Aunt Brigid's help. I'd be only a servant-girl, weighing a few sweets for children, and taking Sergeant out for his daily walk.'

Julia and Mag disagreed with her. Aunt Brigid was well respected by everyone in the town. She had developed her business, and wasn't her shop up to date and a model of cleanliness? And as for money they were sure Aunt Brigid had as much as would buy up half the town at a moment's notice. Indeed, if either of them were free to learn the confectionery business they would leap at the chance. And then, again, if Father applied for a change it might be a change for the worse. He could be sent to the back of beyond where both of them would have time to spare to eat out their hearts in loneliness.

'But Father could be sent to Dublin,' Alice brightened, looking from one to the other for support.

'At Father's age he's more likely to be sent to some goat's shed of a station on the Galway line or exiled to the wilds of Donegal,' Mag countered.

'You'd have nothing to do then except to put out a saucer of milk for the cat or listen to the winds in the telegraph wires,' Julia added. 'Of course it's you we're thinking about all the time. We're foolish to be bothering our heads when you won't listen to sound advice. Aunt Brigid, I'm sure, would take you in with her and teach you the business if you were willing.'

'I'm grateful to you, Julia. I'll think it over. But I'd like to be something better than a confectioner's help.'

'We must work together,' Mag said. 'We must make Father content here and put the notion of leaving out of his head.'

'And, Alice, if you should ever hear him speak of that mad

64

notion you must tell us immediately,' Julia said, 'we must save your life for you. After all we've our husbands.'

'Yes,' Mag murmured, conscious that it was all she had.

Julia drew on her gloves and got to her feet. As she gazed at a few children playing hopscotch on the road outside she rested her fingers on the window-frame and noticed it was edged with dust.

'We must go now and not keep Alice from her work,' she said with feigned consideration. 'I'm sure she's dying to run a duster over this room.'

Left alone Alice felt an uncomfortable silence lie heavy about the house and she jumped to her feet immediately. She opened the window and the cries of the playing children flew in like a flock of birds and dispelled the loneliness. She would dust the house and have it shining from top to bottom for her father coming home. She wouldn't be a mope nor a shop assistant either. She would take her mother's place until such time as her father had other plans for her.

She entered the parlour where her mother had died. It had always frightened her a little but today she felt no fear. She felt that her mother was somewhere near her, helping her, and being pleased with her. The sun was shining into the room and a vase of roses which she had forgotten to water were shedding their petals on a round mahogany table. She dusted the room and opened the window. The corn was cut in the field outside and crows were perched on top of the stooks that stretched in parallel rows up the hilly field. 'Poor Mother would have got some comfort out of watching those black thieves,' she said to herself as she lifted the vase of wilted roses.

Upstairs in Christy's room she found nothing to tidy, not even a dead match in the firegrate. His bed, which he had always made himself — made, she told him, like a gaol-bird's — was now bare, the mattress rolled up and the blankets folded and covered with a newspaper.

The window in her own room was wide open and she saw

from it the weed-covered soil in the garden, the laburnum seeds on the seat and on the roof of the tool-shed, and a clump of unstaked Michaelmas daisies bowed and ravaged by wind and rain. Never had she seen the garden so unkempt. Maybe Julia was right about Father; maybe there was a change coming over him, maybe he was tired of this place and yearned to get away from it. With a hand to her cheek she gazed out at the cornfield where the shiny crows waddled over the stubble. Thoughts formed in her mind: her mother lying in bed plucking at a thread on the pink eiderdown; Christy looking strange without his collar, Aunt Brigid awkward in high-heeled shoes, and Mag lighting a candle at Our Lady's altar as she prayed her heart out for a child.

A shot startled her and she saw the rooks rise in all directions and one flap in the stubble and then lie still like an old rag. The cat pressed under the fence in terror and she ran downstairs to let her in.

At six o'clock when the Angelus bell rang out she saw her father approaching the house, his hat in his hand while he said the prayer, and under his arm his usual roll of magazines and newspapers that passengers had left behind in the train.

'You didn't find the house lonely,' he greeted her.

'I had too much to do to even think of being lonely.'

'That's the spirit! The two of us together will make a brave fist of everything.'

When he had washed and changed into old clothes she had the table laid for him and the cutlery shining like a high-class hotel. He ate in silence for a while, but this did not disturb her for she knew that sooner or later he would tell her what he was thinking without her having to wrest it from him. He pressed down a loose thread on the tablecloth just like Mother, and raising his eyes looked fixedly at her.

'I've been thinking all day that you should study for your matric. You could ask one of the nuns in the convent to give you an odd evening with your work.'

'And what then, Father?'

66

'Go to the university in Dublin or Belfast.'

'And what about you, Father?'

'I've told you before you mustn't think about me in this respect. Your life is just beginning and I want to give you a good education, something worthwhile, something nobody can take from you.'

He advised her to talk it over with Mother Agnes in the convent. It was better for her to have some profession that would make her independent of the whims and wiles of the world. If anything happened to him she would be able to make her own way. He had some money to give her and he would leave it in the bank in her name.

'Now if you run over to the convent and have a heart-to-heart talk with Mother Agnes I'll clean up these few dishes and put that garden in order.'

'But maybe, Father, I wouldn't be fit to pass the matric.'

'You mustn't say that to yourself, girl. Nothing can stop you only your own will. If you have the will to pass you'll pass any exam. It's only the nibblers and the weak of heart that are failures. Have confidence in yourself, and if you do that it will grow and develop the power to do things well. And you mustn't postpone things or keep putting them off — such things paralyse the will and make you slothful. Be off now to the convent. I'll be interested to hear Mother Agnes's verdict.'

'If she suggests that I enter the convent you'll be in a nice fix,' she said jokingly as she ran the comb quickly through her hair.

'Mother Agnes has some sense left in her head,' he laughed, brushing her coat collar. 'A nun the likes of you in a convent would be a heartscald to the community.'

She twirled her yellow beret round her finger: 'You wouldn't like to see me enter the convent because I'd have to have my black ringlets cut — isn't that it?'

'Go on, you tomboy,' he said, opening the door. She kissed him on the cheek and ran off. He watched her go down

67

the hill and when she stopped and waved to him he waved back and closed the door.

He rolled up his sleeves and began to wash the few dishes. He tried to sing but somehow he had no heart for it. All day Christy's parting words — Don't apply for a change till Christmas — had ransacked his mind like an insistent, unsummoned tune; and whatever work engaged him at the station the words beat upon him, distracting and enfeebling him. To quell their remorseless pressure he confronted them squarely on his way home and made a decision. He would let a month pass before sending in his application for a change. He would let the hare sit until then. The final decision would depend on Alice, for if she showed the slightest willingness to continue studying with the nuns and the nuns were keen to take her he realized that no personal reasons of his own should upset her. That was the best he could do, for he could very well be offered a change far away from suitable schools.

He shrugged his shoulders and went out to the neglected garden to do a spell of work before the autumn twilight slipped down upon it. He trimmed the hedge at the side of the tool-shed, raked dead leaves and seed-pods from the lawn, and piling all on a piece of corrugated tin set them alight. The smoke bushed up, and on reaching the hedge-top the evening wind unravelled it and sent it branching in all directions, through the holly tree and into the open windows of the house where he'd continue to smell it if he happened to waken during the night.

He staked and tied his clumps of Michaelmas daisies, turned over the soil and worked till darkness stole upon him and stars shone yellow like a bank of primroses. Two wild duck whirred overhead and he peered over the wire of the fence wondering if they had come to feed at the stooks of corn. But he could discern nothing except the stooks like a queue of shawled women and could hear nothing only the sound of a mother's voice calling home her children.

Alice returned late for she had gone round to Julia's after her interview with Mother Agnes.

'Well, Alice, and what's the verdict?' he asked as she took off her coat and beret.

'That I go back to the convent and do my senior certificate again. Mother Agnes thinks it would be a safer proposition than studying for the matric since none of the nuns could afford time off to coach me for that exam.'

'And would you like that?'

'I'd hate it, Father. I'd hate to go back among a crowd of girls who already knew I had failed.'

'She didn't make any other suggestions?'

'I mentioned doing a matric course by correspondence but she didn't think much of that. She wasn't enthusiastic about anything. She asked what way things were at home and if I returned to school would you get in a housekeeper. A housekeeper, if you please!'

'I hope you told her we could manage all right.'

'I did, but she wasn't convinced. She had everything round her finger as neat as a thimble. You'd have sworn she knew what we had for our breakfast and what time we got up.'

'It beats all how they get to hear everything and they behind closed doors.'

'She even suggested what Julia has already suggested to me: that I ask Aunt Brigid to take me into the shop. Perhaps she thinks I'm a dunderhead and would come a cropper in the exam again.'

'No, that's not it, Alice. She's thinking of me. She thinks if you give a hand to Aunt Brigid you'd have an opportunity of keeping house for me at the same time. That's what's in Mother Agnes's mind.'

Alice looked across at her father stretched out on the sofa, his finger prodding the bowl of his pipe. Red ashes fell from the grate and she saw them cool to grey on the lower bars.

'She should have told me that,' she said in a far-away

69

voice. She paused and gave a broken sigh: 'I'm only beginning to see into the heart of things.'

'What things, Alice?'

'I don't know. It's something I feel rather than know in
my mind. I mean Mother's death and that she's not in the
house any more.'

'If she was I'd know her wish for you — that you continue studying.'

Alice stroked the fallen ashes from the lower grate with
the poker. 'I don't know what to do, Father. Maybe I should
ask Aunt Brigid to take me in with her for a while?'

'If that's your wish, Alice, then I'm agreeable.'

6

THE following evening Aunt Brigid, influenced by Julia, arrived in person to invite Alice to learn the confectionery business under her guidance. With her she carried a pound tin of tobacco for Tom; she usually handed it to him at the wholesale price, but this time she presented it to him as a gift to celebrate the occasion of Alice's first job. It was true her mother would have had a higher ambition for her than a shop-girl but then circumstances alter our desires and we must content ourselves with the lower when the higher is beyond our grasp.

Sergeant wasn't with her; he had injured a paw on the door-scraper and she decided that a rest on the rug at home would be better for his constitution than hobbling through the streets on three legs. Her cheeks were more flushed than usual, for she was carried away on an amiable storm of managing and suggesting both for her own house and theirs. Tom and Alice were to have dinner with her daily for, as she explained, it would be as easy to make dinner for three as for one.

'No, no, Brigid, I cut the rope there. I call a halt and lower the signals. We couldn't do that!' Tom exclaimed, aware of a trespass on his privacy, a disruption of his easy routine. 'That would be imposing on good-nature,' he added. 'No, Brigid, that would never do at all. You may delete that from the agenda.'

'With Mary gone from you all, I thought I could make up for her loss in some little way.'

'You're too good, too thoughtful,' he tried to say with

emphasis, hoping that it would end her managing suggestions for the time being.

She was silent for a moment, and fearing lest she had taken affront at something he had said he interjected tenderly: 'You have plenty to do in your shop without taking in two lodgers like us for full board without residence.'

'Tom, dear, I'd never think of it in that light. Indeed, I wouldn't.'

'I know, I know,' he said, waving his pipe and nodding his head.

Alice made coffee for her, and later when she was going home she handed her a paper bag full of chop bones for Sergeant and left her as far as the main street of the town.

On the following Sunday afternoon on his way to visit his wife's grave he called in to her shop for a box of matches. He told her where he was going, and she decided that nothing would afford her more pleasure than to accompany him and leave the usual selling of Sunday ice-cream to Alice who had developed a real flair for that end of the business.

Their road to the graveyard paralleled the railway embankment where burnt patches of grass were still smouldering, Tom having set them alight yesterday to destroy the encroachment of weeds and whins. Each side of the road had dusty hedges clustered with red berries and streaked with straw where the harvest carts had brushed against them. Motor cars passed frequently, lifting the dust from the road and flittering the fallen beech leaves like a scurry of mice.

'My costume will be grey by the time I get back. Nothing shows up the dust like black,' Brigid said, closing her eyes against the dust and feeling the draught of air left by a speeding car. She linked his arm tightly and kept close to the hedge. He blushed, feeling as clumsy and self-conscious as a schoolboy out with his first girl.

'Do you feel any cobwebs tickling your face?' she asked. 'Maybe it's only my imagination or maybe there's a stray

72

hair hanging from under my hat but I do feel something.'
She halted and held up her face for inspection.

'I see nothing,' he said, giving her face a quick glance.

'But I see something on yours,' she smiled. 'Wait a
minute, Tom.' She took out a lace-edged handkerchief.
'There's just the teeniest fly, or maybe grit, at the corner of
your eye.'

'It makes no odds,' he said gloomily and rubbed it with the
back of his hand.

'No, you didn't get it.' And as she stood on tiptoe and edged
the speck away with her handkerchief the perfume from the
handkerchief dispelled the dry smell of the dusty road.
'There,' she said triumphantly, displaying a pin-head of a
fly on the corner of her handkerchief. 'And there,' she said
again, fluffing from her fingers a cobweb thread she had
picked from his tie.

On reaching the graveyard he sighed with relief and
hurried across the road to the gate where a yard of chain
held the gate open in the middle to admit persons in single
file and keep out stray cows.

After visiting his wife's grave she led him to an elaborate
structure of iron bars, pointed like fleur-de-lis, that enclosed
the family plot where her father and mother and her twin
brothers lay at rest. 'I'll have to get it spruced up a bit,' she
declared, noting the flakes of rust on the iron bars and the
marble slab greened and verdigrised with damp. 'Maybe,
Tom, I should get those iron bars removed altogether. What
do you think? Somehow they're not Catholic looking.' He
agreed with her, and on their way out of the cemetery she
again linked his arm as they faced the low autumn sun that
was now revealing the rainbow colours on the spiders'
threads that looped the hedges. The shadows of the trees
lengthened on the road, the telegraph wires hummed above
on the railway embankment, and swallows gathering on
them fidgeted and filled the air with end-of-summer queru-
lousness.

'I don't believe, Tom, I've ever seen such a crop of haws. They're as glossy and red as blood.'

'My mother used to call those berries Christ's tears. She used to say there was a sermon written on every hedge in Ireland. The red berries on the thorned hedges reminded her of Christ's agony and the purple sloes on the blackthorn reminded her of His blood upon the cross. But she said it was a pity they didn't come during Lent and not in the drop of the year.'

'I'll always remember that, Tom,' Brigid said. 'A thorn hedge will never be the same for me again. Your mother must have read a lot.'

'No, she didn't. But she thought a lot.'

The pressure on his arm increased. What he was saying was drawing her close to him, and he regretted now his moment of confidence. She waited for him to tell her more about his mother but to her regret he relapsed into his usual silence.

She sighed and walked slowly, telling him about her own father and mother and Mary and the twin boys, and how they used all set off on Sunday in the trap, the pony's bell ringing and the harness shining, and how they had permission to drive through the demesne and have a picnic overlooking the lake that at this time of the year would have a swarm of leaves floating at one corner. Now ponies and traps had almost disappeared from the roads and from the chapel gates of a Sunday; people had cars and the saddler in the town was gradually going into the hardware line.

'The old times were quiet times,' she sighed. 'I was the baby so to speak of our family and they are all gone but me. Mary was ten years older than me but we never quarrelled with one another. She was very patient and I'm sure I was obstreperous at times and needed a spank or two. Now she's gone like the rest. We're not a long-lived family.'

Out of politeness he had to make some comment and he remarked that in every family there was always one that lived long.

74

'Maybe so,' she said. 'Maybe so. But I don't know if I'd care to have a long spell of life. It's lonely to be left alone.'

They had reached the new red-roofed houses at that end of the town, and conscious of the people gazing out from their windows he disengaged her arm from his by fumbling in his pocket for his pipe and filling it slowly with tobacco. He'd have to be careful, he thought, for if some playboy saw them linked arm-in-arm it wouldn't be long till some insulting remark would be scribbled up on the wall of the Gents in the station.

'This is where I leave you,' he managed to say calmly. 'I have to pay a call on Mag and I think I see her waiting for me at the window. Alice will be glad to see you for she likes to have Sunday evenings free to go to the cinema or a dance in the parochial hall.'

'I don't hold much with pictures on a Sunday. Better if they'd go to devotions in the chapel than gallivanting to the pictures.'

'Sure, Brigid, they can do both if they've a mind to.'

His answer surprised her, and not wishing to mar her afternoon she replied: 'I suppose, Tom, you're right. You have the experience to speak as you do. The young need a bit of freedom once in a while.'

'If you cage them up too much they become stubborn and sulky, with faces on them like a clap of thunder. Better a silent house than a fractious child.'

'We've had a pleasant afternoon — haven't we, Tom? There's nothing soothes the nerves like a visit to the grave-yard. And nothing would please Mary better than to know we visited her grave together. Call next Sunday if you're going.'

'I'll do that,' he said boldly, but as he strode up to Mag's, his hat in his hand, he was determined not to visit the grave-yard on a Sunday if he could avoid it.

Mag met him at the door: 'You're pale, Father. You haven't a headache?'

75

'No, no, it's the screwing up of my eyes against that sun that's made me pale, if I am pale.'

'Joe's lying down for a bit. He'll get up as soon as he hears you're in.'

'Let the lad rest. Mag, girl, fill me up a good glass of cold water. I've a thirst on me like the scorch of a blowlamp.'

She brought him the glass, and as he drank it noisily at one go her eyes brightened with a secret joy.

'That's the best thing they have in this town — good clear water, water with the flavour of a deep spring.' Having made that pronouncement the repugnant image of the cancerous pike rose involuntarily in his mind, and he shook his head to efface it and stared admiringly at his daughter.

'You're looking extremely well, girl.'

'I feel well, thanks be to God.' She unwound a length of white wool from the ball on her lap and began her knitting again. Then she held the knitting aloft on the needle, gave it a quick glance, and burst out: 'I've great news for you, Father! Yesterday evening the doctor told me I was ...' With her head lowered she rolled up her knitting. 'You're the first I've told it to. I had hoped to see you after first Mass this morning but you must have gone to a later one.'

For a moment he stared at her uncomprehendingly, then he jumped from the sofa, lifted her bodily in his arms and carried her round the room. 'Thanks be to the good God for that bit of news!' — and he kissed her on the cheek and planted her back on the chair.

'Well done, Joe!' he shouted up the stairs. 'Well done, my bonny lad. Come down out of that till I drink your health. Have you anything in the house, Mag?'

'Nothing only cooking sherry.'

'I'll take a dram of it even if it poisons me.'

Joe came down, a newspaper in his hands, his hair tousled and his collar loose. 'Such a racket! I thought it was Richard auctioning the house over our heads.'

76

'Mag told me the good news. Spruce yourself till we drink to the good health of what's to come.'

He sat down on the sofa and recalling to himself the story he had heard of a barren twin he assured himself that it was an old wives' tale and dismissed it for ever from his mind.

'Man, Joe, if you had a decent job now or a shop of your own you'd be on top of the world. Why don't you suggest to your boss to buy a car and let you peddle tweed about the countryside? There's money in that side of the business and better health than stuck eternally in that ill-lighted shop — that mausoleum of dark drapery.'

'I've never felt better since that holiday you gave us at Blackrock.'

'By all events the sea air has done you both a world of good,' he said, laughing mischievously.

'There's a paragraph in the Sunday paper might interest you,' Joe said, handing him the paper and slapping the paragraph with the back of his hand. 'Seizure of poteen in Monabeg. Isn't that your home-place?'

As Joe fixed the tie round his collar he watched him read, the paper shaking in his hands.

'I went to school with two of them that's caught. I did that.'

'Have they no shame in them to be making stuff that every priest has condemned?' Joe winked at Mag.

'I'll say this in defence of the culprits. There's no other place in the country where they make it as pure as in the islands of that lough. Do you know that St Patrick made his bed in one of the same islands. I've done pilgrimages to it in my time.'

'I suppose you'll be telling me he bequeathed them the secret of illicit distilling.'

'I will not. Like many of the Irish saints St Patrick was too ascetic, too fond of praying and fasting, to think of hilarious living. But I'll say this: if the good man had had a bottle of the Monabeg stuff hid in his garments it would have

77

saved the poor soul from many a foundering — I'm sure of that.'

'His fasting and praying didn't leave much of a mark on them heathens.'

'Ah, Joe, if I were back among the same heathens I'd bless every day I lived. I would indeed.'

His voice fell as he talked to them of the little place with its river and its loughs. With startling vividness he marshalled his sundered memories of it, turning now this colour and that like a child with a kaleidoscope. There was Monabeg railway station, no bigger nor longer than a few shop fronts, where he began his apprenticeship under a lame station-master. There were no flower-beds or roses at the ends of the platform; there were plain red brick walls with fresh mortar, and the stationmaster's house had a yellow chimney pot with a drip of tar on it like a sooty crack. But there were trees around it, a rookery, and to see those branches bend and swing in the windy months of March, and the nesting birds unperturbed by the pother was to learn a lesson about creation every time you lifted your head from your ledger and gazed out the office window. There was a demesne there, too, and he told them of a windy October night when branches were wrenched off trees and the moon flying through the tatters of the sky he, and his brother that's dead, with a wide net and two quiet dogs bagged thirty rabbits; and if the gamekeeper had come on them that night, so mad were they with excitement they would have flung him into the lake. And the lough too was a storm of wild duck in October: many a night he and a man by the name of O'Hara lay in a flat-bottom boat among the reeds, and with two hammerless guns banging till the barrels were hot they had a tough job rowing home with their cargo against the stream. There was cockfighting, too; his brother reared and fought them, and sold clutches of eggs to men in the far states of America where their strain is still talked of to this day.

'But all that's behind me now, Joe. We go away. The

78

road does not lead back. We follow desires and the desires elude us.'

'No, Father, that's not true. Look what I have prayed for and got,' Mag said.

'The flesh and the spirit are faithful allies on that score. Isn't that so, Joe? Prayer builds itself on nature.' They laughed loudly at that till Joe got him started again on Monabeg.

The sun had set when he was leaving them, and as they stood at the door commenting on the garden he had laid out for them the wing-rush of starlings heading for the spire attracted their attention.

'Rain's not far off,' he said, 'the starlings are making for the roost before their usual time. And I think I'll make for mine because Alice will be waiting for me and wondering what's keeping me.'

As he shut the gate and waved his hat to them Joe told Mag that her father was a lonely man and that his heart was not in the station beyond, in spite of all the care he lavished upon it. At the turn of the road he waved again, pleased to see them still standing at the door.

In order not to pass Brigid's shop he took the by-road home, the road he took with Christy on his return last June. The streets were quiet, the sun-shadows gone from them, and a thin mist flowing in from the fields and piling up in alleyways where people were now closing their doors against the sudden chill.

His own door was open, the table laid for tea, and the rattle of crockery coming from the scullery.

'Alice, come quick. Great news!' he called out, and his lower lip hung loose when he saw Brigid sail out from the scullery with a plate of salad in each hand.

'A surprise for your tea,' she said. 'I got a present of two lovely trout and I wished to share them with you.' She noticed the dashed expression on his face and she asked quickly what was the good news he had to announce.

'Oh, it was a bit Mag's husband showed me in the paper about a seizure of poteen in my home-place,' he said and gave her a summary of what he had read.

Thinking he was glad to hear of the seizure of poteen she began to condemn the making of it and lambaste those who encouraged them to make it, and she hoped the whole pack of them would get gaol instead of the customary fine.

'If the magistrate had a dram of it in him at the trial he would neither fine them nor gaol them.'

'If you were caught hob-nobbing with the likes of them ruffians it would cost you your job. It would indeed.'

'It would be the excitement to be out on the windy lough with them that would attract me. Now and again there rises in a man an urge to break out.'

'I'd like to see you with that urge in you,' she said, pouring out the tea, and explaining she had put the trout to cool on the outside window-sill after she had cooked them. 'They taste better with salad when they're cold.'

'They taste sweet,' he said after sampling a forkful. 'And where's Alice did you say?'

'The two McKenna girls called for her to go to the pictures. I told them it would suit them better to go to devotions first.'

To her surprise he agreed with her, and that emboldened her to attack the selfishness of the young girls that were going nowadays, and as he remained silent during this tirade she veered off to Alice and praised her management of the shop during her visit to the graveyard. He nodded and interjected an 'Aye' and 'Good' in an effort to keep her talking, for if he let her talk the piece out now she might go home early and give him an opportunity to read a few chapters of a book before bedtime.

After the meal, and in order to manœuvre her speedily from the premises he dried the dishes for her despite her vehement protests, and when they had finished, to his dismay she sat in front of the range staring defiantly at the purring cat that had finished the leavings of the trout.

'What about Sergeant?' he asked, and she started as if he had read her thoughts. 'He'll not be fretting and you away so long?'

'Maybe now that you mention him I should toddle off. You don't know the great comfort he is to me, Tom. Before I got him I dreaded going into the silent house at night. But now he's always there to greet and comfort me.'

To atone for any abruptness or ungraciousness about her sharing of the trout he arose to get her a bunch of his late-flowering roses.

The rain was falling, the garden was dark and wet. He called to her to switch on the light in the parlour, the light that shone out on the garden, as it would enable him to see what he was doing. He pricked his fingers a few times as he snipped off the finest blooms, and shaking the rain from them he smelt their perfume, rejoicing with pride in his own cultivation.

'What a bouquet for this time of year,' she exclaimed, 'and not a brown speck on any of the leaves!' She held them against her breast. 'How well yellow roses look against black.'

'The same roses would look well against anything,' he said in haste, unconscious of any satire.

'Well, well,' she said dolefully, 'you're not called honest Tom Magee without good reason.'

'Did I say anything out of tune?'

'Oh, nothing,' she answered, rubbing off the shining raindrops that had dribbled on her jumper.

Embarrassed, and not wishing to revert to the unwitting retort, he strove to make amends by offering her an old umbrella of Mary's and proposed to leave her home and maybe meet Alice coming from the pictures.

They set off together down the hill, she linking his arm, he holding the umbrella on which the rain rattled like bird-pecks. The lighted windows of the houses reflected on the wet road, and all the doors were closed and no one abroad.

At the bridge over the stream the footpath narrowed, and becoming aware of the cushiony softness of Brigid's arm against his he hurried her breathless across the bridge and up to the deserted main street where the lamp outside the police barracks stretched a spine of light on the wet road. Past the parochial hall they went, hearing the noise of the dancers and the music issuing loudly as the door opened to admit a few latecomers.

'A penny for your thoughts,' she said. 'You haven't spoke a word since we left the house.'

'I'm keeping an eye on the puddles.'

'Mary loved you for your quietness.'

'I suppose you heard the good news about Mag,' he tried to say casually. 'She's expecting.'

'She is not!' she cried, halting him in the street. 'God be praised!'

Her noisy excitement embarrassed him and as he took her arm to move off she unreeled a litany of praise. 'God never closes a window but He opens another. It's great news, great indeed. It's a pity no man ever appealed to me or I would have married years ago. Somehow I always thought them rough and headstrong and I was always afraid of being hitched all my days to some drunk that would upset the peace of the home. I always liked quiet men. Poor Julia, I often think, deserved better than she got. But we'll not discuss that amidst such joy — we'll not indeed.'

They reached the house and shaking the rain from the umbrella he glanced down at the cinema with its line of cars shining wet in the lights from the entrance. Sergeant barked on hearing the key in the door. 'Now, now, Sergeant,' she called soothingly. 'Hush, hush, do you not know your friends yet?' She invited Tom inside for a while, for Alice would probably call on her way from the pictures for the loan of an umbrella or a mackintosh.

The interior was snug, the range shining, coloured rugs on the floor, and a little square of glass covered with flowered muslin looked into the shop. She immediately moved over an armchair towards the fire, hung her coat on a hanger, arranged the roses in a cut-glass vase and pinned one to her breast.

Since the day Alice had come to help in the shop it had given her time at last to do a bit of cleaning and she now drew forth a box of photographs she had discovered, and placed them on Tom's knee. They were in bundles clasped with tape. There were photographs of himself and Mary on their wedding day; Christy in his clerical clothes; Julia and Richard and their two children, and one of Richard standing at his car with one hand resting proudly on the bonnet; there was a picture of Joe and Mag standing at the door of their new house; a photo of the family plot in the cemetery, and even one of the station embankment with the name of the station printed in daffodils; there were many of Sergeant and one of himself holding a large pike in each hand.

'An interesting collection, Brigid,' he said. 'There's one of Mary I like very much — could I have it?'

'That's not Mary,' she laughed, sitting on the arm of his chair. 'That's me. We were very like one another at one time.'

'You were indeed,' he said, glancing politely at it again before placing it back in its accustomed bundle.

A motor honked outside and Brigid went to the door and saw cars moving off from the cinema through the rainy streets. People hurried by on foot and boys called out to girls, and then Brigid's voice was heard ringing out: 'Alice, yo-ho!'

A few minutes later Brigid with Sergeant in her arms stood at the door to see Alice and her father move off, the father's arm around his daughter's waist, and the umbrella poised above them. The last car hissed along the wet road. One by one the lights in the cinema went out, and hugging Sergeant tightly she closed the door against the rain-chilled air.

THE following Sunday instead of going to the graveyard he went to the lakeside to watch the lads fishing, and on the succeeding Sunday he took out his own rod for the first time since his wife's death. He fished for an hour or so but somehow his heart was not in it and after catching a few roach he folded up his gear and left early. He had intended to call on Julia on his way back but some impulse veered the intention from his mind and without considering it further he arrived home. The house was silent, and Alice had left a note on the table to say she had gone cycling with the McKennas.

After stowing away his rod on top of the wardrobe he sat down to smoke, and immediately his conscience about Julia began to disquiet him and he realized he would never ease his mind unless he went at once to her and paid her a visit, no matter how short it might be.

He grew to detest visiting her. He could always get on well with Mag and Joe, but with Julia and Richard he never felt relaxed, never could make a simple remark without pondering on it beforehand. For some reason Julia always crossed him, and her fits of unreason always floundered and perplexed his spirit for days on end. She didn't intend to do it, but then there were some people with whom it was impossible to carry on polite conversation. Idle talk always flowed into dangerous whorls of argument, and it was better for both of them, he excused himself, that they saw little of one another. Not that he didn't love her: he did. He wished everything good for her and Richard and nothing ill to befall them, and he sorrowed as much over Richard's periodic misfortunes as Julia did. He couldn't, as a father, turn his back on what he had brought into the world, and no matter how much she disappointed him it was his duty not to isolate himself completely from her.

As he walked slowly up the concrete pathway to her house he saw the doors wide open on the empty garage, and though he half expected and half hoped they had gone for a drive he rang the door-bell timidly, and, presently, to his dismay heard someone descend the stairs. It was Julia herself: she had been putting Marie down for an afternoon nap in her cot; Richard was out in the country on a bit of business and she was alone except for little Dick who was sprawled on the sitting-room floor with his toy engine.

She took her father's hat, and little Dick on hearing his voice threw down the engine and ran to him with outspread arms. Julia, flustered at the unexpected visit, began tidying up the room, folding up the scattered sheets of newspaper, lifting Marie's heap of clothes where she had undressed her on the hearth-rug, and, while excusing herself for the state of the place, rearranged the sleeves of a frock that were inside out, lifted white socks that were soiled at the toes and placed all in a neat pile on top of the sideboard. Dick, in his granda's arms, explored the orifices of his ears and began to pull at the fine hairs that grew there until his mother told him to behave himself. He drew out his granda's watch that hung by a chain to his waistcoat, and placing it to his own ear he smiled attentively, held it to his granda's ear and called out to his mother to come and hear the tick-tick. The granda said he had something nice for him and he took out a thin bar of chocolate he had got from the slot-machine at the railway station. Placing the child on the floor he slowly peeled the silver paper from the chocolate.

'You shouldn't bring him a messy thing like chocolate,' Julia protested, going for a towel to tie under the child's chin.

'I forgot, Julia, I forgot. Next time I'll bring him butterscotch. I must remember that,' he said apologetically, sensing that Julia wasn't in a good mood.

He waited for her to speak again, but she sat with a hand to her cheek frowning at the child. How to make compassionate contact with her he didn't know, and already he could feel a tangling spirit of discord come between them.

Melted chocolate streamed from the corners of the child's mouth and he held up his brown fingers and smiled with full-rounded cheeks.

The granda looked away from him to the window, endeavouring to take Julia's eye from the child.

'That's great news about Mag,' he ventured.

'Hm, God help her, she doesn't know what's before her!'

There it was again, the growing hardness, and he found himself chastising her: 'Julia, Julia, for the love of God don't be so cynical! Try and face the world more brightly, more patiently.'

'How can I!' she cried and flung her arms wide with a despairing gesture. She would dearly love to know what she had to be bright about. Hadn't she two children and another unfortunate on the way, and wasn't her poor Richard hanging around with a set of card-players and gamblers who imposed on his good-nature — a set he had to hob-nob with for the good of his business. And it was a strange thing to say, but it was true, that a set like that could extend his business. They were regarded, if you please, as the highly respectable.

She finished her outburst with a long sigh that almost broke into a sob. And then there was great silence in the room and into it there dropped like pebbles the pout-pout of his pipe between his lips. The child looked up and swallowed audibly the last flavours of the chocolate.

'And then there's the extra worry about yourself,' she pursued.

'Worrying about me?' He took the pipe from his lips and looked puzzledly at her. 'I've fine health, thanks be to God, and myself and Alice are blazing along in champion style.'

'That's not what I'm referring to, and right well you know it. Your desire to apply for a change from this town is what vexes me. Not knowing when you may do it is a living torture to me. And furthermore you won't give any of us the satisfaction of knowing what's going on in that mind of yours.'

'I don't know myself what's going on in it.'

'The last letter I got from Christy he inquired if you had mentioned to any of us your idea of going away.'

'Mmmm,' the child said, wiping all his fingers at once on the towel, and then wincing away from the firm wipe his mother applied to his mouth, a wipe that made his skin burn.

'I haven't applied for any change.'

'But will you? — that's the point. No tantalizing equivocation, please.'

'That I do not know,' he answered quietly.

'There!' she exclaimed, and her voice, thin and shrill, made the child stare in sudden fright.

That he would even think of applying for a change was beyond her reason and didn't make sense. Hadn't he everything here a man could wish for? He had an easy pleasant job at the station beyond; he wasn't hard wrought except when he took it upon himself to make a flower-garden on the embankment — a thing he wasn't paid for or even thanked for. And hadn't he his family around him and didn't everyone in the town respect him and have a good word for him? And wasn't Alice nicely situated with Aunt Brigid, and if she behaved herself in the right way it could all happen that a day would come when her name would appear on the signboard above the window: Alice Magee: Confectioner and Tobacconist. To drag the girl away from such a prospect, or even to make her one jot dissatisfied with her job, would be a sin crying out for vengeance.

'I'm not making her dissatisfied,' he defended. 'Alice made her own choice, and if she has expressed regret to anyone about it she has done so off her own bat. All the

87

complaint I've ever heard from her was about her pay. She thinks, and I agree with her, she isn't paid enough.'

'If Alice bides her time she'll get a nice hansel.'

'Live horse and you'll get grass.'

'Of course there's another aspect of the matter we've forgotten. It's quite possible Aunt Brigid might take it into her head to get married.' She paused and studied her father. 'The man that would get her would be fortunate. She's attractive for one thing and she has plenty of money forby.'

'If she married I hope she'll be lucky in her choice. I wish her well,' he said evenly.

The child had climbed on to his knee and had taken out of his pockets a ring of keys and rosary beads and had thrown them on the floor. His mother and granda didn't seem to be aware of his rummaging until he discovered another bar of chocolate, and immediately his mother took it from him and told him he had had enough and that he must go out and play and leave Granda in peace. She lifted the articles from the floor and dragged the reluctant Dick to the front door and put him outside.

'Let me in,' he said and thumped at the door. 'I wanna play with my granda.'

'Maybe, Julia, you should put an extra jersey on him. It gets cold quickly at this time of the year.'

'Don't worry yourself — the same child is as hard as nails.'

She saw him glance at the window and then lower his eyes as he slowly refilled his pipe. What he was thinking about her home, her role as mother, she would dearly love to know. If only she could rouse him! But that slow shredding of the tobacco and the slow ceremonial movement of his fingers told her he was beyond her control.

She hated to live in an indefinite world. She always wanted things straight and clear as daylight, and wished for no mystery to exist among members of the same family. At times she felt that her father was beyond caring how they lived or on what they lived. For instance, since his arrival, he

88

hadn't asked about Richard, and she supposed he just didn't care what way he was. If he was smoking his pipe now in Mag's he'd behave differently. At least Mag never found anything to challenge him with or anything in him to criticize. But then that was Mag — meek and mild like a leaf on a tree. It's well Christy didn't leave him in Mag's hands — a bad job she'd make of it. Indeed, a bad job she herself was making of it. But, then, how on earth could she organize a man like her father who was so detached and so cold, and, since Mother's death, had grown a bit odd. She recalled the evening in the garden when she had approached him for the loan of money. She had certainly roused him that evening, but she had also stirred up a hatred for him that she had to pray against when she found it settling insistently on her heart.

Her father got up from his chair and went to the window. He was getting restless now, she thought. He was ready to go but she'd just detain him and make him stay in spite of himself.

She put the kettle on the stove.

'Don't be making any tea for me, Julia.'

'You're not thinking of going, surely. Just a cup of coffee, I'll not be two ticks.'

From the window he saw the child pulling at a spade that stood upright in a dug-up circle of sods. There was rust on the blade of the spade, evidence that it hadn't been used for days.

'By the way, Father, Aunt Brigid tells me that when she calls at the house, as she always did in Mother's day, you are seldom at home now.'

'Ah, good boy, he's got it out at last,' he said, smiling at the child who had wrenched the spade from its moorings.

Determined not to be sidetracked Julia repeated what she had said and added: 'Where do you be? You certainly don't give me much of your precious time.'

Without turning from the window he told her in a casual

manner that he went out for a shot on a few occasions and went round to Wilson, the stationmaster, for a game of chess.

'The chess is a new departure,' she commented.

He could hear the cups rattling noisily on the tray behind him.

'I do hope you're not avoiding Aunt Brigid so as to make her displeased with Alice and give you a virtuous excuse to apply for a change of station.'

He still did not move from the window. His back was to her and he felt an angry race of blood flush his face. He must be careful, must try to control himself.

'If you're avoiding her say so and I'll tell her not to bother calling at a house where she's not wanted,' Julia pursued.

'Surely, Julia, you wouldn't hurt your aunt's feelings like that.'

'And what, pray, are you doing? You're hurting her, but not in a direct and manly way. You do it in a slinking way. Surely it's better to kill the heart at one stroke than to kill it by inches the way you're doing.'

He didn't reply and pretended to be more interested in the antics of the child in the garden as he straddled the spade and rode it over the lawn. The child was free and happy, while he himself, it seemed, was trapped by an implacable judge whom he could not circumvent except by giving place to anger.

'Ah, you rascal,' he said, putting his head close to the window pane. 'That's a fine horse you've got.'

Julia shook her head and poured out the coffee.

'Thanks, Julia,' he said, subduing his real feelings and sitting down. 'I'm glad of this.'

'I thought you would as long as you have nowhere else to go. At the same time I think you should drop in to see Aunt Brigid. You were always a great stay-at-home man and she might think it queer at not finding you at home the last few times she called. After all, Father, she's Mother's only sister.'

'I know she is.'

'Aunt Brigid is pleasant company. Indeed I've heard people praising her companionship with you already. "Mother's perfect deputy," one said to me recently.'

'People talk and jabber to no purpose.'

'Would there be any harm in visiting Mother's sister?'

'None in the least. It's just that I desire the company of men,' he said and to her surprise held out his cup for more coffee.

'So then I take it that you are deliberately avoiding her.'

'I hear a car,' he said. 'That must be Richard back.' Getting up he glanced out of the window. 'I was right. It's him.'

Richard came in carrying little Dick in his arms. He shook hands with his father-in-law and turned to Julia: 'It beats all you hadn't a coat on the child a day like that. The grass is cold and even a goat has the instinct not to lie down on it at this time of the year.'

'I didn't know it was as cold as all that,' Julia said.

'Sure you know the grass is wringing wet with dew these mornings.' He looked across at Tom: 'It's a wonder a knowledgeable man like you didn't advise her.'

Julia eyed her father, waiting for him to say that she wouldn't listen to advice, but her father forced a smile and without looking in her direction said cheerfully: 'The last time I looked out the window the child was having the time of his life riding on the spade. Galloping around like that would ward off any cold.'

'I hope you're right.'

'Don't be fussing about nothing, Richard,' Julia said and glanced tenderly towards her father. She poured Richard out a cup of coffee and took little Dick in her lap beside the fire. He was as warm as toast except for his legs, and as she rubbed them with her hands and picked bits of grass from his wrinkled knees she heard Richard announce that he had bagged the sale of two farms on his little outing.

'Not bad sailing for a Sunday,' he said, clapping his hands. He took a pipe from the mantelpiece and unscrewed the shank. 'And yourself: how does the old vessel sail?'

'Sweetly enough, thank God, sweetly enough.'

From upstairs came Marie's awakening cry. Richard nodded towards Julia and she put little Dick on the hearth-rug and went up.

'Shush, Marie,' she said, entering the bedroom, 'Mamma's here,' and she saw the child standing up in the cot and holding the bars.

She let up the blind to the evening light. There was a mist on the window and she rubbed it off, and beyond the shining railway lines mist leaned against the hedges, and in the fields cattle moved through it, up to their knees as if in smoke. The leaves on the trees were turning brown, and the swallows alight on the telegraph wires made her think of a sheet of music. The cries of crows foraging for acorns in the oak trees were sharp and clear.

She sighed a long deep sigh and in her eyes were tears. 'God, my God, what's wrong with me,' she said. 'Why do I cross my own father — why, why? Why do I show him the worst side of my own nature? He's good and I won't admit it to myself. I'm proud. He said nothing in his defence when Richard rounded on him about the cold evening, and yet it was he who advised me to put an extra jersey on the child. And why did I refuse to take his advice when I knew in my heart and soul that he was right and I was wrong? I'm perverse — and that's the truth. God forgive me. Mother of God help me to be humble, help me to drive the things out of my heart that I shouldn't do, help me to do the things that I should. Help me, O God, to control my rotten temper, and forgive me for what I said to Father about Mag. I didn't mean it, really and truly I didn't. Don't let the sun go down upon my anger.'

She heard Richard and her father laughing and smelt the smoke from their pipes. She lifted the child from the cot and hugged her in her arms and brought her to the window. 'Look at the cows, pet. Moo, moo,' she said and covered her warm cheek with kisses. 'We'll go down now and see Granda. We'll take the train — shush, shush, shush, shush!' And the child smiled in her arms.

AUNT BRIGID ceased calling at the house and Tom ceased to expect her. He stayed at home in the evenings and often stood at the open door, smoking his pipe, waiting for Alice coming from her work.

One evening she was very late. It was dark and windy and he gazed intently down the hill, fastened his eye on the one electric lamp-standard that dropped its cone of light on the little bridge. It was cold and he pressed his back against the jamb of the door to keep warm, listened to a train's whistle honing itself sharply on the lean air and saw the moon speeding past the flying clouds.

'I'll put on my overcoat and go for her,' he decided and was ready to turn in when he spied her yellow beret pass quickly under the lone light on the bridge.

In a few minutes she had arrived breathless beside him.

'A terrible thing has happened, Father,' she exclaimed.

'Nobody dead, I hope,' he said humorously and followed her inside.

'No, no, but I've had a row with Aunt Brigid, a terrible row!' Her eyes were bright with anger and her cheeks red from the wind.

'Now, now, Alice, that's nothing. Sure everybody has rows some time or other in their lives.'

'But this has been going on for a long time, and I didn't want to torment you about it for fear you'd be disappointed in me.' And she began to tell him in broken sentences what had happened.

Aunt Brigid had been nagging at her for days, finding

fault with everything, and deploring the way regular customers were leaving since the unfortunate day she had taken her into her employment. And that was only the half of it. She accused her, no less, of eating too much chocolate, and during the warm weather in the past few months of gorging herself with more ice-cream than she sold. And her manners were not what one one would expect from a convent-school girl. She was abrupt with young children and old women, but was all sweetness and plaster with customers of no importance.

On listening to this tearful outburst her father tried to look serious and now and again interjected with forced gravity, 'Dear, oh dear, that's a libellous accusation.'

'But what brought it to a head, Father, was Sergeant. Oh, how I'd love to have the drowning of the same Sergeant from the bridge below and the water so nice and cold!'

Her father turned from her and put a pipe-spill between the bars of the grate; his hand shook, the tip of the spill smouldered and didn't light, and he had to use another.

'Go on, pet,' he said, lighting his pipe and obscuring his smiles with big puffs of smoke.

'I always had to take the blasted dog for a walk.'

'Easy, Alice, don't use nun's language.'

'Oh, if you're going to laugh I'll not go on at all.'

'Laugh!' he said, raising his eyebrows. 'Laugh! I'm very far from laughing, I may tell you. Very far, indeed.' And complaining of the stinging of the tobacco smoke he rubbed his eyes with his handkerchief.

'Well, anyway, I took that nasty ornament for his daily constitutional. And he ate grass or something or maybe a seed got in his throat and he choughed and houghed like a goods train. And when I got him into the house Aunt Brigid fondled and deared all over him and he seemed to get worse, and then as he lapped up a bowl of water she hit me a slap with his lead. "You've deliberately tried to choke him," she said. "You wouldn't give him time to smell around and be a dog." And then I said what I shouldn't have said: that nobody would slave from morning to night and walk a toy dog all for a miserable pound a week. And one word added to another. And here I am.'

'Aunt Brigid will be up to apologize, you'll see. She'll be pleading with you to come back. She thinks the world of you — I know that.'

'But I don't want to go back. You'll not make me, Father, sure you won't. We could go away from here and I could work for my matric.'

'You mustn't fall flat at the first burst of hailstones. You must have courage.' He crossed his legs and blew out the smoke in perfect rings.

'You don't know her, Father, the way I do. She can be as sour as a crab apple. And she can be sly too into the bargain. The curtain on the little window that looks into the shop from her sitting-room has a permanent curl-up in one corner. She was always lifting it to peep in at me and it was getting on my nerves so it was. I pretended to you I was happy but I wasn't.'

'Put it from your mind, Alice, and when she calls we'll settle it in a friendly way.'

'But I'm not going to face her again. I'll make myself some tea and go to the pictures with one of the McKennas. Sure you won't send me back, Father? You could apply for a change of station and we could go away from here. Promise me you'll not send me back.'

'I'll not, Alice,' he said, and as he saw her hurrying to get out he got up and laid the table for her tea.

Later when he was alone Brigid came as he expected. Her side of the story was similar to Alice's except that she emphasized the fact that Alice flirted outrageously with every boy that came into the shop. 'I wouldn't mind at all, Tom, if they were valuable customers,' she explained, 'but most of them only come in for a mangy box of matches or change of a sixpence and she gives them her whole attention.'

96

'That's how you build up custom: being courteous to everyone.'

'Courtesy within reason. Not when more valuable customers are jigging from one foot to the other, awaiting their turn.'

'In her romantic moments she doesn't see them,' he smiled.

'She's not in my shop to indulge romantic notions and make eyes at the boys,' she said, lapping Sergeant's lead round her wrist.

'Sure, Brigid, if she didn't do that she wouldn't be a young girl at all. I'm sure you made eyes at them yourself.'

'I've more respect for myself.'

'But I mean when you were in your teens. Come now, Brigid, admit it.'

In a few minutes he had her smiling and accusing herself of her lack of understanding, and, she supposed, of being a little hasty in her temper. She stroked Sergeant who lay on her lap, and when she ceased stroking him he pushed his head under her hand in a coaxing manner. It was really Sergeant, she explained, who was to blame for the row, for she honestly believed he was jealous and disliked going for walks with anyone except herself; and the fit of coughing he had had when out with Alice may have been only an act on his part.

'Isn't that so, Sergeant? Aren't you an old actor?' And the dog raised his eyes and brushed her lap with his soft tail. 'Tell Alice to turn up as happy as Lazarus in the morning — won't you, Tom? We'll never mention it between us again. Tell her that.'

Tom regarded her with sympathy; what he was ready to say embarrassed him and he felt it might offend her. His pipe had gone out and as he relit it he told her between the puffs that Alice didn't want to go back and that he himself was sending in an application for a change of station.

The colour rose to her face and she pushed the dog from her and stared at Tom with a stricken expression that made him flinch. Their easy conversation broke apart and the free

97

flowing evening seemed to stop and knot itself in a tangle of discord. Surely, surely, a little meaningless row wouldn't be the means of driving two people away from the town. He assured her, as calmly as he could, that the row had nothing to do with his intention of going away. The intention had been in his mind for a long, long time — even when Mary was alive it was there. Her death had strengthened it, and now that Alice had failed in her attempts at shop-keeping it would be better for her to try her hand at something else, and as there was nothing in this town for her she might fare better somewhere else.

'But, Tom, you'll reconsider it? Oh, don't go away whatever you do!'

He looked down at the dog and playfully touched it with his toe.

Brigid sighed a long sigh, and without looking at him she said slowly: 'All I can say is that I'm sorry, sorry from my heart that this has occurred. And I'm sorry for the unpleasant scene I had with Alice. If she were here now I'd humble myself before her — I would, truly I would.'

He raised his head. Never until now had he seen her so resemble his dead wife. People had often remarked the resemblance that existed between them, but he himself could never see it, and what brought it to his mind now he could not say: perhaps it was her tone of voice or the way she smoothed the backs of her hands as if tightening a glove on them.

On the range water tumbled from the spout of the kettle and he got up and pushed it aside. The wind was rising and he could hear it rumble in the chimney like a lumbering train. The fire hummed, and flaky ashes, thin as a moth's wing, sifted from it on to the grate.

'I'm sorry this has happened,' she said and rose up to go. Without a word he pulled on his overcoat, but she told him not to bother coming out as she'd find her way home all right.

He didn't heed her for he knew she didn't mean it, and anyway it would be the last time he would ever walk down the hill with her. He'd try to rid her mind of the idea that his leaving the town was her doing.

The dog trotted at her side, its bell tinkling. Tom took her arm, pressed it firmly and assured her that the little tiff with Alice was a thing to forget about at once.

At the bridge they halted and for some reason they moved away from the lamplight that wedged the darkness. Below them they saw the river run coldly with borrowed light from the sky. The wind put a curl upon the water, roughening it like the bark of a tree, and then the moon slid out and livened the water with fins of light.

'Tom, I don't know what to say about all this,' she said with deep remorse. 'This unexpected break … It'll break.' Her voice stopped suddenly, and he put his arm round her shoulder and once more pleaded with her not to worry about what had occurred between herself and Alice.

She gripped his hand. Did he not understand what their going away would mean to her? She was used to Alice's company, and now that the long nights were dropping down they would be lonelier for her than ever. It was different when her sister was alive: she had company then and understanding, but now all that was changed.

His pity for her drew him towards her. He patted the hand that held his and told her that they would come back often on visits to the town. She mustn't forget, that however far away he might be sent, he was held fast to this place by his children and by the memories of his dead wife. If he didn't go away now he would never go. It was his last chance.

'But, Tom, must you go?' She raised her head to him and shuddered as if with cold.

'I must,' he said.

The wind tore at the trees, dry leaves dropped darkly into the river and some falling on the road made the dog start in fright.

'I know you're fond of me,' she went on. 'Not only because of Mary but because of myself. Julia knows it and I know it. But never until tonight did I realize how deep it was.'

He could make no effort to draw his hand from hers. He wished to be away from her but some hidden pity held him fast.

'I want to comfort you all,' she went on. 'To help you as Mary would have wished. You know what I'm going to say.'

'Alice will apologize. She will indeed. I'll make her do it,' he said, pretending he did not understand her.

She held his sleeve and he could feel the warmth of her breath on his cheek. 'It's not Alice I'm thinking of — it's you. I don't know how to say it. I love you, Tom; I love you. And now that I've said it I don't regret it. I love you. Do you hear me?'

'Hush, Brigid, hush for goodness' sake.'

The moon freed itself from the clouds and shone out brightly.

'I love you!' broke from her again, but perceiving the crumpled expression on his face she plucked at the dog's leash and fled from the bridge. He stared into the tunnelled road between the moonlit trees. Above the noise of the wind he heard the dog's bell for a moment, and then heard it dwindle and vanish in the distance.

He didn't remember coming up the hill to the house nor did he remember opening the door to let himself in. All he knew was that he was alone in the kitchen, and the fire burning redly as the wind whipped up the draught.

In God's name what had he done to encourage her or to give her to think that he would ever marry again. And to his wife's sister at that! And what made Julia think he'd ever do the like. Had she lost her senses since she married Richard Colton? Was her own father a puzzle to her? Time and again she had accused him of indecision but tonight, please God, he'd rid and rinse her mind of that problem. He would send in his application at once. Uncertainty was smothering the life in him, making him lazy and indifferent. He had sacrificed his own ambitions for his family but tonight he'd free himself once and for all. Alice had liberated him.

Henceforth he would live for Alice. In another town he would work his last years to make her happy. He would fire her with ambition. He would establish self-confidence in her, the lack of which withers the best in all of us. Once she had the will to work, nothing would stop her from passing any exam and making something worthwhile of her life.

He poured himself out a glass of whiskey and as he sipped it he raked his mind for some flaw in his behaviour that would have caused this misunderstanding with Brigid. He was always distantly circumspect with her: not because he ever thought she felt like this towards him but because he didn't want the gossips to talk maliciously about what didn't exist.

She often took his arm but there was nothing in that. And even when he took hers this evening to comfort her he was sure it wasn't that that set her affections ablaze. No, it was Julia who was at the back of it all. And it was she that his going away would hurt most. Mag would be pleased and Christy would approve once it was done. Brigid would be relieved, too, and he would write her a note pledging her to say nothing of what had happened this evening to anyone.

An hour later when Alice had come home he had three letters written and they were standing side by side on the mantelpiece in front of the clock: one was his application to the railway company, one was to Christy, and the other to Brigid.

'You've been working hard, Father, I see,' she said, scrutinizing the addresses on the envelopes.

'I have, girl, I have. After Christmas we'll probably be away from here. That one to the railway company is my application for a change. I have mentioned Monabeg but it may not be available.'

'I'll be glad to go from here. I will, Father, I will!' And the brightness of her manner gladdened him.

THE following morning Alice told Mag about Father's application, and then she called on Julia and broke the news to her.

'You're only joking,' Julia said incredulously on hearing it. 'It's not true, Alice? Tell me it's not true!'

'It is too true. I posted the letter for him myself.'

'Here, mind the children for a minute or two till I talk it over with Mag.' And lifting a coat from the rack she went out, pushing her arms into it and buttoning it as she hurried to the gate.

'Isn't it dreadful news, Mag!' she declared, rushing into Mag's sitting-room where Mag was hem-stitching little cot-sheets and nappies for her baby due six months hence. 'It's heart-breaking, Mag, and I'll do all in my power to block him from going!'

'Relax for goodness' sake or you'll have me as bad as yourself,' Mag said calmly, and continued her work at the sewing-machine.

'Stop that machine and give me your attention for a few minutes, please. You'd think you were expecting your baby before mine, the way you're toiling. You've as much clothes made as'd do an infant school.'

For the sake of peace Mag obeyed her and snipped off the thread with her scissors. Then she began to fold up the sheets and the nappies, but her slow, meticulous foldings so enraged Julia she had to look away from her to the window to restrain herself. She saw a train leaving the station and heard a glass tinkle somewhere on the shelf as the train rumbled past. Her eyes rested momentarily on the caterpillar of smoke that stretched above the carriages and disappeared among the hedges on the road. She sighed and turning to Mag helped her to manœuvre the cover of the machine into its slots. After much fumbling and pulling against one another the cover was securely fixed in its position and the machine pushed into its corner.

'Whatever you have to say, Julia, say it quickly for I've Joe's dinner to get ready for him.'

'Maybe I shouldn't say anything and let things take their course.'

'Maybe you shouldn't.'

'But I must do my duty. When Christy was going away he left Father in my charge. I've tried many ways to prevent Father from taking this mad step but I've failed. Both of us now must work together to protect him. A change at his age will break him.'

'If he gets a good change we can spend our holidays with him — that's the way to look at it. His heart, Julia, is not in this place.'

'It should be. His family is here. Times, I think, he should have joined an order of contemplatives. He lives within himself too much. Last time he called — and he seldom calls — he never told me about this departure. Indeed he tells me nothing. He's as deep as a draw-well and just as cold. He's not like a father at all.'

'He's too good for us, Julia. Why can't you be content by seeing others contented. Why do you want to probe into Father's mind. You've no right to do that. It's like trying to read his soul.'

'Oh, you'll stick up for him no matter what folly he plans.'

'Julia,' she said, slowly plucking bits of thread from her lap, 'there should be respect for differences in a family. You shouldn't try to mould everybody to your ways.' She looked tenderly at her sister but Julia stared at the window, at the leaves falling from the trees near the railway embankment. Whether she was listening to her or not Mag could not say though she sensed contempt in the way Julia covered her side face with her hand. The gesture irritated her, and it reminded her that when they were growing up together it was Julia who always selected what clothes they should wear — clothes of the same design and colour — and what hair-style they should have in common.

Julia still kept her eyes averted and her face half-hidden by her hand. She made no comment as Mag uncovered this strong-willed trait in her character. But when Mag accused her of not allowing her to have an opinion of her own and even advised her against marrying Joe she took her hand from her cheek and told her Joe was not strong, and that was good enough reason to warn her against him.

'You're speaking of what was, Julia, and not what is. He can work hard now, and though we haven't much we are content with what we have and with each other. And God withheld this child that's growing up inside me till, I suppose, He saw we were in a more fit condition to rear it properly. I was impatient about it. I prayed for my own way and now I ask God to forgive me for that dictation. Oh, Julia, if we only have patience and not want our own way all the time we could make our lives easier.'

'Really, Mag, you've missed your vocation!'

'You're very cynical and it roughens everything you say. It'll be a long time before I speak my heart to you again.'

'The family is certainly taking to the rafts and leaving the helm of the sinking ship to a man not fit to steer a rowing-boat.'

She was speaking in Richard's voice now, Mag thought, and though it gave her an opportunity to be cynical she silenced that urge and said simply: 'We can't always have Father with us and we must accustom ourselves to that change. After all, when birds have reared their brood the brood is allowed to go and fend for themselves.'

'Birds have no reason and we have.'

'Unfortunately we reason things out for our own ends.'

'Mag, child, you've as much sense in your head as the birds you speak of. You don't suppose for one moment that I harbour any selfish reasons against Father's going away. I am only concerned with his good and with Alice's good.... You've hurt me very much by your insinuations.'

'I didn't mean to be hurtful. I only wished to be reasonable.'

'Father, at his age and in his loneliness, is not liable to be reasonable,' and she stood up to go, buttoning her coat and looking out of the window.

'Each day that passes the trees get barer. It won't be long, Julia, slipping by to Christmas and to Christy's homecoming.'

'Each day that passes will be a torment to me. I'll write to Christy at once.'

'He'll side with Father. I'm sure of that.'

Julia shook her head: no use talking to her — she's so content in her own future she has no thought for other people. She left her without another word and didn't look back as she closed the gate to see Mag standing expectantly at the open door.

The following morning as soon as Richard had gone to his business Julia put Marie in the pram, and taking little Dick by the hand she set off for Alice's to beseech her not to go should a change be offered to Father. Alice gave her no satisfaction, and displayed no weakness in her determination to go away with Father, no matter where that might be.

Three mornings later she was back again and Alice was able to tell her that a letter had just arrived offering Father the job as stationmaster at Pettigo.

'And where in the name of God is Pettigo?' Julia exclaimed. And Alice drew forth an atlas that she and her father had earlier scrutinized, and with the point of her hair-clip pointed out the town of Pettigo on the borders of Donegal.

'So there's where you're going!'

'There's where we're going!' Alice brazenly answered back.

'To the wilds of Donegal.'

'To the hills of Donegal.'

'Do you know, Alice, I'd just love to slap your bold little face!'

'I've grown up now, Julia. And I'm going to direct my own life in my own way.'

'I'll go before I lose my patience. Oh, it's well poor Mother isn't alive to see that cheeky face of yours.' She strapped Marie in her pram and called to Dick who was playing with the cat on the hearth-rug. 'It's no wonder poor, patient Aunt Brigid couldn't put up with you!'

She pushed the pram down the hill, little Dick toddling alongside and gazing at the tracks made by the wheels of the pram on the wet road. At the bridge he tried to pick up a wet leaf and throw it into the river but he tripped and fell and dirtied the breast of his new coat.

'Oh, what a heartscald of a child!' she cried, wiping his hands and his coat and dumping him into the foot of the pram. 'I wish you were going to Pettigo,' she added, and as she pushed off, the wheels seemed to rumble out like a child's game — To Pettigo, To Pettigo. It beat into her brain like the fall of the rain on the hood of the pram, and at the post office she halted and telling Dick not to move till she'd come out she went inside. She scribbled out a telegram: PETTIGO NOT ACCEPTABLE — MAGEE. With stiffened calm she saw the postmistress count the words, write the charge on the corner of the telegram and stamp it.

Quietly she went outside where Dick was catching with his tongue the drops of rain that hung from the handle of the pram. She hurried up the main street, past Richard's office where she heard the tap of a typewriter coming through the partially opened window. A few yards above the office she halted with one hand on the pram. She glanced back at the open door, hesitated for a moment, and then went on, the wheels hissing on the wet pavement. Later on she'd tell Richard but not now. She need not worry about what she had done. She'd have Christy on her side, and Richard on her side, and later on Father would realize that she had saved him from absolute desolation.

In the house as she prepared the dinner she tried to hum a tune but her efforts soon dwindled to silence. Her impulsive action in the post office pursued her with a powerful slyness, and as she struggled to escape from it the struggle wearied her and sent her heart pulsing wildly. Whatever else she'd do she must remain calm, mustn't allow herself to brood on what she had done.

Her mind throbbed and thronged for notice, and she momentarily eased it by concentrating on the vigorous scrape and scrub she gave to the potatoes and carrots that lay in a basin in the kitchen sink. As soon as Richard would come in she would discuss it with him and he'd advise her what to do about it. That would soon quieten her conscience.

But an hour before Richard was due for his dinner his typist arrived with a note to say that he wouldn't be home till the evening as he had to drive at once into the country to bag a sale of hay and the letting of land. She turned on the radio, gave little Dick a box of blocks to play with, and after making a light dinner she put Marie and Dick into the bedroom for their afternoon sleep. 'You'll take care of Marie,' she said to Dick, 'Mamma's going down to Aunty Mag's just for a minute. Be a good boy and Mamma will bring you some nice chocolate.'

She raced down to Mag's. But no one answered her ring at the door. She looked in at the windows and tried the latch on the back door, but the door was locked. Where on earth would she be at this time of the day — she that never goes out. She hastened to the chapel but Mag wasn't there. She tried to pray, her lips moved but she could not concentrate on the words, and felt her whole soul soured and unclean. She was out in a minute. The rain was falling in long thin strings and as she glanced down at the railway station she saw its roof polished with rain and a post office van driving up to the entrance. It was for Father's good she had sent the telegram but he wouldn't understand that if she went and told him now. She'd go to Alice and tell her — that would be her best plan.

She passed the school, heard the hum of the children inside and presently reached the main street. It was the town's half-holiday; all the shops were closed and the street was deserted except for a shambling cart that was halting at the heaps of sweepings at the edge of the kerb. There was a reek of turf smoke in the air and the houses were mirrored in the wet road.

She found herself outside her father's house, and as she was knocking at the door a neighbour shouted across to her that Alice had gone off on her bicycle. The whole town seemed to be going away, she thought, and, as for Alice, could she not find something useful to do at home without gallivanting about on a bicycle on a wet day? She glanced at her watch: she was an hour away — a whole hour — where had it gone! She must get back to the children. She must keep calm. On her way back she called at Brigid's, but no bark from Sergeant answered her knocking. Had everybody left? Is the town smitten with plague? Where in God's name have they all gone to?

At the open gate of her own house she saw little Dick with his head out through the window calling to her and asking for his chocolate. She ran upstairs and pulled him back from the window. 'If the sash cords had broken, your head would be off. Never do that again!'

'I wan' my chocolate, Mamma.'

'You're too bold. You're lucky your head's not off.' She looked at Marie in the cot. The child was asleep. She looked at her again, closely, and saw that her face was covered with blood-red scratches. 'What have you done to my child!' she screamed, lifting her bodily from the cot. The child, wakened from her sleep, cried loudly. She saw Dick's hands and fingers as red as dye, and then on the pillow of the cot saw her lip-stick case.

'Hush, Marie, hush, my pet!' and to keep from falling she gripped the bars of the cot, and when the dizziness passed she carried the child to the bathroom and gently sponged away the lipstick-markings from her face. She dabbed her own forehead with the cold sponge, and as she raised her head from the wash-hand basin she felt a tightness in her breast and a burning upthrust in her throat. The mirror in the bathroom seemed to sway. 'Be calm, be calm,' she said to herself, and sitting on the floor rested her forehead against the cold side of the wash-hand basin. 'Dick, be a good boy. You and Marie go into Mamma's bed. I'll be in in a minute.'

She got to her feet and retched into the basin. She struggled back to the room, closed the door and lay down on top of the bed. She lay still. Her breathing was short and quick. She listened to it and to the children running about the room. She tried to call to them but her breath was smothered and she seemed to choke. She clasped her hands, and in her mind she asked God to forgive her, to spare her, and to spare her baby that was still unborn. She wanted her baby, no matter what she had said. She wanted it. She did, she did, though she deserved to lose it. She breathed loudly and called on God to give her strength till someone came.

The hair on her forehead lay flat with sweat. The bed seemed to tilt, and as she gripped the clothes to keep from falling off, she heard Dick's voice from far away, a tiny twirl of sound making towards her. Her right hand hung limp over the side of the bed and for a moment she felt Dick turn the wedding ring on her finger, and then she seemed to sink and be covered with avalanches of air shelving and tumbling down upon her.

Mag, bathing her forehead with cold water, drew her back to consciousness.

'Oh, Mag, Mag, how did you come here?' she said and

grasped her hand. Mag told her she came in by the back door when she saw the children at the window and no one answering her knock.

'Pray, Mag, that I don't lose my baby. I feel limp and without any hold. This temper of mine is my undoing. I want my baby as you do yours! You know that, Mag, don't you?'

'Of course I do, Julia, of course I do! Lie still till I run up for the doctor.'

'He'll be away. The whole place is away. Get Father O'Brien for me. He'll be away too. Oh, Mag, I've done a dreadful thing. I've stopped Father from going to Pettigo. I sent a telegram. Tell Father I'm sorry and don't know why I did it. I feel I'm going to die and have done nothing good for anyone. I'm not worthy of anyone's kindness. Oh, if I could live for another while yet.'

'Shush, Julia, you're better than all of us,' Mag said, undressing her and getting her into bed. 'Lie still and pray till I come back.'

'And the children?'

'They're playing in the sitting-room. I'll take them with me. Don't move. Lie quite still, Julia, and don't worry. We'll be back in a few minutes.'

She left the front door ajar, and taking Dick and Marie with her in the pram she set off to the presbytery for Father O'Brien, and on her way seeing two boys on roller skates she gave them a shilling to go to her own house for Joe and then to go on for Alice. 'And let me see how quick you can go,' she called after them.

Father O'Brien was in and said he would go immediately. She told him that there was no one in the house and he was to push the door open and go right in. She was going to call right now for the doctor.

About ten minutes later the doctor and Joe arrived at the house just as Father O'Brien was descending the stairs. He announced that she was feverish but he didn't see any immediate danger. Should they send for Christy? He himself didn't see any urgent reason why they should do that, but it would be better to let the doctor decide.

Mag went upstairs with the doctor, and after he had examined Julia he asked if anything had upset her, asked if she had fallen or had something frightened her. Julia told him about the lipstick that Dick had plastered on the child's face and which she thought was blood. She gazed at Mag and then added she had been worrying a little about other things, things she didn't want to talk about now.

The doctor wrote out a prescription, left some tablets for her to take, and told Mag that he would call again in the evening and would be able to tell her then whether or not she should send for Christy. Her health, he explained, was always good during her last pregnancies and he didn't really see any reason why she shouldn't pull through this as long as she didn't worry. They must keep her warm, keep her quiet, and for a few days at least not let her have too much of her two children.

And when the doctor was gone and Joe and Mag were alone in the sitting-room with the children, Joe besought her for the sake of their own child to get Alice and Aunt Brigid to do the bulk of the nursing.

'But, Joe, I must do my duty by my own sister. Do you not see that all this will be good for our own child? Its character is being moulded now, even before it is born. If I become selfish and easy on myself our own child will have the same selfish nature.'

She put on her coat and told him to hold the fort and mind Dick and Marie till she'd come back from the chemist's — she'd only be a few minutes.

On returning she saw that he was still seated dejectedly in the armchair and she appealed to him to have courage. 'We must have faith, Joe. We must believe and do our duty even if it does cause us a little bit of annoyance. If we do what is right for others nothing can break us — I am sure of that.'

'Just when everything was going well with us we get this.'

'But, Joe, think what it means to poor Julia. And think what it will mean to Richard and Father when they hear it.' She paused and looked at him with tender disapproval. With his elbows resting on his knees he ran his fingers through his hair, not looking at her or paying any heed to Dick who was pulling a handkerchief from his pocket. She asked him to go down to the railway and break the news quietly to Father, and on his way he could call on Aunt Brigid before she'd hear it from the neighbours.

He got to his feet and put his arms round her: 'You'll not do more than your share, Mag?'

'I'll not do more than my share,' she smiled, and smoothed back his tossed hair with her hand. 'Don't look so hangdog or you'll frighten the life out of Father.'

Shortly after he had left the house Alice arrived and immediately arranged to take the two children home with her till Julia was better, and going about the house quietly, filled a suit-case with the children's clothes, put Marie in the pram and told little Dick they were coming to live with Aunty Alice for a whole week.

'Tie a scarf round Marie's head and put up the hood of the pram,' Mag advised as they were setting off. 'Don't let them get cold whatever else you do.'

A few minutes later Joe and the father came in and the father went upstairs to Julia. She lay still, like one unconscious. There was no light in the room except the glow from the electric fire. He put his hand on her brow. It was moist and hot, and a swollen vein beat slowly. He made the sign of the cross on her forehead with his thumb and slipped quietly from the room.

'How did it happen? What brought it on?' he asked Mag as they stood around in the firelit sitting-room, the darkness dropping down outside and no one thinking of switching on the light. Joe sat at the fire prodding the coals with the poker.

'I don't really know what brought it on,' Mag said, not wishing to tell him yet about the telegram. But she'd have to do that soon — before the railway company would reply to it.

'And the doctor? What does he think, Mag?'

'He's to call back again later. But he think's she's very strong and that we'll not have to send at all for Christy. And Father O'Brien thinks the same.'

He asked them about Richard. Neither Joe nor Mag knew where he was except that he was somewhere in the country looking after a sale.

Brigid came in, offering to do anything, even to the minding of the two children. Alice had seen to that end of it, but Mag would be glad if she would take turns with her at sitting-up with Julia tonight. As they were discussing the best means of doing that, Richard's car swung in at the gate and its headlights fled across the walls of the room.

Mag and her father went to meet him so as to stem his usual boisterous entrance. His face was red under the light from the hall door, and his breath smelt of whiskey. They told him that Julia was unwell but that there was no need for alarm.

'And why was I not sent for?' he blustered, and then realizing the foolishness of his question he ascended the stairs and Mag went with him, restraining him from making a noise or switching on the light in the room.

'Julia!' he cried, kneeling down at the bedside, and kissing her hand that lay on the eiderdown. 'Julia! Julia!' But Julia lay as quiet as one on the threshold of death.

'Come, Richard,' Mag whispered. 'The doctor gave her something to make her sleep.' As she plucked his sleeve she saw the steam rising from his shoe that touched the guard of the electric fire.

'I broke her, Mag,' he faltered, crying like a child. 'I broke her. God in heaven forgive me. I broke her and I deserve to lose her, I do indeed.'

113

She led him out to the landing, and as he dried his eyes he asked about the children and where they were. She told him and he sighed, and not to embarrass him she left him and went down to the sitting-room.

In a few minutes he came down after her, and not speaking to anyone they heard him open the front door and go out. They thought he was away to his car for something, but after a while Tom strolled outside to look for him. He wasn't in the car or in the garage or about the garden. Tom came into the house and told Mag he'd walk up through the town and find him.

'He had a queer look on his face, Tom,' Brigid said. 'It was a look that boded no good. I hope he wouldn't do any harm to himself.'

'Why do you say that, Aunt Brigid?' Mag asked in alarm.

'She's a foolish woman – that's why she says it!' Joe exclaimed, and the suddenness of his outburst startled them. 'She's a fool!' he said again when no one answered him.

'Joe, Joe!' Mag said. 'What's wrong with you?'

'Only for the girl that's above,' Brigid said, 'I wouldn't stand here and let you insult me like that.'

'Aunt Brigid, please, he doesn't mean it,' Mag said, laying a hand on Joe's shoulder.

Tom held back at the door, and pretending not to notice the suppressed tension he said calmly: 'Lay the table, Brigid, for the supper and I'll have Richard back here before the kettle's boiled. Come on, Joe, and help me to trace him.'

When they were outside the house he told Joe he should have more sense than exchange words with women at a crisis like this.

'I couldn't help it. I didn't want Mag upset by a lot of nonsensical fears and old womanish talk.'

Tom reeled off at random a number of Richard's friends that Joe could call on, and if he found him he was to bring him back to the house.

They parted outside Brigid's unlighted shop. A black wind

was blowing through the wet streets and no one was abroad and no youths standing at street corners. Tom made his way to the church half expecting to find Richard there, but when he opened the door and peered into the grey silence he saw nothing but the glow of candles from a candelabra and an old woman praying with outstretched hands near the high altar. She did not turn when the kneeling-board clacked under him or, later, when he genuflected and a pencil fell from his pocket on to the aisle. As he lifted it it fell from his hands again and rolled under a seat where he let it lie and hurried on tiptoe from the church.

The wind seemed colder and he could feel it penetrating through his thick coat. He went inside the four pubs in turn, silently scanning the smoke-filled air for Richard, unperturbed by the hubbub of talk or the faces that glanced at him. He spoke to no one and no one asked him his business.

He crossed to the hotel and glanced in at the lounge where a few ladies were sipping sherry and having a game of bridge. Richard wasn't there. He wasn't anywhere he could think of, and he only hoped that Joe had found him.

He stood for a moment in the wide street, undecided where to go. He walked a few steps towards home, stopped, and then went on again. Unsought and unmanly fears clambered for notice, but at the bridge over the river he deliberately quelled them by thinking of Brigid's declaration of love, a declaration he never wished to dwell upon.

He opened the door of his house with his key, and there in front of the range was Richard with little Dick sitting on his knee in his pyjamas, a teddy bear clutched in his arm.

'That night would frizzle the life out of you,' Tom said, controlling the joy that edged away his fear. He rubbed his hands together, held them near the bars of the grate, and playfully began to box with Dick and his teddy bear.

'Bed, bed, bedsy-bed!' Alice called out as she descended the stairs. She lifted Dick in her arms. 'Come now, Marie's asleep. Say night-night to Daddy and Granda. Up we go!' Half way upstairs Dick threw his teddy over the banisters. 'You're a rascal,' she said, and retrieving the teddy she chased after Dick as he scrambled laughing to his room.

Tom went to the sideboard and took out a bottle of whiskey and two glasses.

'You'll take a spot, Richard, it'll steady your nerves?'

'No, Tom, I'll not,' and he shook his head and covered his face with his hands.

'You must pull yourself together, man. Julia's strong and, please God, she'll get over this in a day or two.'

'I've been a poor father and a worse husband. Drink has ruined me and broke her heart. On my knees at her bedside tonight I promised God I'd try to give it up and turn a new leaf.' And as he spoke he did not once look round to where Tom stood against the sideboard.

From upstairs came the sound of little Dick singing out his prayers and then the sound of the bed creaking as he jumped into it. He began to giggle and they could hear him plead with Aunty Alice not to go away till he was asleep.

Not wishing to drink in front of him Tom stowed the bottle away quietly. Richard blew his nose with a handkerchief and held it clenched in his fist. 'I lied to her today. I didn't come home for dinner. I told her I was out letting land. I wasn't. I went to the race meeting at Dundalk with a few of the lads. That's where I was. I brought this on her. I did it. No one else did it but me. She's too good for me and that's the truth.'

Alice came down, folded up Dick's clothes, and poked the fire under the kettle. Her father explained that he and Richard would have supper at Julia's and that she needn't wait up till his return. He'd be back about twelve or before one, but if he weren't back she wasn't to worry as he didn't know what arrangements would be made for the night at Julia's.

Richard had no overcoat with him and Tom gave him an old one of his own and a coloured scarf that Christy would have no more need of. They went down the hill together, silent, united by a common sorrow, the ground under their feet already glittering with the year's first frost.

The doctor had called again while they were out, and he was pleased that she was still sleeping and her pulse becoming normal. Brigid had the tea on the table and after they had taken it Tom sent Mag and Joe home and said that he and Richard would sit up that night and in the morning Brigid could take over. After a little wrangling they agreed to that arrangement and when they had all gone Tom banked up the fire and while Richard fell asleep on the armchair he unlaced his boots for him and spread a rug over his knees. With his rosary beads in his hand he tried to pray but his mind kept wandering from the words he was saying, and on hearing a stir from the sick-room he would steal upstairs and, as in the days when his wife was dying, ask in a whisper if she needed anything and on receiving no answer he would slip downstairs again to where Richard lay with his mouth open and his chin buried on his breast. Richard was dead beat, and scanning the face in repose he saw the strained corners of the mouth, the cheeks blotched and swollen — a face disfigured and loosened by drink.

At dawn Brigid came in, the edges of her shoes white with frost.

'How is she? Had you to give her her medicine?' she asked in a whisper.

'No, Brigid, she slept all night, thank God.'

'Wrap yourself up well for there's been a heavy frost. And there's a nip of brandy I brought for you. It'll keep the life in you on your way home.'

'Thanks, Brigid, you're very kind.'

While sipping the brandy she did not look at him but threw her coat on the back of a chair, and stooping down at the fire gently raked the ashes with a glance at Richard snoring

117

on the armchair. As he drew on his heavy coat she still did not look at him and he realized how easier life would be for him and for her when he went to Pettigo; and as he thought of Pettigo he remembered he had not yet acknowledged their letter and accepted their offer. There would be plenty of time to do that when he was sure that Julia had turned the corner.

He raised the collar of his coat and set out into the white frost of the early morning. The path to the gate was white with it except where Brigid's footsteps had broken it, and as he opened the gate the needles of frost clung to it like filings on a magnet. His breath smoked in front of him and he plunged his hands in his pockets as he hurried through the grey deserted streets. A squashed cigarette packet was frozen in a cellophane of ice, and ice lay white at the edges of the river and in the channels of the road that led to the drains. His coat was grey with frost when he reached home, and as he stamped his feet at the doorstep he looked up at Christy's room where little Dick slept and was glad to see that Alice had closed the window. He sneaked upstairs to see if Dick had kicked the clothes off himself, but the child slept without a stir, and against the bed Alice had placed two chairs to keep him from tumbling out.

He didn't go to bed. He lit the fire, made some porridge for the children and placed it at the side of the range, and when he had his own breakfast taken he wiped up the melted frost from the inside window-sills and went up and wakened Alice and told her Julia had a restful night.

All that day Julia continued to improve and when he called in the evening Richard was sitting beside her bed and signed to him to keep silent as he entered the room. With his finger to his lips Richard rose, tiptoed towards Tom and taking him by the elbow led him quietly from the room.

'A while back she was asking had you called, but now that she has gone into a sleep it's better not to waken her. The more sleep she gets the doctor says the less likely will she take a turn for the worse. I'll stay up with her tonight. I think she's over the worst of it. But if anything happened during the night I'd send Joe for you at once.'

That night, shortly after Alice had put the children to bed and there was no sound from them, Tom himself felt tired and went to bed about nine. He went to sleep immediately but wakened after a few hours. He sat up in bed wondering if a knock at the door had wakened him, and as he listened wakeful in the darkness he heard a loud wind bumping against the gable and whining round the corners of the house. Then he heard the whistle of the goods train, the rattle of its couplings and he knew by the bluntness of the sounds that the frost was gone. He heard a lid clattering on the garden path and then the crumb-board that he had put out for the birds was hurled against the back door. He couldn't sleep. He blessed himself and taking his rosary beads from below the pillow began to pray for Julia, and because it was November, the month of the dead, he prayed for his wife, his parents, his dead brother and sister and all the nameless ones he had ever met or spoken to in his life. The wind continued to rise and keep him awake, and at six o'clock, though it was still dark, he got up and lit the fire.

After he had shaved and was taking his breakfast he heard the postman drop a letter through the letter-box. He slit the letter open with the corner of the knife and read it slowly. It was from the railway company acknowledging the receipt of the telegram and regretting his inability to take Pettigo. He was puzzled by it, and thinking that someone at the station had played a joke on him he remembered that he had told none of them about the offer or his desire to leave. He pushed the breakfast things away from him and read the letter again. He could soon find out at the post office who sent the telegram. But first of all he'd ask Alice if she knew anything about it.

He brought the letter upstairs to her and as she read it her face burned, the letter trembled in her hands, and in the grey daylight that struggled through the window she saw the beaten look on her father's face. She told him — had to tell him — about Julia's threat the day she heard they were going to Pettigo.

'And do you think, Alice, she'd stoop to the like of that? Surely to the good God no child of mine would do the like!'

'Oh, Father, I hope she wouldn't. But she was in a bad mood that day I told her you were offered Pettigo.'

He took the letter from her and put it in his pocket. 'Don't breathe a word about this to a living soul till we get to the bottom of it. If Julia did it we'll have to hide it and keep it to ourselves.'

It was half-seven; he would go to Mass at eight and then call to see how Julia was. He went out, walking quickly to quieten the throbbing in his mind, and because it was early he took the road that fringed the town. He came out by the lakeside, now deserted, where a squally wind scattered handfuls of shadow on the water, and coots, disturbed by his presence, jerked like wound-up toys towards the shelter of the reeds. He tried not to think of the letter in his pocket, tried not to accuse Julia, and as he did so the image of the cancerous pike filled his whole mind. He shook his head, and on hearing the bells of the church pounding above the sound of the wind in the trees he hurried into the streets of the town and saw the thick smoke from the first fires falling like a blue fog over the roofs of the town. A post office van was stationed outside the closed post office, and he glanced at it and thought bitterly of what they didn't know and would never know.

Inside the church at the back he knelt among the scattered congregation and tried to give his mind to the prayers of the Mass and to the movements of the priest. But his thoughts wandered to the letter in his pocket and he drew them back to the sacrifice on the altar, and because the priest wore black vestments he tried to think of his dead wife and all who had gone before him and now slept the sleep of peace. He bowed his head and prayed silently that God would direct him what to do and what to say; that whatever he would do, now or in the future, would be for his own spiritual good and that of his family.

After Mass he went over to see how Julia was and as he opened her garden gate Mag ran to meet him.

'Julia's in great form, Father. She was speaking about you this very minute and asked if you had called yet. But, Father, I want to tell you something, something that I should have told you before this, something Julia told me to tell you and I didn't. It's about Pettigo. Julia didn't want you to go there. She thought you'd break your heart there and she … '

'She sent a telegram to the railway company,' he said and put a hand on her shoulder. 'She only did what I was thinking of doing myself.'

'Oh, Father, wait till I tell her that I have told you,' and she ran into the house ahead of him, and when he ascended the stairs he met her coming out of Julia's room with the breakfast tray. She smiled and closed the door after him as he went into the room.

Julia was sitting up in bed in a lilac jacket, her black hair combed back, her face like wax in the low sunlight that shone into the room.

He put his arms around her and she cried on his shoulder.

'Mag has told you,' she said.

'Put it from your mind, Julia, like a good girl. I'd have written rejecting Pettigo but you forestalled me.'

'Is that true, Father?'

'Does Richard know?' he evaded, hearing him in the bathroom.

'No, Father, he doesn't. And I don't want him to know.'

'Then we'll keep it among ourselves — a secret between Mag and you and Alice and me. We'll not let it leak outside the Magee family.'

'And Christy?'

'We'll keep it from him too. What he doesn't know won't give him a grey hair.'

'Oh, Father, what made me do the like to you and you so good to me and Richard. And God is good to me and I don't deserve it. The doctor told me this morning I'm not going to lose my baby, the danger is passed. The haemorrhage has stopped.' She sighed a long deep sigh and clasped her hands tightly together. 'Promise me one thing, Father! Promise me you'll go away if another place is offered to you.'

He smiled but could not look at her, and joy flushed his heart, not from what she said but from the fierce strength in her voice that told him she was getting better.

'Promise me you'll try to get away. Say yes!' She pressed her two hands on his and made him look at her. 'Say it, Father. You'll go away where you'll be happy and where Mag and me and our children can go on holidays. See how selfish I am. You'll go — won't you? In God's name say yes before Richard comes in to disturb us.'

'To Monabeg — if that's possible.'

Tears of joy glittered in her eyes. 'I'll get better now. I know I will. Look at those hands.' She held them out, palms downward. They were bloodless, and the veins showed on them like pencil-marks. 'There!' she said and clenched them slowly. 'I've strength. I know I have it. I'll change. It will be a hard struggle to straighten the twist in me, but I'll manage it.' She knew she had much to atone for and that atonement would come by helping him to go away and then bear the pain of his going.

'Mother used to tell us what was in your mind. She held you here, held you for us, for the family. Isn't that so?'

'I suppose it is, Julia. But we can't have everything we want in this life and even if we do get it it often disappoints us.'

'The Christmas that's coming might be our last together in this town. It will be Christy's last with us and we must make it a happy one — as happy as we can make it without

122

Mother. And next year, please God, we'll spend it with you in your new place if you invite us.'

Richard came from the bathroom wiping the shaving-cream from below his ears. 'Well, Captain,' Richard greeted. 'I think she has weathered the storm. What do you think?'

'I think she's a great girl, that's what I think,' Tom said, and Julia closed her eyes and shook her head sadly.

As he withdrew from the room he rejoiced in the real goodness he had seen in Julia, and realized that there was nothing like misfortune to reveal one's true strength. It was strange that he was only now beginning to know her.

He descended the stairs and ambled off to the station, tapping the school-going children on the head with his rolled-up morning's newspaper. People are far better than we know and better than they themselves know, he mused; sorrow is growth, the seed of character. And what if her resolutions, like many of our resolutions, have only a short life they still showed that she desired to help and not hinder him. If he went away from here it would hurt her — there was no doubt about that in spite of what she had made him promise. He recalled Christy's words: that when a man has a family he is no longer a chooser of where he should go and of what he should do, that the family, no matter what age they were, would tug him at every turn. Perhaps Christy was right. He had seen in Julia's sickness a glimmer of what his son had meant. He had foolishly thought that all his love for Julia had withered since his wife's death.

He had tried to get away from this town and his attempt had failed. Maybe a change wasn't destined for him and that he should now leave the future to chance and live out each day as he had lived it when Mary was alive. That's what he'd do, and he'd start right away and make his peace with this place by work.

Of late he had done his work in the office perfunctorily. Now he would revert to the enthusiasm of other years. His books and entries therein would henceforward be free of blotches and slovenliness. And the other duties that he voluntarily took upon himself — the flower-beds, the climbing roses, the shelving bank with the name of the station printed with plant or flower — he would attack with earnestness and pride. He would straw the roots of the roses against frost, he would make new strips of leather to fasten his climbers to the station walls, and he would get a few loads of dung and next year, as a change, he would have the name of the station printed in aubrietia, aubrietia that would flower in blue for many a long month, and when the flower would fade the cushiony rosettes of leaves would still flaunt forth the station's name throughout the winter months.

He braced his shoulders and set to work as soon as he hung up his coat at the back of the office door. With ink eraser he removed the blots and smudges from his ledgers, rubbed off the columns of telephone numbers pencilled on the wall above his desk, and from the inside of his desk swept out the pencil-parings and litter of string and squeezed-up balls of paper. He tidied the cluttered pigeon-holes, and reprinted the names of stations below the ticket-holders in the large frame. With passe-partout he rigged up four coloured prints that had come from a tourist-agency and hung them on the bare walls. And though it was the wrong time of the year to put in plants he sent an order to McGready's nursery in Portadown for six dozen aubrietia plants to be sent to him by return if possible.

Within a week the sluggish indifference that had burdened him since his wife's death had gone, and one sunny morning after a light frost had evaporated from the soil he pulled on his dungarees and replanted the name ROCKCROSS with the aubrietia plants, regulating the size and space of the letters by string and rod. He began to clip the grassy edges of his rectangular plot, his long shadow stretching across the railway lines, and melted frost dropping from the telegraph wires on to his back. He whistled to himself and teased the dunged straw round the edges of the aubrietia. Resting on his spade and gazing through the bare hedge at the traffic in the town he was startled to hear a man speak to him and looking round was surprised to see a railway inspector from head office shading his eyes from the sun and staring at the flower-bed.

Tom wiped the mould from his hands on the grass-clippings and drying them on his trousers he jumped down to meet the inspector and to shake hands with him.

'You'll have a nice display there in the spring of the year, Mr Magee.'

'Not bad, I hope. It'll be a change from the geraniums.'

'You take a great interest in this work. Yesterday I was admiring a photo of your embankment that's hung on the wall in head office.'

Tom smiled: 'I wouldn't call this work. It gets me out in the air, and since Mr Wilson gives me all encouragement I may as well enjoy myself at the company's expense, so to speak.'

'Your work inside in your office is just as neat as the outside.'

Tom smiled again, roguishly aware that if the inspector had called a week ago he would have found the place as untidy as a tinker's caravan.

The inspector sympathized with him on the loss of his wife and assumed that that was the reason he had applied for a change.

Tom nodded and gazed at the dirt embedded in his finger-nails.

'We wish to do our level best for you,' the inspector continued, 'and though it is our opinion that Monabeg is a rather small offering for a man that has given long and excellent service to the company we have written to the Monabeg stationmaster to see if he would be willing to exchange with you.'

'But, but ... ' Tom fumbled, 'I wouldn't wish to force my way into Monabeg over another man's head.'

'The exchange if effected will be mutual,' and the inspector stared at the coffee-coloured sleepers and said with feigned casualness: 'Mr Wilson will be retiring from here shortly.'

'I know; he told me so.'

'Yet you wish to leave?'

'Well — yes, I suppose I do.'

The inspector shook hands with him again and as he turned away, walking along the edge of the track, Tom stumbled after him and asked him not to mention his intention of leaving to Mr Wilson.

'I have no call to mention it, Mr Magee. He has guessed it long ago.'

Left alone on the embankment he was disquieted by the alternate moods of joy and regret that struggled for dominance. Now that there was a possibility of getting his desire he did not know if he wanted it. His deepest impulse swung him towards it, the thought of Julia swung him back from it.

He lifted the fork and plunged it into the soil. He sifted out the strings of weed on the tines of the fork and spread them on a heap of paper he had gathered from the litter baskets. No use waiting to talk it over with Christy; it would be too late then. To write a letter of withdrawal would not be the action of a balanced man. He set a match to the heap at the edge of his plot and watched the smoke rise up and scatter through the moist hedge. The smoke watered his eyes and burned in his throat. He moved away from it and gazed at Julia's house and the washing hanging white on the line. He sighed and listened to the soft hiss of the burning weeds. The flavour for work had gone from him and he shouldered his spade and fork and got down from the embankment.

What would he do? Whom could he turn to? He would do nothing, make no stir one way or another — that's what he'd do. If Monabeg was offered to him he would go, if it wasn't it might all be for the best. And anyway there would be no upheaval till the New Year. He would at least have time to enjoy Christmas.

On his way home in the evening he called on Julia as he usually did now for a short visit, and those evenings were free from strain, and though they talked of her illness and how Richard was scouring the country to get her goat's milk to drink no reference was ever made to the telegram. And sometimes, too, Richard called to see him of an evening and he would endeavour with calm patience to teach Richard chess, allowing him to win a few games. But Richard displayed no real interest in the games, moved the pawns haphazardly, and in a morose and grudging silence would yawn and smoke endless cigarettes. And one night when ten o'clock struck he looked sourly at the clock and struggled to his feet: 'The pubs are shut! Another victory for old Ireland! I'll steer my barque home on an even keel. If I haven't pawned the Queen, at least I haven't pawned my watch. Drink, Tom, is a disease, a pleasant disease that I wouldn't mind contracting at this moment, despite all the rooks and crooks and knights and kings that I have handled. Good night, it won't be long till Christmas.'

Tom saw him to the door and stood listening to his flagging footsteps descend the hill. As he closed the door and cut out the laneway of light that stretched from it he suspected that Richard's enforced abstinence from drink would have a short life.

In a week's time Christy would be home and a week after they would all be enjoying Christmas together. On those two things he would allow his mind to dwell. And as of old he would dig up the little fir tree in the corner of the garden and drag it into the parlour in a bath of mould and let Alice string it over with lights and top it with a star as was done when Mary was alive. It would give pleasure to Julia's children, and on his way home at night he would see it shine out from the narrow window in the gable-end of the house.

ON the day Christy was due home Tom awoke early, and before he threw aside the blankets he knew by the watery brightness on the walls that snow had fallen during the night. The window was open, the air in the room thin and fresh, and the sun shining on the snowy roofs of the houses opposite. He made the sign of the cross and as he pulled on his trousers he looked down upon the hushed road. No one was abroad except two dogs playing in the snow, sneezing and shaking their heads, their shadows long and sharp on the hill slope.

He went downstairs, and when he had the fire blazing brightly he wakened Alice and began to shovel the snow away from the front door. He had it all cleared away by the time Alice called him for his breakfast, and before sitting down to the table he crumbled bread on a board for the birds and went out and left it on the garden seat. And when he came in again Alice suddenly asked him if it would be all right for her to go to a Christmas dance with the McKenna girls and their brother who was home from South Africa.

'And why wouldn't it be all right, Alice girl?'

'Christy and Aunt Brigid may object.'

'In what way object?'

'Mother's not so long dead and they might think it unseemly.'

'Your mother's happier than any of us and she'd want you to be happy too. Have you a frock?'

'I have an old one of Mag's that I could fix up.'

'Get a new one in Joe's. Frocks go out of fashion and I don't want you to look like someone out of a pantomime.'

He gave her a five-pound note and as she took it she said that that would be her Christmas box and that she wouldn't expect another thing.

'We must make a good Christmas this year,' he said, 'and we must rope them all in as usual, including Aunt Brigid and your old friend, the Sergeant of the canine grenadiers.'

The door was knocked and the postman dropped in a card. It was from Christy to say he would arrive by the afternoon train.

Humming to himself he put on his best jacket and Alice helped him into his heavy overcoat, and as he sauntered off down the hill the sun reflecting from the snow watered his eyes. Three boys were sleighing down the slope, the snow gushing from the runners like spray, and the two dogs barking at each side of it. Tom passed them as they trudged back up the hill, dragging the sleigh by a snow-covered rope.

'Enjoying yourselves?'

'Yes, Mr Magee,' they answered.

Nice lads, he said to himself, and just then a snowball flew over his shoulder, and without turning round he hurried out of range, hearing the snowballs ploof behind him. At the bridge he glanced round and seeing the sleigh whizzing down the hill he quickly made a few snowballs and fired them among the lads, and losing control of the sleigh they fell off and rolled in the snow, the sleigh coming to rest against a boulder at the edge of the stream. Laughing to himself Tom stumbled quickly away and was well out of range by the time the lads had recovered themselves.

He called at Julia's but as she wasn't up yet he dropped Christy's card in the letter-box and went on his way, past Aunt Brigid's unopened shop where he noticed the window decorated for Christmas, tinsel on the chocolate boxes, and a green cord looped across the window holding Christmas stockings, their silvery contents and pink sweets showing through the net. It reminded him of Marie and little Dick and he made a note in his diary of what to buy them, and because Brigid was sure to present him with a pound-tin of tobacco he made a note of asking Alice to buy her a scarf or a handbag. It was his custom also to give Richard a bottle of wine, but remembering Richard's pledge he decided not to put temptation in his way and would give him a rug for his car instead.

In the afternoon when Christy's train drew in, Julia and her two children, dressed like rabbits, were on the platform and with them was Mag looking more advanced in pregnancy than Julia. Steam escaping from underneath the carriages clouded them like a fog, and as the wet-streaming doors opened and shut no one spotted Christy. But when the train pulled out and the steam cleared away he was standing quietly at their backs, studying their disappointed attitudes. Tiptoeing forward he put his hands over Julia's eyes saying: 'Guess who?'

'Oh, you rascal!' Mag said. 'We thought you hadn't come.'

He embraced them all, and lifting a child in each arm he hugged them and buried his face playfully in their warm furry coats. He noticed Julia's pinched and pallid face and he shook his head gravely and told her to take good care of herself.

'And Mag' — and he stood away from her and smiled. 'Upon my word you're looking extremely well. Joe's more than good to you.' She blushed and rubbed drops of water from the shoulders of his coat with her gloves.

'Come on, Christy,' the father said and lifted his case. 'You're foundered and we must take a car.'

'We'll take no car. I want a spanking good walk, snow or no snow.'

Outside the station his sisters parted from him, and as father and son walked through the snowy streets it reminded them both of his last homecoming and the death of his mother.

Alice was at the window on the look-out for them, and she watched them, two black figures, trudge up the hill, while little boys hauled the suitcase on the sledge, and women came to their doors to hail Christy and shout greetings after him — a young man, their young man, on the threshold of ordination. Neighbours stood at both sides of the street, gazing after him till he had passed into the house, the father staying behind to give the sleigh-boys a shilling each and telling them he had jobs apiece for them at the railway.

Winter darkness dropped early and with it the snow dripped from the roofs like a broken gutter and streamed down the channels of the road into the river. There was no sense in going out on such an evening so Christy sat in an armchair in the warm firelit parlour, his feet on a pouffe, and a pipe held delicately in his mouth. His father shuffled in with the chess-board.

'Maybe you're too tired for a game, Christy?'

'Are you keen?'

'Not if you're not.' He put away the board and handed his son an unopened tin of tobacco.

'Brigid's at wholesale price, Father?'

His father arranged cushions on an armchair, sat down, but didn't answer him. He hadn't bought it at Brigid's. Since the incident at the bridge it embarrassed him as much as her when they met face to face across the counter of her shop. He often walked home with her from Mass on a Sunday, but save for these meetings, intentional on his part, they seldom met. She ceased to call at his house and this abrupt cessation of her weekly visits Alice attributed to the little tiff she had had with her on the day she left her employment. But now that Christmas was approaching and Christy at home the father hoped she would come up as usual for the Christmas dinner.

As he lit his own pipe he glanced across at his son, at the neck shrunken in the Roman collar and the black clothes hanging loosely upon him.

'I hope, Christy, they give you plenty to eat beyond.'

131

'We get lashings of stuff but you need the digestive capacities of an elephant to enjoy it.'

'You'd think they'd feed you like prize fighters and get you into good shape for the African bush.'

'They do their best and I do the best with it when the old tummy permits.'

'You weren't ill?'

'Not at all. I'm as fit as a fiddle.' He lifted his legs from the pouffe and pushed it under the armchair. 'But I'll tell you, Father, who was ill, and very ill — Julia!'

The father admitted that she was worse than they had said in their letters; and he unfolded in detail how little Dick gave her the fright of her life the day he plastered Marie's face with lipstick.

'When I read that in one of your letters I wondered at it,' Christy remarked. 'I was thinking that maybe your desire to change had a part in it or maybe Richard's fondness for a drink or a gamble at the cards.'

'Richard's given up the booze.'

'Since when?' Christy exclaimed. 'This is the first I heard of it.'

'Oh, he hasn't shipped a drop for some weeks now.'

'Good man for him. I hope his ship, as Richard might say himself, weathers the Christmas season. It'll have a tough passage but we must hope for the best.'

'It was Julia's illness decided him on that course.'

'And her illness decided you to turn down Pettigo?'

'That was one reason, and the other was my disappointment at not being posted to Monabeg.'

'And you'd go back there if it were offered to you?'

'Sometimes, Christy, a great longing comes over me to get back there. But lately I often wonder would it be a wise move.'

Sensing his father's indecision it braced him to toss out advice, for often in the college he had dwelt upon his father's eventual move and the more he pondered it the more freely was he convinced that his father could never recover his former life in Monabeg.

He leaned forward in his armchair, and taking the pipe from his lips he assured his father that the only road that leads back was one in memory only, and that it was better for him to live with that secure illusion than to return to Monabeg and find that what he sought was no longer there. The station would not be altered in appearance, the rooks would still nest in the trees and the river flow from the lough — all these would be the same, but his own mind would be irrevocably changed, changed utterly from what it was when he lived and worked there thirty years ago. Roads lead on; nothing goes back except memory and it would betray him.

'Do you not realize, Father, that what I say is true?'

'What I seek is small and reasonable. I would work hard and that would bring me the little contentment that I want.' Stretching his hand to the coal-scuttle, he lifted a lump of coal, dropped it in the fire, and wiped his fingers on his socks.

Christy pointed out to him that Julia and Mag would always have difficulties of one kind and another and it would be easier for them to bear them if they had a father near at hand to share them with.

'I'll let things take their course, Christy, that's what I'll do. If Monabeg is offered to me in exchange I can't refuse it.'

'But you must act and use your reason and not be like a sheep on a hillslope.'

'I may as well tell you that Julia wants me to go and so does Mag.'

'And if you go away and Alice gets married?'

'I'll not cross that bridge till I come to it. You needn't worry about me being lonely. I'll not be lonely. Keep that in your mind.'

Christy sighed, and fearing lest he would rile his father by harping on Monabeg he lowered his voice, and on inquiring if Aunt Brigid still visited the house as usual he learned that since Alice's row she hadn't visited the house much,

133

but now that Christmas was approaching they all hoped she would come up as usual for the Christmas dinner. Christy demanded that she be left to him; he would manage her and bring her along, by force if necessary.

And on Christmas day, shortly before dinner, Brigid hadn't arrived and he hurried away for her, leaving Richard and Joe in the parlour, both hoping she wouldn't hold up the dinner. They were standing at the window, gazing at the bare garden with the rain drenching the holly bush when suddenly Joe clapped a hand to his breast pocket and fished out an envelope.

'I nearly forgot about that, Richard. My boss asked me to deliver it to you in person. A Christmas box, I suppose?' he added jokingly.

'Oh, I know all right what it is. He's posted it to me a few times already.' He gazed vindictively at the address on the envelope: per hand to Mr Richard Colton. 'Look at the insulting way he addresses it. I'd like to crush his bald little head between two bales of his bad tweed.' He tore it open with his forefinger and read: 'Fourth application: Stock-taking — an early settlement of the account would be appreciated.' He tore it in smithereens and showered the bits into the fire. 'You can tell him what I did with it. And tell him I'll pay him when I'm ready. God knows he made me wait long enough for the two damned suits, suits that are too short in the yard-arms and too narrow in the beam for comfortable cruising. I declare to me God I'd need to go on a strict diet to wear them in comfort. Upon my word I should sue him for damages for the constriction they put on the old heart.'

'You'll not pay him?'

'I'd have paid him long ago if he hadn't been so damned persistent and insistent. When my ship comes home I'll pay him.' And he gave Joe a slap on the back that took the breath from him.

'Oh, I'll pay him all right,' he went on with emphatic

134

irony, and eyeing the holly tree and the rain shining on its leaves he wished at that moment to be flinging Joe's boss amidst its prickling branches.

'Your debts put me in an embarrassing position,' Joe remarked timidly, and pointed out that they were related to one another by marriage. Richard couldn't see what on earth that had got to do with the case, and his mood suddenly changed to irritation and defiance.

'It has a lot to do with it,' Joe said firmly. 'The boss told me he didn't think a relation of mine would treat him with such disrespect.'

'You should have told him to go to hell.'

'And lose my job over it?'

'Sure you're almost working for nothing as it is.'

'Mag and me are able to live on it, not sumptuously, but in decency.'

'Only for old Tom helping you now and then you'd be out gathering scrap iron like the tinkers.'

'He paid for a holiday we had at the shore — that's all. Thank God we can stand on our own feet.'

'I know, and Julia knows, that he helps the two of you and settles your accounts occasionally.'

'It's a lie! That's what it is. Only it's Christmas I'd call in Mag and her father and make them prove it to you.'

At that moment they heard Aunt Brigid and Christy arrive and they moved away from the window in bitter silence, Sergeant rushing into the room, shaking the rain from himself, and hopping on to a cushion on an armchair. Christy joined the men in the parlour, and presently the father came in carrying a tray with three glasses of sherry and a glass of orange juice for Richard.

'I'm going to celebrate Christmas like a Christian,' Richard declared and waved back the orange juice offered to him. 'I'll give myself a dispensation for one day. Christy can tell you my ethics are above board.'

They all smiled and Tom handed him a glass of sherry.

Richard held the glass up to the light. 'Here's luck to everybody' — and plumping down on an armchair he sat heavily upon the unnoticed Sergeant who yelped madly and brought Aunt Brigid racing to the room.

'It's well he didn't give me a nick in the backside and branded me for life,' Richard said as he wiped the spilt sherry from his trousers.

'Oh, Richard!' Brigid exclaimed, stroking Sergeant in her arms.

'It'd be a nice "oh" if that had happened. Anyway I couldn't have better luck.'

Tom refilled the glass for him and they sipped at the sherry till Alice came in and told them to take their seats, Julia directing them where to sit, and at the same time propping cushions on chairs at each side of her for Marie and little Dick. Tom, at the head of the table, sharpened the knife on the steel, little Dick watching the sparks scamper from the blade. Before carving the turkey, and while the others drank their soup, he said aloud words that he had heard when he was young, 'God grant we'll all be spared till next Christmas.'

Alice put turkey and ham on each plate and Brigid spooned out the vegetables and handed the plates round the table. Tom poured out some whiskey for himself and as he did so Richard demanded in a loud voice that he be given a thimbleful to celebrate, and by the time the dinner was half over he had stretched out twice to the whiskey and his face was flushed and swollen.

The plum pudding crowned with a twig of holly was carried in from the range and as Tom sprinkled it with whiskey and set it alight, all eyes watched the blue cold flame spread calmly over the pudding and then a sudden crackle and spurt of flame as a holly leaf burnt and shrivelled, filling the room with a pleasant smell. Tom dipped his finger in the burning whiskey and held it out to little Dick, but the child winced away from the bright blue flame that wavered on the tip of the finger. 'Look, son,' Julia said and she touched

136

her father's finger in an attempt to catch the flame, and for a moment, as their fingers touched, father and daughter exchanged a secret, tender look, he thinking of the evening in the garden she had refused to hold out her hand to him, and she drawing now from his touch a feeling of confidence and security. In the rush of joy that now flushed his soul he dipped three fingers in the flame and as he held them out to her he watched her take them and hold them aloft on the tips of her own fingers where they flowered for a moment like bluebells and then shrank and went out.

After the pudding-dishes had been cleared away and the coffee cups sent round Richard struggled to his feet and despite Julia's protests he attempted to make a speech of thanks to Tom Magee. The honestest man in the town, he asserted, and thumped the table; a man who stood up for his own, in storm or calm, come rain or shine; a man who came to your rescue when you hadn't a spar; a man who kept the old ship on her course through gale and over rocks.

'And over the desert and the mountains,' Joe put in.

They all laughed and shouted 'Hear, hear' — and in the noise and clapping of hands little Dick struggled down from his chair and went over to the Christmas tree in the corner, touching the balloons and tracing his fingers over the big white letters stretched upon them.

In spite of the applause and Julia's tugging at Richard's coat-tails he went on with his speech, praising Tom for the good Irish whiskey that he kept and never spoiled by diluting it with water like a doctor's prescription. ('Hear, hear.') For a moment Richard glanced at Christy and Christy smiled and hung his head. 'And to his son across the table who'll soon be across the sea we, gentle folks, say God speed. He is ready to face the blacks in the bush and the bushes in the black. Goes forth to civilize the heathen — ah, friends, there's nothing like civilization when all is said and done. That's the motto for your banner, Christy. Civilization every time.'

'Hear, hear,' they all said and clapped their hands, and then suddenly little Dick burst a balloon, and Sergeant barked wildly and in the excitement they all began to sing 'For he's a jolly good fellow' and Julia succeeded in pushing Richard down on to his chair. And while he sat there and rubbed his face with his hand little Dick ran over to him with a wrinkled bit of the burst balloon and asked him to blow it up again.

And when dinner was over and they were all seated round the parlour fire and Richard sound asleep in an armchair, Alice, who wished to get a rest before going to her dance, suggested handing round the presents from the Christmas tree earlier than usual, and when Christy and Joe had dragged the tree into the centre of the room, and the big parcels too heavy to hang on the branches were arranged round it on the floor, Julia gave out paper hats and fitted a green one on Richard without wakening him, and going to the piano, which had not been played since her mother's death, she began to play carols while Mag and Brigid and Alice and the two children joined hands in a ring and skipped round the tree to please the children. And when they had had enough Alice stood on a pouffe and clipped off the parcels from the branches and gave them to Dick to hand round. There was even a present for Sergeant, and as Brigid unwrapped the papers that covered the parcel, and as sheet after sheet fell on the floor, she at last reached the core of it and discovered a tiny brass bell wrapped in tissue paper.

When all the presents had been handed round and admired Marie climbed on to her mother's lap and when she had fallen asleep Tom suggested to Julia that she should put her down on his bed for a while. Julia shook her head and said she would go home soon for she was afraid Richard would take more drink and be in no condition to drive the car. Scarcely had she spoken than Richard wakened, yawned, rubbed his face with his hand and discovered the paper hat on top of his head. He smiled stupidly and seeing Marie asleep on her mother's lap he stretched out a hand and patted the child's knee.

'Maybe we should go home, Richard, before the children get past their sleep?' she whispered.

'Whatever you say, Julia,' he answered, shaking his head. 'I broke my pledge but only for the Christmas season. You'll see I'll be all right by the time the New Year comes around.'

Mag helped little Dick into his coat and Julia wrapped Marie in a new rug and carried her asleep to the car, and after they had driven off Alice went upstairs to dress for the dance and was ready by the time the McKenna girls and their brother had called for her.

Their brother was a year or two older than Christy, had been at the university in Dublin for two years, had been in South Africa for seven and was now back in Rockcross to help his father, the veterinary surgeon. As they stood around in the parlour he talked to Christy about South Africa and continually loosened his neck as if the collar were too tight for him, and when Alice came into the room holding out her white frock with the tips of her fingers he took her playfully by the arm and striding up to Christy he drawled: 'How'd you like to be saying the words: "Do you, Aloysius, take Alice here present for your lawful married wife." ' Alice, laughing, struggled free from him and Brigid, going over to her, teased out the velvet bow that had been crushed.

The two McKenna girls took off their coats to display their frocks, Christy telling them that Rockcross was not behind in style.

'A pity you're not coming with us,' they teased.

'My suit's all right, but my collar's all wrong,' he said.

'And that reminds me of what the big chimney said to the little chimney,' Aloysius put in. 'Some day I'll leave you my old suit.'

'And that suit would be just as black as my own,' Christy said and noticed how he lifted a scrap of tinsel from the floor and placed it on Alice's hair.

'I wish, folks, you were all coming. Brigid and dog and all,' Aloysius declared and twirled his white scarf round his neck. 'We could pack you all in that old bus of mine outside and still have room for the two gorgeous bank clerks that are to partner my beloved sisters. Come, Alice, take my arm and we'll lead the way.' He winked at Christy: 'I'll be over some day to give you a tip or two about the African climate.'

They all stood at the door to see them off but the car wouldn't start and Christy and Joe had to come and give it a push towards the hillslope, and when it was half-way down the hill the engine started and a cloud of smoke came from the exhaust.

'I'd have more peace of mind if Alice were going with some other boy,' Brigid announced when they were seated round the fire again. 'That Aloysius McKenna is not her sort.'

'What makes you say that?' Tom probed.

'Oh, I've plenty of reasons for saying it.' She looked at Mag and Joe for corroboration.

'He's a bit light-headed, a comical fellow,' Tom said. 'That's all I see wrong with him. I know too that he was in South Africa for some years — that's all.'

'What drove him off to South Africa in the first instance?' Brigid pursued. 'There's the question, and there's more than me in this room knows the answer.'

Tom looked from one to the other. Christy was sitting with his eyes closed, Joe twirling a piece of string round his thumb, and Mag tidying away the wrapping paper that was scattered over the floor. No one spoke, and Brigid folding her arms and tapping the floor with her toe stared grimly at the fire. She shook her head and said: 'I'll say no more. After all I'm only her aunt.'

'Do any of you know anything about him?' Tom asked.

'He's a bit of a scamp,' Joe said.

'Christy, what do you know?'

'I suppose he's all right in a way.'

The father regarded him puzzledly and asked what he meant by 'in a way'.

'Oh, nothing much,' Christy answered. 'There was some bit in the paper about him a long time ago — something that happened in the university. He threw a book at the dean.'

'He threw a boot at him,' Brigid corrected. 'But there was more than a boot in it.'

'Ah, forget about the poor fellow,' Christy said, annoyed. 'It's Christmas. I'm sure he's well settled after his sojourn in Africa.'

'Leopards don't change their spots when they change their country,' Brigid persisted. 'We can't forget he's out with Alice, a young and innocent little girl.'

'In God's name,' Tom said, rising to his feet. 'Will you tell me what kind of a fellow he is or do you want me to go down to the dance hall and bring Alice home right now.'

They all spoke then, hesitatingly, glancingly, but never directly. But there was no let-up now with Tom and he tore through the confusion of each answer till he had discovered that some years ago Aloysius McKenna had been drunk and disorderly in the college, had thrown a boot at the dean, and had been involved in stealing silver cups from a show-case in the students' union and had been expelled and had gone to South Africa in disgrace.

'Don't take it too seriously, Father,' Christy advised. 'Look on it as a bit of student pranks and high spirits.'

'The spirits he had in him were too strong when he did it. Sure the account was in the newspaper for all to read,' Brigid said. 'How else would I have heard of it?'

'He was young then and we can let him begin again,' Christy said.

'Poor Mary wouldn't have allowed her to go to a dance with the likes of him,' Brigid went on, and turning to Tom: 'I'm surprised at you allowing it.'

'I knew nothing about the lad except that he was a brother of those decent McKenna girls and that he was home from South Africa.'

'Sure he has been the talk of the town since he came home.'

'I never hear the talk of the town.'

'Indeed that's true,' Brigid said drily. 'You never took much interest in us. And it's a pity you didn't.'

'I'll take less interest in it when the New Year comes around,' he said in sudden anger. 'It'll not be long now till there'll be a good distance between me and it.'

'Oh, Father,' Mag exclaimed, 'don't take these things so much to heart. Alice will be all right. Aloysius isn't a bad sort.'

'It's a great pity we haven't all forgotten about his student days,' Christy said quietly. 'Our memories for these things are too strong and too long. When a lad's at a university there's more swagger in him than malice. Forget about him.'

'What if he gets drunk and drives the car into the river on his way home?' Brigid said.

'The river's the right place for it,' Joe said, 'or failing the river it could fill up a nice gap in a hedge.'

They all laughed heartily at this except Brigid, and when they had finished she stood up and to the surprise of all she declared she was glad they were so happy, and glad that they could see so much fun in a young girl being out at a dance with a rake of a fellow that was drunk before they set out and would be drunker before the night was much older. And as for the car: she couldn't for the life of her see what was amusing to laugh at if he drove it into the river on his way home and the young girls had to wade through mud and slush in their frocks to get to dry land. She was sorry, too, that she had even spoken about the McKenna fellow, for after all she was only Alice's aunt and it wasn't her duty to interfere and admonish.

She put on her coat, hooked the leash on Sergeant, and though they tried to persuade her to stay till Mag and Joe were going home she wouldn't unbend, and while Christy was getting his coat to go a piece of the road with her she set off without him and he had to run to overtake her.

AFTER Joe and Mag had gone home Christy and his father were alone in the parlour. They were tired after the day's over-eating, and each was wearily watching the fire burn low in the grate and each reluctant to drop more coal on it to prolong the night. Out of courtesy neither was inclined to make the first move towards bed and bring the long day to a close. Christy smothered a yawn once or twice, but after the clock had struck twelve the father rose to his feet, stretched his arms and said it was time they were shutting the shop for the night. He told Christy to go on up to bed for he was sure he was not used to late nights in the college. He himself would tidy the room, bring in coal and sticks for the morning's fire and leave the back door unlocked for Alice's return.

Half an hour later on climbing the stairs he noticed a crack of light below Christy's door and he knocked and asked if he was all right. He got no answer, and opening the door he saw his son on his knees by the bedside. He spoke to him, touched his shoulder and wakened him.

'I fell asleep, Father,' he said, and shrugged his shoulders.

'With the window wide open you could get your death falling asleep like that. God doesn't expect long prayers when the mind is jaded. Hurry into bed and I'll bring you up a hot water bottle.'

In spite of his son's protests he went downstairs again, filled up a hot water bottle and carried it up to him.

'Out of obedience to your father and as a little penance you must put it at your feet,' he said with a smile.

'Do you know, Father, you'd have made a better priest than ever your son will make.'

'I'm afraid, Christy, you're still asleep or suffering from the effects of it. The best priests are the ones who think they're no good. Good night now and talk sense.' And he switched off the light and went across the landing to his own room.

He undressed slowly and when he was in bed he was surprised that the drowsiness he had felt at the fireside had now forsaken him. His mind was clear, his eyes no longer heavy. He lay on his back, his arms under his head, and pondered Christy's remark, wondering if the lad had anything troubling his mind. He retraced every movement and every word of Christy's since his homecoming but could find nothing to support his worry or make him suspect that his son was tortured by scruples. No, no, no, he said to himself, the strange fancy is in my own mind and not in Christy's. There are some people you can be sure of in this life, people who are always constant: Christy is one of them and Mag is another.

He turned on his right side to sleep. He wondered if he was sure he had left the back door unbarred for Alice's return, and to pacify himself he went down the stairs quietly and saw that everything was all right. Anyway, she would be home soon. But it's a great pity she hadn't a nicer partner to go with than Aloysius McKenna. Strange that he had never heard anything about the lad until Aunt Brigid started the hinting and the nudging. It all shows the little interest he ever took in the town's gossip when not only could he not recall the lad's expulsion from the college but he couldn't even remember ever seeing him before. And yet he must have been around often with his two sisters and played at the field at the back of the house when they were all young. From the remarks passed tonight he doubted very much if Aloysius was the sort of young man that would attract Alice. Surely she would prefer someone less light-headed, less mad. But he mustn't think too much about him: if he were really as bad as Aunt Brigid made him out to be Christy would surely have dropped a hint or two. And when he was under fire Christy defended him. He mustn't think any more about the lad. Anyway Alice has enough common sense to know sense when she meets it.

He heard the clock strike two, and he was still awake. Three struck, and shortly afterwards came the explosive noise of the McKennas' car as it surmounted the hill. Voices called out cheerily in the night: 'Everything all right, Alice?' — and in a few minutes the back door was pushed open, the key turned in the lock, and the rustle of Alice's dress as she ascended the stairs. The father breathed easily, turned on his right side and was soon asleep.

Christy was first up in the morning and the creak of the front door opening as he went out to Mass wakened his father, and he rose at once, lit the fire and had Christy's breakfast ready for him by the time he came back from the chapel. Then he put Alice's breakfast on a tray and brought it up to her. He drew back the curtains and standing at the window waited for her to waken. A misty drizzling rain was falling on the dishevelled garden and falling on a flock of starlings that were foraging noisily in the stubble field. He pulled down the window to let in more air and the sound startled the starlings and they rose up like a puff of soot and settled in the trees at the head of the field. The sound also awakened Alice and he brought the tray over to her while she pulled on her bed-jacket. He propped pillows at her back and sat on the edge of the bed and asked her about the dance.

'Oh, Father, it was great and Aloysius was the best of fun. He had me in stitches laughing all night.'

Not wishing to annihilate her joy he let her talk on without interruption, and he learnt that Aloysius had told her all about himself even to the throwing the boot at the dean and his subsequent expulsion from the college.

146

'You'd think, Alice, there must have been a graver reason for expelling him than that.'

'Indeed you would. But he told me the college authorities in Dublin are far too strict. And I'm sure they are. They shouldn't have expelled the poor fella as if he were a common criminal.... This is lovely breakfast, Father.' Laying down her knife and fork she began to laugh so much that the tea jabbled from the cup on to the saucer. 'Excuse me for laughing so much. But I'm laughing at a funny thing Aloysius told me.' And wiping her eyes with her father's handkerchief she began to tell him of the incident that was making her laugh.

One evening for devilment Aloysius carried a live hen in his attaché case into the college library. All the students were seated round the tables hard at their books, and in the deep silence Aloysius, unnoticed by anyone, released the hen. It was a white leghorn and it trotted across the polished parquet floor and flew up on to one of the tables, and when the students, Aloysius among them, tried to grab it, it flew from their hands and perched on a marble bust of Goldsmith, not on his shoulders, but on top of his bald head where it sat down and looked for all the world like a lady's hat. In the commotion that followed, the librarian came in and gave the students ten minutes to clear the library of the fowl pest otherwise he would see that the building was closed to them for a week. They all sat up then, girls and boys, and swiped at it with rolled up sheets of paper till at last someone got a feather-duster and poked it off Goldsmith's head and it flew up and settled on an electric standard hanging from the ceiling. A step-ladder was brought in and Aloysius volunteered to catch it if they would switch off the lights for a second or two. He caught it and the librarian told him he was the only fellow with brains in the whole place.

'And what happened the hen in the heel of the hunt?' the father said.

'Oh, the librarian took Aloysius and the hen in his car

147

and they drove out to the country and at the first field they came to he told Aloysius to throw it over the hedge. And when they were driving back the librarian kept saying that he only wished to the good God that he knew the fellow who brought poultry into the library and he would make it hot for him. Oh, Father, if you only heard Aloysius telling it you'd double up with the laughing. I must really get him to tell you it the next time he calls. He thinks the world of our Christy and he'll be calling soon to have a long chat with him. And by the way he has asked me to go to a big New Year's dance in Newry and I've agreed to go. Won't that be all right?'

'If you've agreed to go, girl, it'd be better to keep your promise. He doesn't drink — does he?'

'I wouldn't care for him if he did. When he was dancing with me last night I would have known it. He chewed a clove most of the night and though I disliked the smell of it I didn't tell him so.'

'No, you couldn't do a thing like that,' he said, smiling at her naivety.

She smiled back at him, a smile of joyful recollection and as he lifted the tray words he didn't wish to say came out with an abrupt rush: 'I'm expecting news one way or another about Monabeg these days.'

'And you'll go if an exchange is offered to you?'

'I suppose I will. And you?'

'I'd have to go wherever you go, Father.' And she lowered her head and broke off a hanging thread from her bed-jacket.

He told her to stay in bed for a while yet, and going downstairs he discussed Aloysius with Christy, and Christy advised him not to thwart her at this stage, not to object to her going to a dance with him for it might only drive her too close to him.

'If Monabeg was offered to me tomorrow I'd set off without a qualm. I would indeed.'

'Alice would not be fascinated by a foolish fella the like

of Aloysius if that's what's in your mind. The same fella would laugh himself into hysterics if he thought he was responsible for driving you from the town.'

'One daughter married to an unreliable husband is enough for any parent to stand.'

'Alice has sense.'

'We thought Julia had — and look where it has landed her.'

Before the week was at an end the half-expected letter from the Monabeg stationmaster arrived. He and his wife intended to visit Rockcross before deciding on the exchange that head office had offered to them. Tom waited their coming and when they did arrive they called first at the station where they were shown around. Then they called on Tom. He showed them through his own house and garden and complained that owing to its position in the shelf of a hill the soil was inclined to be heavy and that some spots of ground damp were for ever appearing in certain corners of the house. But as he enumerated its faults they were already comparing it with the narrow-waisted house in Monabeg and with the fine house in Rockcross station which they would inhabit as soon as Mr Wilson retired. Tom's manner puzzled them and the more they sensed a reluctance on his part to leave the more eager they became in their own minds for the exchange. At last he asked them directly if they thought they would like the place, and for a moment man and wife looked at him and then at each other and nodding their heads they thought it would suit them all right.

'Then in God's name you can have it. We'll settle it at that and write to head office accordingly.'

He shook hands with them and wished them many happy years, and as he watched them set off down the hill a sudden heaviness came over him and he turned into the house and filled himself a good measure of whiskey.

Christy realized that this move would mean the break-up of the family, the family that his mother had striven to hold together, who from her death-bed had passed on this constant resolution of hers into his keeping. He had tried to carry out her wish but he had failed, and listening now in the evenings to his father praising Rockcross he knew that the imminence of the leave-taking was not going to be the happy venture his father had anticipated. Deep in his father's heart he knew there were unconscious attachments ready to spring forward and block his leave-taking; he had foreseen this long ago but now that the decision was made there could be no rejection or cancellation without a complete breakdown in his father's health. In the few days that were left to him before his return to college he would urge his father to go forward hopefully and throw away all shreds of regret. He had made the change or rather the change had been thrust upon him and he must make the best of it.

'But I feel I'm deserting Julia and Mag,' the father would say to him, unconsciously quoting what Christy had said to him months ago.

'You'll be no distance away from them,' Christy would counter with words his father had used in their long-ago discussion. 'A few hours' journey in the train and they're with you or you with them.'

'But I'm taking Alice away from her friends.'

'She's better away from Aloysius McKenna. She'll find and fare better in Monabeg.'

'You think I'm doing the right thing, Christy?'

'Of course you are. Change is good for us all.'

And after Christy had returned to college in mid-January his father held that conversation in his mind and repeated it often to himself when he found his own mind emptying itself of all the prejudices he had nurtured against Rockcross. Men and women spoke to him, people whom he hardly knew, and expressed regret that he would soon be leaving them. They had often set their clocks by him as he went to his work, they told him; and they reminded him of occasions when he had held up the train for a couple of minutes on seeing them hurrying along to catch it — they'd never forget him for his consideration.

Why had he been so incurious about people? he asked himself; curiosity of the right kind came from a deep interest in people and he had none. He had friends, many friends in this town, and he hadn't known it or gone out of his way to know it.

'Maybe at this last minute we should cancel it?' he said to Alice one night.

'But we couldn't do that, Father. Most of our furniture is sent on ahead of us. And I'm looking forward greatly to going away,' she added, for Christy had warned her what to say.

'And Aloysius McKenna?'

'I like his sisters but not him. I discovered something the last dance I was with him in Newry — he drinks like a fish. One of his sisters had to drive us home or he'd surely have landed us in the ditch. I can tell you that now.'

'You're a good girl. You're all good — Julia, Mag and Christy — every one of you. In this life we think we always know what is best for us but we don't. What is closest to us, our own selves, we do not know.'

Two days before he was due to leave, a note came from Joe's boss and with it the unpaid bill for Richard's two suits. Richard had asked that the bill be sent to his father-in-law. He tore the note in pieces and threw it in the fire. Richard was dragging himself down and dragging them all with him and sooner or later he would lose everything if he didn't pull himself together. Monabeg would be an escape from the likes of that fella, he thought; and then he shook his head at the selfishness of that thought, for an escape from Richard was a desertion of Julia and in neither way was there contentment. It'd be better for him to go round at once and pay the damned bill if only to relieve Julia of a little worry. That's what he'd do — he'd pay it and ask that the receipt be sent to Richard without comment.

The following day was his last in Rockcross and as he didn't wish any of them to come to the station to see him off he decided to visit them in turn. He called at Richard's office and though he knew that Richard had already received the receipt for the paid bill no mention was made of it. Richard did all the talking, shaking hands with him several times, slapping him on the shoulder, and promising him that if the next child was a boy he would be called Tom.

He called then on Julia but on arriving at her house Aunt Brigid was with her and since she put a constraint upon their meeting he told Julia to be sure and call up to see Alice in the evening as she had some things to give her. He stayed only a few minutes and when he said that he was going on to see Mag Aunt Brigid proposed going with him as far as the shop.

'This is the last time we'll see each other,' she said as they walked off together from Julia's.

'No, not the last,' he said. 'I'll be back in Rockcross often I hope.'

'Tell me this, Tom, and tell me honestly. Am I responsible in any way for this change?'

He knew what was in her mind but not to embarrass her he did not revert to it, and just told her that his desire to get back to Monabeg was always in his mind since the day he married.

'There'll be many people miss you in this town,' she said. 'Julia and her children and Mag and Joe. But none of them will miss you as much as I will. Do you hear what I'm saying to you?'

He nodded his head, and misinterpreting his silence she again declared her love for him and asked him to write to her should he ever find himself alone in the world.

'You're good and kind,' he said, 'and I know the children will always have you as their friend.'

'And so will you. I feel Mary would have wished that.'

'Thanks, Brigid, thanks for all your goodness.' And as he

shook her hand firmly she ran away from him before he'd see her cry.

He called on Mag. Joe was not in and because it was cold she had a large fire burning in the grate. He sat with her for a long time and as he spoke she sensed the heaviness on his heart that burdened and saddened him. She knew that he had always lived for them and now when he was on the verge of living for himself, in his own home-place, he could not rise to it. If he were less selfish he could go from them with a smile, and after what Joe had told her yesterday about paying Richard's bill he could, if he were any other man, be glad of the chance to get away from his relations.

'Father, you're doing the right thing,' she kept saying to him, 'not only for yourself but for Alice and for us all. As I've said often before we'll have a place to visit for our holidays.'

'You and Joe and what's to be born will always be welcome — always. I prayed for direction but to my shame took little or no part in the direction. I wanted to go to Monabeg and now that the time has come I feel I don't wish to go at all.'

'You were always respected here. People might not know you as well as they knew Mother and Aunt Brigid but they always respected you and up to now respected everybody belonging to you.'

She looked at him tenderly and he knew what was in her mind and knew too that she'd never come out with it.

'Oh, Father, you'll do well for your new place! I know it, I know it! You are going back where you were reared and going amongst your own. I know too when we visit you after my big event we'll see your hand upon the station. It will be bright with flowers and paint. It will be something that passengers will look out at and admire.'

'It will, Mag girl, it will. I will have it ready for your coming. And I'll give you the brightest room in the house. The rooms are small but you and your baby that's to come will have the sunniest room in it. And you needn't get Joe to lug a cot. As soon as I hear the good news I'll make a cot and carry it up to your room.'

'Oh, Father, I feel great joy in your going. I do, I do!' And to ease the joy that weakened her like a release of pain she rose slowly and stood at the window, wiping the mist off it with her handkerchief, and gazing at a slowly moving freight train hurtling its white smoke through the bare trees.

He stood beside her and lifting her hand he squeezed it tightly. She turned and put her head on his breast and wept.

'Don't heed me, Father, they're tears of joy — joy that we're both getting what we yearned for.'

ON the last Saturday in January in the late afternoon Alice and her father came to Monabeg where their furniture, having arrived ahead of time, had been placed by the outgoing stationmaster in positions already designated for them. The day was cold, sharpening to frost, a low orange sun hanging in a bruised haze, and a dark wind blowing in from the river and flitting the labels on the empty bread-hampers stacked on the station platform. Alice stood without speaking, appalled at the smallness of the place, her father appalled at its obvious neglect: white palings casting flakes of paint, windows in need of a douse of water, and doors gloomed in the dark brown common to all railway stations. 'Well, well,' he said, and lifting the suitcases entered the house by a side door on the platform.

The porter, having already lighted a good fire for them, had gone off, leaving the room as warm as an oven. Two steps led down to the scullery and after Tom had filled the kettle he opened the stiff door that led into the garden, and walked across a cindered path and down steps made of old railway sleepers to where four apple trees crouched like umbrellas and beehives rotted against the northern hedge.

'It's a long time since that garden had a loving hand laid on it,' he said, shaking his head at the broken panes in the greenhouse and staring into the distance at the rusty rushes and the trenches of wrinkled water. Alice put up the collar of her coat, and silently counted on the fingers of her hands all the houses that comprised the village and wondered to herself what possessed her father to leave Rockcross for a place so small as this. But not wishing to upset him she put to flight all the belittling comments that overran her mind, and as they turned back into the house she began to say things in praise of it.

'Oh, Alice, I'm glad you're not disappointed in it. At this time of the year with no growth or greenery it's looking its shabbiest. But wait till I get my foot on the lugs of a spade and you'll see a change in that garden out there. You will indeed.'

They went upstairs and inspected the rooms, and after making up two beds Alice went down to the kitchen and prepared their first meal at a little table placed against the window through which she could see the storage sheds and three tarpaulin-covered wagons with their destination marks chalked up on their sides. As she waited for the tea to draw, her fingers nervously tugged at her necklace of beads and the string broke and scattered the beads over the floor.

'I trust in God that's not a bad omen, child.'

'It's the sign of a bad string, Father, that's all.'

As they sat at the table the last freight train clanked slowly past, tinkling the crockery on the table and disturbing the starlings lined four-deep on the telegraph wires. They heard the signalman open the level-crossing gates and the held-up cars bumping on to the main road, and then the signalman passed the window, knocked at the door and handed in his keys to Tom. Alice heard them talk for a while, and when the signalman had gone off the starlings ceased their orations and flew to their roosts under the scalloped eaves of the sheds. Silence closed in upon the station, darkness dropped down and the firelight fluttered in the window pane.

Neither of them rose to switch on the light, and the father drawing his chair round to the fire filled up his pipe and spoke of Julia and Mag and Christy and wondered what each would be doing at this very moment.

'Ah, Alice,' he sighed, 'the heart can lose its allegiance without our knowing it and I'm thinking I did wrong to

156

leave Rockcross the way I did to come back here where I thought my heart lay. I've got my desire and already it's falling short of what I hoped.'

'You did right to leave Rockcross. I know it. We all know it.'

'When a man brings a family into the world they are always on his mind no matter where he goes or what they do or how often they disappoint him. You might think there's no sense in what I say but when you're married — and I hope you will be — you'll see the truth in what I say.'

He got up and paraded the floor. The room now seemed to him no bigger than a box, and yet when he was in it thirty years ago and drinking tea with the old lame stationmaster he was uncritical of it, seeing it then with the free friendly eyes of youth.

'You think you'll like this place?' he asked suddenly.

'I'll like what you like. And I'll join a correspondence course and study for my matric.'

'Yes, and when we get settled and things running sweetly you'll have to go back when Julia's time has come and help to mind little Dick and Marie or maybe bring the two of them along here and give poor Julia a chance to recuperate.'

They cleared the dishes from the table and putting on their heavy coats strolled through the village in the frosty air. Light from a few shops laid squares on the roadway and a bright light above the pub door reflected on the white walls where a group of men were sheltering from the wind. He bade the men good night and though they answered his greeting none of them knew him or they would have added 'Tom' or 'Mr Magee' to their reply. Perhaps they were children when he was here last — here at a time when there was no electric light and one stumbled through the village in a cavern of gloom.

They reached the roadbridge that spanned the river and under the lamp-standard that illuminated it he brushed the frost needles from the parapet with the sleeve of his coat and gazed down at the strong current flowing away into the flat darkness of the countryside. In late September or October he had often rowed down it to its little islands to have a crack at the duck and then at daybreak pulled back against the strong current. The thought now shuddered him for he felt somehow the rawness of the cold on his hands and the realization that he would be no longer fit for it. Catching a few pike on a summer's day would have to content him now. Yes, that would be the height of what he could do and as he mused at that the memory of the ugly pike he had caught in Rockcross came back to him and taking Alice by the arm he hurried from the bridge on to a path along the river bank, their feet muffled by the sand where the sand-barges were unloaded. They reached the railway track that smelt of tar and their feet pinged on the iron bridge that carried the railroad over the river, and against the sky a signal stood erect, its red eye aglow and one arm raised stiffly like a scarecrow.

'Listen, Alice,' he said holding her arm.

'To the wind in the wires?'

'No, no, listen to the rumble of the falls. That's the river tumbling out of the lough. In summer it will be all different. You'll have boating and picnics then, and you can swim the whole day long in the lough and play tennis with the Miss Walshes. Oh, Alice, you'll not be at a loss for friends I may tell you.'

'I'll not need them.'

'Of course you will. You'll not be lonely. Every young girl needs heaps of friends and a bit of brightness. But you'll make your own way and you'll study in the evenings and be something worthwhile.'

They came into the village again and saw in the light from the shop windows a man in the middle of the road leaning on the back of a chair and pushing it in front of him for support. Alice smiled. He was heading for the pub and at every ten yards or so he halted, sat down on the chair for a rest, and then got up and continued his shuffling journey. Tom recognized him. He was Ben Brady, a man who taught him chess years ago, a man whose two legs were now stiff as gate-posts with rheumatism. Tom went after him and Alice could hear Ben's loud voice: 'Ah, be the holy sure I heard you were here and I went up on my Rolls Royce to the station-house and damn the squeak could I get from it. I'm going now on low gear over to the pub. Sit now on the front seat and I'll give you a lift,' he laughed loudly. Tom hurried back to Alice, gave her the key of the house and told her he'd have to go with Ben to the pub and stand him a drink or two.

Alice didn't wait for her father to come home but went to bed early and in the morning he came into her room and wakened her for Mass, wakened her to a world of Sunday whiteness, every bush and tree arrayed in frost, and the railway lines like long white ladders lying flat across the fields. At breakfast they heard the fists of the church bells pound and ground the air and as they wheeled out their bicycles to cycle the two and a half miles to the church they were surprised to see by the unmarked frost on the road that they were the first to leave the village. They took their time, pedalling cautiously, the frost striking their faces like flying needles of glass, and the turf smoke from the houses trying to take the sting from the air. A man polishing his boots at an open door called out to them for the correct time and going inside shouted to his children to hurry or they'd all be late.

They had time to call at the graveyard before Mass and as he showed Alice where his people lay at rest he lifted a piece of slate and scraped off the frost from the headstone and read the names aloud. And as he said a prayer for all their souls he recalled the visit he had made with Aunt Brigid to his wife's grave in Rockcross and knew, in his inmost heart, that his own name would never be engraved on the headstone in front of him.

'My brother John is the last name on that headstone,'

he said sadly, 'and I suppose it is the last name that will ever go on to it,' he added and turned away. As their feet crunched over the frosted grass he pointed through the hedge to the house where he was reared and to a little gate in a field where he had often run as a boy to serve Mass. 'A James O'Hara is in the house now and I must have a look out for him after Mass.'

The last bell sounded from the bell-tower and the people who were round the graves began to move away. Some of the older women recognized Tom, shook hands with him and welcomed him back, praising the fine lump of a daughter he had with him.

Inside the church it was as cold as a vault, their fingers so numb they had to blow the pages of their missals apart with their breath to turn them, and when the priest began to preach Tom squeezed his back hard against the seat to warm himself.

After Mass the men congregated in groups outside the church, lighting their pipes and exchanging the latest news and the highest prices to be had for hay. Alice stood aside while her father mixed with the men but when she saw a poster hanging on the chapel gates she went over and read that the Monabeg Dramatic Society would give a performance of *Autumn Fire* by T. C. Murray in the Hall tonight at 8 p.m. She made up her mind that she would go to it.

The sun came up and scattered the haze and hung silver on every twig and branch. The groups of men broke up and she saw her father talking and laughing with a small man about his own age. Her father stared across at her in a strange way and then suddenly he called her over and introduced her to James O'Hara, his greatest friend, one of the old stock. Shyly she stood while James looked her up and down, saying at one moment that she was a true Magee and then contradicting himself by saying she must take after her mother's side.

He invited them up to the house, and leaving their bicycles

160

against the graveyard wall they ambled along the frosty road, the two men talking of their schooldays, of poaching for rabbits, of setting long lines for eels and shooting duck, and they would occasionally draw up on the road and laugh at some incident that occurred to their minds simultaneously. And all the time Alice walked along unnoticed, following them up a lonin that led to a slated farmhouse where two dogs ran out to greet them, and two youths appeared at the front door for an instant and hurried in again, nowhere to be seen when the three entered the big kitchen where a woman with her hat and coat still on after Mass was endeavouring to tidy up the Sunday morning untidiness from the table and chairs. And there Alice had to sit near the wide fire and take tea on her lap and baked bread that had a thick mortar of butter while her father talked with unconcealed joy of his eldest son that, please God, would be ordained in June, and of Julia who would soon be having her third child and of Mag that would just be in in a photo-finish with her first.

'You've done well for them by all accounts,' Mrs O'Hara said, having taken off her hat and coat and tidied her hair. 'And this is a fine girl you've brought amongst us and just as shy as them two boys of mine that fled like hares through the back door as you came in the front.'

She put some turf below a big pot on the fire and standing with a hand on her hinch declared that it must have been a hard wrench for him to break away from Rockcross and leave his family behind.

'It was, I suppose,' Tom said, rubbing a hand along his cheek. 'But when Monabeg was offered to me I took it. I trust in God I did right.'

'The railway company did right to bring in a good man. The poor man that's gone hadn't his fair share of health since he stepped into it and if Rockcross agrees with him as it has with you he'll live to draw a good haul of pension money from the company. And may God prosper you, Tom, the way He has prospered us since we bought this farm of your poor brother that lies beyond in the graveyard. We haven't lost a beast since we first put a foot across the threshold. Isn't that so, James?' she addressed her husband.

'It is, it is,' James said. 'When you've a good woman at the helm anything will prosper.' And at the mention of helm Tom smiled, thinking of Richard and his nautical terms.

James took Tom around the outhouses and going into a stable he barred the door behind him and in the light that filtered through the cobwebs on the window he kicked straw away with his feet, lifted a trap-door in the floor and descending a ladder whispered to Tom to follow him; and then in the underground darkness he lit a lamp and when the lamp globe had warmed and the wick was turned up Tom saw against one wall a grey poteen still and the ashes of a dead-out fire below it.

Tom whistled his breath in surprise: 'I never saw the beating of that in all my born days. Never!'

'She hasn't been in action since Christmas,' James said in a low voice. 'The wife's dead set against it and I only make a drop at Christmas and Easter and sometimes at the turf-cutting. But I make it well. I always give it the three runs, and I've some matured stuff in a corner for my best friends, every tint of it five-year-old — that's the God's truth I'm telling you. You'll have a bottle away with you never fear, and in hard weather the like we have now a few drops of it would bring warmth into a cork leg.'

He crouched behind the still and showed how he had joined the flue with that of the kitchen-chimney and how he had a supply of cold water coming from an overhead tank and the outflow going through a pipe below ground-level and trickling away into a stream at the back of the house.

'A masterpiece of engineering,' Tom said and he patted him on the back and hoped he wasn't being sacrilegious in asking God to keep it safe for him.

James rummaged behind a load of turf in the corner and

producing a bottle wiped the dust from it with a rag and held the bottle against the lamp. 'As clear as a drop of rain on a thorny hedge. Man, Tom, a cupful of that in a bride's cake would keep it fresh for a year and make all who ate it happy for a week. It would do more than that; a spoonful of it would chase in one night the heaviest cold that ever lay on an Eskimo's chest. Not that I should praise the produce of my own fields or the work of my own hands.'

'A powerful contraption entirely,' Tom said, looking into the barrel where the worm disappeared. 'And to think of the poor fellas down in the islands frozen to their skins at night making it out in the open.'

'I wouldn't compare their stuff with mine. Theirs is the colour of skimmed milk and it would poison a regiment of rats and come back for the commanding officer. I wouldn't have stuff like that lying on my conscience.'

'No, nor lying on your stomach.'

'Not a whimper to the wife about it, Tom,' he warned as they climbed the ladder to where the ammonia smell of the stable quenched the smell of the still-house. 'Not a word to her for when I run off a gallon or two I never let on, and what she doesn't know she won't have to confess to the priest.'

It was near midday when Alice and her father arrived back at the station and he kept apologizing to her for staying so long and holding up the making of the dinner. To make amends he washed the potatoes for her and scraped a few carrots and made up his own bed. And because the sun was bright he knew the evening would turn cold and he lit the fire in the station's waiting-room in case there would be passengers arriving or departing by the train in the evening. And after dinner he wrote letters to Julia and Mag and laid them open on the window-ledge in case Alice would wish to enclose a line or two of her own.

That evening it turned bitterly cold and though he was reluctant to leave the comfort of the house and go with her to the Hall to see *Autumn Fire* he realized that it was only her

163

second night in Monabeg and the place, God knows, dull enough for any Christian that it would be better to help her to seize every bit of brightness or interest that would attract her.

They hadn't far to walk, for the Hall was situated beside the pub and as they climbed the steps and entered by the brightly lit door they were early enough to get seats in the third row. Alice glanced in front of her at the heavy wine-red curtains and turning her head to read posters on the side walls announcing forthcoming films she was conscious of a young policeman staring at her from a seat in the second row. Wherever she turned he looked at her, and to avoid the pleasurable embarrassment of his constant stare she lifted her programme and fixed her eyes on it, aware in her own mind of the freshly shaved face of the policeman, the tracks of the comb in his brown hair, the white handkerchief tucked in the sleeve of his uniform and his gloves lying inside his cap that lay on his lap. She yawned deliberately and tapping her mouth politely with the programme gazed in his direction and watched him light his pipe and stow the matchbox in the breast pocket of his uniform. The flap of the breast pocket lay open but after crossing his legs he buttoned it, tapped it delicately with his fingers and threw a smile towards the corner of the stage where Alice could see nothing to smile at. Music from a gramophone played from somewhere at the front of the hall and the curtains bulged as someone passed by on the inside. The hall was filling up quickly and those who were last to arrive had snowflakes on their shoulders, and women who were already seated were whispering to one another and saying: 'It's snowing outside. Dear, dear, and me coming out without an umbrella.'

Alice's father filled his pipe and as he tapped his pockets he exclaimed that he'd forgotten his matches, and the young policeman turned sideways in his chair and handed the box to Alice, who was sitting nearest to him.

'Thank you very much,' she said, handing them back after her father had lit his pipe.

'Thanks for nothing,' the policeman said, and opening the box he gave her half of them for her father.

There was a loud clear voice at the entrance door and everyone turned round, laughing, as they heard Ben Brady demanding admittance at half-price because he had fetched his own seating accommodation. After much discussion and loud laughter Ben shuffled up the side-aisle pushing his chair in front of him, and to the amusement and hand-clapping of the audience, he reached the front row, planted his chair at the side, took off his cap and shook the snow from it and before sitting down announced: 'You can begin now! His Excellency has arrived.'

'The best performance of the night!' Tom said.

'He's a caution!' the policeman said, smiling at Alice.

'He's a heartscald,' a women commented. 'He gets every-thing easy including a dose of the cold on account of his poor legs.'

The gramophone ceased playing, the lights dimmed, went out, and the heavy curtains parted to reveal a farm-kitchen and an old-young woman knitting near a window. A young girl enters and Alice follows her closely but later as she is described as 'a flighty bit that would throw eyes at a tomb-stone' she lowers her head fearing the policeman would turn in his seat to look at her.

Her father let his pipe go cold as he followed the theme of the play, watching a widower marrying a young girl scarcely half his age and foolishly bringing her into his family where his grown-up son is already in love with her. And as the tragedy truly unfolds itself: jealousy, discord, love and anger clashing one upon another he draws comfort from the thought that he had never any inclination to remarry, and now and again he repeats to himself: 'A man isn't as young as he feels.'

His pity goes out to the young wife and son who are both striving hard to do right though their hearts are tugging the other way and inwardly he admires the greatness that is

165

in both of them, and at the final moment of the play — when the lights are dimmed upon the stage and the broken old man takes his rosary beads and says: 'They've broken me ... son ... wife ... daughter.... I've no one now but the Son o' God' — Tom closes his eyes to keep at bay the emotion that sweeps over him.

And as the audience applaud, the policeman turns excitedly to Tom and says: 'What do you think of that for a play! He's writing about a bit of the country I know well. He knows his people all right.'

'There's things in all of us it's hard to fight against. He's speaking to the common heart that is in all of us.'

'He has another play I hope you'll see some day,' the policeman went on. 'It's about a young lad that turns back from the priesthood on the eve of his ordination.'

'I'm afraid it wouldn't be as good as the one we're after seeing. I mean its story isn't a common one like that of an elderly man marrying a young girl,' Tom commented, and though he was mechanically clapping the players who were taking their final curtain his mind was not on them but on what the policeman might say next.

The audience rose to leave the hall and as they moved slowly towards the exit Alice walked in front of her father and the young policeman.

'That other play you were telling me about,' Tom said, 'does the lad go back to the college when he sees the foolish thing he has done?'

'No, he doesn't. His poor mind gives way under the strain.'

'It'd be a sad play that, I'm thinkin'. I don't think I'd care to see it.'

'If you once saw it you'd never forget it.'

They had reached the exit. It was snowing heavily outside and a sharp wind was blowing snowflakes through the door-way, and as Alice put up the collar of her coat and tightened her belt the policeman was advising Tom to get her into the dramatic company for there was nothing that would give her a greater interest, and if ever she'd think of joining it he would be glad to speak for her.

'We're very grateful to you indeed, sir,' Tom said, and introduced himself as the new stationmaster and told him he'd be welcome to a cup a tea in the house any evening he was off duty. The policeman thanked him and after shaking hands with Alice he gave her a friendly smile and raised his peaked cap to her.

They ran down to the station through the suffocating whirl of snow, and once inside the house and the snow shaken from their coats Tom talked of nothing but the young policeman.

'He's a friendly sort, Father,' Alice said. 'Nice of him to talk to us.'

'The poor fella's probably lonely and is glad of somebody to talk to,' he replied and took a hurricane lamp from a hook on the wall. As he lit the wick he told her she should think seriously of joining the dramatic club.

'Sure I might be no good,' she said, combing her hair at a shaving mirror and looking sideways at the pink glow on her cheeks. 'Or maybe if I turned out a success you might lose me to some film-company.'

'As long as I don't lose you to an old man,' he joked back, 'I won't mind.'

Putting on his cap with the word 'Stationmaster' in gold braid above the peak, he noticed the two open letters on the window-ledge and he asked her to put a note in each of them for Mag and Julia and he himself would write to Christy after he had locked up for the night.

He went out to the platform and saw the sleepers already obliterated by the snow, the telegraph wires thickening to ropes, and the glow of the lamp-heads shrunken to the size of a yellow moon.

All the doors were locked except that of the waiting-room and he stuck his head round the door and stared across at the fire dying out in the grate. He closed the door and was about to lock it when some unconscious urge made him open it again, and on switching on the light he saw lying on a bench along the wall a ragged tramp, his head on a bundle, the nail-heads on his boots shining brightly. Tom strode across the bare floor and asked him what he meant by lying there.

'For the love of God, sir,' the tramp groaned, 'don't turn me out. I'll do no harm, sir. I'll leave at break of day; I will sir, as God's my judge.'

The bare window rattled in the wind and the patches of snow on the panes gave back the light.

'Do you make a habit of this?' Tom asked.

'No, sir, this is my first time. I couldn't get out to the Walshes' barn for the snow was choking me.'

Tom put the lamp on the round table and going to the fire threw on a few lumps of coal from the scuttle and went out, leaving the door unlocked.

He said nothing to Alice about the tramp and after warming his hands at the fire he sat down at the table and began to write to Christy, telling him about the months ahead that were going to be full for everybody: Julia's third child, Mag's first, and then, please God, the greatest day of all, ordination day, the Magees there in full strength and with them Aunt Brigid and her beloved Sergeant with the superior's permission. He sealed the letter and wrote the address across it with a satisfied flourish, and after leaving it on the window-ledge he once more opened the door on to the platform and looked out at the white vacancy of the station, the snow drifting on to the footplate of the weighing-machine and the dark footprints that led to the waiting-room door.

'I'll let him stay. I'll close my eyes to it.' Turning inside he closed the outside door with a bang, shaking the snow from its panels.

From his bed he could hear the snowstorm rubbing itself like heavy cattle against the walls of the house, the sound arousing memories of Rockcross, memories of storms bumping against the gable and whining down the hillslope and across the little bridge to the town. Everything would be white there with this weather, and he supposed that in the morning Julia's garden would be a tablecloth of white until little Dick would come out riding on a spade and call to his daddy to make a snowman. Yes, that's what will happen; and sighing loudly he stretched his feet and was soon asleep.

But in the early hours of the morning he wakened and heard a stumbling noise like a horse in a stable. Then it ceased, broke out again, and he raised himself on one elbow and listened. The storm had spent itself, and thinking that the noise came from snow tumbling from the roof he was about to lie down again when once more he heard the strange rumbling and the voices of men in anger. He threw aside the bed-clothes and striking a match he stared at his watch hanging by its chain to the bedpost. It was after two and he pulled on his trousers and jacket and thrust his feet into his unlaced boots and made off down the stairs in the dark and out towards the waiting-room that pounded like a boxing-ring. He rushed inside and switching on the light saw the table upturned and two tramps struggling on the floor one on top of the other.

'Get up to hell the pair of you and clear out of here!' Tom shouted. 'This is a nice how-do-you-do. And sweet God look at the state of the place.' He glared at the crumpled newspapers, crusts of bread, and a blackened tea-can lying on its side on the floor.

The two tramps sat up, glaring at one another, and panting heavily.

'Don't blame me, sir,' said the tramp whom Tom had allowed to stay in the waiting-room. 'I was sleeping on the floor fornenst the fire and when I woke up I seen the window open, the light on, and my bold bastard putting a can of tea on the fire for himself. I told him to switch off the light and behave decent-like and he asked me who in hell I was talking to and did I think I was the director of the bloody railway company. I said nothing to vex him, sir. I wanted to behave like a Christian and told him the new stationmaster was a damned good sort.'

'Is he indeed! He can be a right nasty sort when he's roused. The two of you pack up at once and get to hell out of here before I step up to the barracks.'

'But, sir, he put coal on the fire and I beat back my temper. I turned off the light and I told him if he'd lay a finger on it I'd brain him with the tongs.'

'That's a damned lie, stationmaster.'

'It's the Lord's truth, sir.'

'I haven't time to be listening to the pair of you blackguarding one another. Lift your bundles and march off.'

The tramps eyed one another with impotent ferocity, and as the polite one set the table upright and gathered the newspapers from the floor he pointed to a slash of tea leaves on the hearth and declared with outraged decency that it was the tea leaves that set him mad.

'I tholed him, sir, while he ate and drank as ignorant as a horse and flung crusts about like an overfed rat. But I could stick him no longer, sir, when he dashed the dregs of his can on the floor. I told him he was no gentleman and I went for him.'

'It's this way, stationmaster.'

'I don't want to hear another word from either of you.

Clear off to wherever you're going and count yourselves lucky that I don't report you to the barracks.' And shrugging his shoulders against the cold he shooshed them in front of him and as he did so the young policeman appeared in the doorway.

'I see you've trespassers, Mr Magee. A nice welcome to Monabeg. Just sit down in the room till I get a statement or two.'

'Let them go, Constable,' Tom said, his mind working rapidly to extricate himself from the dilemma that was approaching.

The two tramps began to speak simultaneously and the constable appealed for order as he put his notebook on the table.

'Don't bother tonight, Constable,' Tom entreated, 'we'll get our death of cold sitting around like this.'

The policeman advised him to go and get on a heavy coat or two and leave the statements to him and he'd assure him that he'd be troubled no more by unauthorized persons trespassing on the property of the railway company.

Tom nodded grimly at one of the tramps and going out to the kitchen he put on his heavy socks, a woollen vest, his heavy coat and his stationmaster's cap. He took a dart of O'Hara's poteen, and chewing some toothpaste to quench the smell he ambled out to the waiting-room where the policeman was adding the final words to the two statements. He read the statements aloud and Tom was surprised to hear that each of the tramps had asserted that he gained admission to the waiting-room by way of the window.

'And now, Mr Magee,' the policeman addressed him, 'maybe you'd give me a word or two to fill in the missing details.'

'Ach, there's not much I can add except that I heard a noise in the waiting-room and coming down as you see to investigate I found the two men struggling on the floor.'

The policeman wrote something down in his book and

Tom jingled the ring of keys in his hand and then sat down at the table and pushed the cap back from his forehead.

'Yes,' said the policeman.

Tom rubbed a hand over his face, shook his head bemusedly and said: 'Leave it to the morning, Constable, my mind is all throughother. We'll let it drop on account of the wild night. They'll never come here again — they'll promise us that.' He looked mournfully at the tramps and they nodded in agreement.

The policeman ordered the two tramps to stand outside on the platform, and when they had gone he warned Tom that he was doing a foolish action in allowing men like that to break by-laws and regulations set down by the railway company.

'I never liked taking anybody into court, Constable, and I don't want to go next nor near the place.'

'Do you not see that it will add to your reputation. Many another stationmaster would have slept through the commotion.'

'Maybe so,' Tom said not looking at him. 'But I don't like the idea of having to go into court and give evidence. I'd have to take an oath.'

'That's easy.'

'Laws can be cold and harsh, Constable. We have to be merciful when the need arises and not carry out to the very letter every frittery bit of a rule and regulation.'

'We're obliged to keep them and not to break them. That's what they're made for.'

'If we only do what we're obliged to do we can often run counter to what our hearts bid us.'

'You can't be soft with men like that roaming about the countryside and making themselves a nuisance to everybody.'

At that moment there was a scuffle outside on the platform and rushing out they found the tramps struggling in the snow and one trying to lever the other on to the railway lines. The constable gripped them and jerked them to their feet and calling out to Mr Magee that he would call first thing in the morning he led the tramps out of the station to the barracks.

Tom brushed up the floor of the waiting-room and as he did so he decided that when the policeman would call again he would tell him the whole truth. Come what may he was certainly not going to go into any court to perjure himself. And despite the statements he had heard he was certain, because of the footprints he had seen in the snow, that the first tramp came through the open door and not through the window. And the more he pondered it the more it was borne in upon him that the tramp was lying not to save himself but to save him.

In the morning while Alice was washing up the breakfast dishes and gazing through the window at the patches of snow slithering from the slates she heard a polite knock at the door, and wiping her hands on her apron she admitted the young policeman whom her father had told her to expect. He stepped into the kitchen-sitting-room, smiling, his hand-kerchief in his sleeve, his red face freshly shaved. She asked him to take a seat till she'd fetch her father who was in the booking-office. There was no hurry, he told her, and to detain her for a while he asked her about the play and asked if she'd really care to join the dramatic society. Yes, she would love to join it but doubted very much if she could afford the time off from her studies, explaining to him that she intended to do a matriculation course by correspondence. He was glad to hear that and promised to bring her a trunkful of old books that he had beyond in the barracks, mostly old school books of his that she might find of some use. She thanked him and skipped off to her father, and returning immediately by the side door she discovered the young policeman combing his hair at the little shaving-mirror on the wall, admiring his profile, and pulling down his tunic till every wrinkle was erased. She coughed politely and in his embarrassment he dropped his comb, lifted it quickly and began dabbing his eye a few times with his handkerchief.

'A bit of grit has blown into my eye, Miss Magee. But for the life of me I couldn't trace it in the little mirror.' He blinked his eye at her, blew his nose, and added: 'It's going away now. Yes, it's gone.' And he smiled at her and shook hands with her father who entered at that moment.

'I'll only detain you for a few minutes,' the policeman said as they sat down at the little table opposite one another. 'All I want is a few words about the two playboys.'

'No, Constable, I don't want to go on with the thing. If I went into the court the magistrate could ask me an awkward question or two. He could ask me was everything in order when I locked up for the night.'

'And wasn't it? Didn't the pair of boys gain access to the premises by the window? They probably levered back the snib with a penknife. You wouldn't have to take an oath that every snib was fastened.'

'I'm not good at prevaricating, Constable. I'll tell you the blunt truth. One of the tramps was in the room when I went to lock up and I let him stay.'

'But he didn't mention that in his statement. He says he came in through the window.'

'I don't know how he came in. I only know that I didn't order him out.'

The policeman tapped his pencil on the table and looked out at the melting snow dripping like a broken gutter from the eaves of the storage shed. Then the porter passed the window, whistling to himself as he brushed the snow from the platform with a stiff-bristled brush.

'Your porter doesn't mind the extra bit of work,' the policeman said as if it had some relevance to the pages in his notebook; and drawing his pencil crosswise over some pages in his notebook he added with a smile, 'The case for the crown is now dismissed,' and stowing his notebook in his breast pocket, he fastened down the button and gave the pocket a sartorial pat.

Tom stared at him in gratitude, and some instinctive

sense of correct behaviour withheld the thanks that hovered at his lips, and each understood the other without a word being spoken. And they sat on, talking about how quickly the snow was melting and of the touch of warmth in the air that promised an early spring, a spring that Tom insisted he would be glad to see for he was dying to put the place into respectable shape and to tidy up his garden before his married daughters would come to visit him. And the mention of the married daughters drew further questions from the policeman and drew from Tom an account of his years in Rockcross, his marriage, his family and the death of his wife. He spoke of them in such a regretful tone that the policeman inquired why he had exchanged Rockcross for a place like Monabeg that was really on the downgrade, and Tom confessed that some urge to get back to his home-place continually nagged him; and then, after the death of his wife, the desire to get away grew so strong he couldn't resist it.

'I trust you'll never regret the move,' the policeman said. 'It's all right for the likes of me. I'm unmarried and don't like to be kept too long in the one place and wouldn't like to be kept here beyond the normal span.'

'You're young and it's the life of a young man to be on the move. But for a man of my years it's the life of him to be back where he was reared. I'm like the swallows.'

'And this is the youngest of the flock?' the policeman said, gazing straight into Alice's eyes as she laid a tray with tea and biscuits on the table.

'The youngest, the kindest and the best,' the father said as Alice whisked away in pleasurable agitation and took a seat by the fire.

The policeman sitting sideways at the table silently admired her and wondered if her eyes were grey or green.

'Are you not having a cup?' he asked her, smiling.

'No, thank you,' she answered, and to avoid his constant stare she went down the steps to the scullery and took dishes from the shelves and replaced them again, one by one, till the policeman had finished his tea, moved back his chair, and stood up dusting the biscuit crumbs from his tunic.

At the door, which she held open for him, he held out his huge hand to shake hers, thanked her again for the tea, and promising he wouldn't forget the books he strode off dabbing his lips with his handkerchief.

A few evenings later, being off duty, he returned dressed in a tweed suit. He had a carton of books under his arm, but on entering the sitting-room was discomforted to find Ben Brady and Tom installed at the table in a game of chess.

Alice smiled with a finger on her lip and the two men at the table raised their heads and bade the constable good evening. The policeman rested his hands on the back of Tom's chair, peered confusedly at the chess-pieces and announced loudly that it was a game he could never make head or tail of.

Ben Brady winced, coughed and sat back with his arms folded, a sign that he had ceased for the moment to ponder his next move. Tom took out the pipe and lit it.

'Go on with the game and don't let me disturb you,' the policeman said.

'Plenty of time, Constable O'Brien, plenty of time. The night is young,' Ben answered. 'It was a nice night for a walk when I was coming in. I hope it's still holding up fine.'

'It is, Ben,' the policeman said and moved away from the table. He lifted the carton of books and sat beside Alice near the fire and carefully untied the string. Ben with his shoulders hunched, his lower lip hanging loose scowled at the chess-board, and tapped his black-nailed fingers on the table. To ease matters Tom lifted a few books that the policeman had piled on the seat of a chair and pushed one over to Ben. They were mostly school-editions of Shakespeare, Wordsworth, Keats and Burns and some ink-splashed copies of mathematical books and on the flyleaf of each was written: Francis Joseph O'Brien. To make conversation Tom asked about the schools he had attended and from his replies learnt that he had lived for a while in Limerick, joined the police at the age of twenty, and a few months ago sat an examination for promotion.

Of his own family he did not speak, nor did they ask him, for he spoke so politely and courteously that they feared he might have run away from home and because of his height and width of shoulder had joined the police force. Tom liked his shy hesitancy, the handkerchief in his sleeve, and the red face that seemed to be always freshly shaved; and he liked the careful way he handled the books and arranged them with Alice on two small shelves that had a cretonne curtain covering them. And when the books were stored away the policeman said that if no one objected he would like to take Alice with him as far as the schoolmaster's and make arrangements for her to join the dramatic society.

'That'd be a noble action,' Ben said. 'The judge and the jury are in entire agreement.'

'We won't be long, Mr Magee,' the policeman called from the doorway.

'You needn't hurry yourself,' Ben said. 'It's a glorious night for a walk. I wish to the good God I could walk and have a nice young girl for company.'

They went out laughing and Ben and Tom turned to finish the game. Ben gave a significant cough and declared that the peeler had certainly an eye for a good-looking girl and that she'd not study much if he took her under his wing.

'They're a class of people I'm not particularly fond of, Ben, though I make an exception in this case.'

'They're a breed I don't trust till they're seven years dead. But I must say O'Brien's a good chap and a cut above the ordinary run. He's well liked around here though that mightn't be to his credit.'

'It's your move, Ben, we mustn't take our mind from the game.'

Within an hour the game had ended and Ben having won was demonstrating Tom's fatal move when Alice and the policeman swept into the house again, laughing and jostling, and bringing with them the windy freshness of the night air. They had had their walk for nothing for the schoolmaster wasn't at home and wouldn't be back until late.

Alice took off her coat, put on an apron, and began to prepare the supper. Ben told her not to include his name on the list as he couldn't wait to take a crumb, and despite all their coaxings he rose up stiffly from the table and Tom escorted him to his own chair that he had placed at the front door. He walked alongside him till he reached the road and Ben said he'd be back on the evenings that O'Brien was on duty. He pushed the chair in front of him till he reached the light from a shop window and with that light to aid him he crossed the road in safety and shuffled on home in the darkness.

When Tom returned to the house Alice had the table laid and in a short while had cooked a mushroom omelette, and when the policeman had finished his share of it he confessed it was the best supper he had tasted since he came to Monabeg and he was afraid that Alice was taking the wrong turn if she didn't go in solidly for a domestic economy course and become a teacher of that subject.

'It beats all, that that never crossed my mind,' Tom admitted. They discussed then how one would go about it and the policeman said he'd make all inquiries in Belfast tomorrow as he had a day off, or if he wished Alice could come with him and they could set the ball rolling without any dilly-dallying or shilly-shallying.

'You're very kind,' Alice said. 'I'd love that.'

'Or maybe she mightn't have to go to Belfast to study it at all, Mr Magee. She might be able to do it in Ballymena and travel in and out by bus every day. But I'll see, I'll see. Just leave it to me and I'll make full and adequate inquiries. I'll call tomorrow and we'll set off to Belfast for a start.'

They were grateful to him indeed for all the trouble he was taking, and when he had gone off to the barracks for the night Tom told Alice that although they had met many kind people in Rockcross none of them had the beating of this new friend.

'And look at all the books he has given me,' and she took a few from the shelf and leafed through them. Some smelt of damp, and on the flyleaf of one was the skeleton of a spider and in another a leaf of grass that had faded and left a stain. And as she held them too near the fire the pages stiffened and buckled and the smell brought her mind back to the laburnum tree that she used to climb as a child in the garden at Rockcross. She sighed, stared into the fire, and returned again to the book on her lap. She scrutinized the signature on the flyleaves and whispered: Francis O'Brien, Francis Joseph O'Brien. She wiped the covers of the books on her apron and leaning her elbows on them listened to the hum of the range.

'A teacher of domestic economy alias cookery,' her father said. 'That would suit you down to the ground, and the little money I've put by for you might see you through the course and make you independent. And even you get married and were ever widowed, like many another poor girl, you'd still have your job to fall back on.'

'Your mind, Father, has seven-league boots. You've pushed me through a lifetime in one short sentence.'

'Sometimes I think life's just as short as that. It's short but a good deal happens in it both joyful and sorrowful. But no matter how old we get or how hard life has hit us we'd all relive it again. Be in love with it and make the best of it. You've a new friend in O'Brien and I like the look of him. You need have no fear in travelling to Belfast with him for he'll take good care of you. I'll issue two return tickets free of charge seeing he's going on our behalf.'

Yes, she'd be all right with him, she said to herself, deliberately recalling him to her mind, seeing his great big hands, powerful hands, hands that wouldn't know their own strength. Again she sighed, languidly put the books away and tidied up the scullery before bedtime.

Early next morning Tom was handed a telegram: JULIA'S SHIP NEARS PORT SEND ALICE TO HELP WITH CARGO — RICHARD. Within half an hour of its receipt Alice was out of bed, had breakfasted, had packed her bag and was off to Rock-cross by the first train, and when Francis Joseph O'Brien arrived in the forenoon to take her to Belfast Tom explained all and the policeman nodded his head in tolerant understanding.

'We can't arrange these matters, Mr Magee, and though I'm sorry Alice can't come with me it can't be helped.' As he spoke thickly and with disappointment Tom noticed he had a bad cold hanging on him and he advised him to take a day in bed and leave the Belfast expedition until Alice's return. He shook his head and wouldn't alter his plans and confessed it'd be better to spend a day in gaol than a day in bed in the barracks with a resentful housekeeper.

The train came in and Tom opened a first-class carriage with his key and handed him his ticket, and later in the evening when the train returned, all her windows alight, he was on the platform to meet him and bring him into the house for a supper he had cooked. The policeman had all the particulars about Alice's course, and as they leafed through the prospectus they concluded with dismal reflection that she'd have to work very hard, not only to gain admittance to the course but to get a certificate at the end of it.

'You'd wonder why the poor girl would have to learn all that about physics and chemistry and stuff and she only going to teach girls at the heel of the hunt to bake cakes and all that.'

'Ah, you'd wonder,' Tom agreed. He noticed that the policeman's cold had worsened, and he advised him to take a good hot dart of whiskey before rolling between the blankets.

'I'll have a smoke of the pipe first and you can be writing out Alice's address for me as I want to send her the result of my findings.'

180

He lit the pipe, took a few pulls at it, and put it in his pocket. 'It's no good, Mr Magee. The cold has a bad grip on me. I think I got it the night of the snow.'

'Wait a minute and I'll give you the cure as long as you don't ask questions.'

Tom went into the scullery, and in a few minutes the constable heard the squeak of a cork and the run of liquid from a bottle. Then the kettle was taken from the range and presently a warm bowl with the smell of lemon coming from it was in the policeman's hands. He took a sip and coughed a few times.

'I know what this is and if I were caught taking it I'd never be allowed to put on the uniform again.'

'To hell with the uniform. If you don't shift that cold pretty quick it'll be a brown uniform you'll be wearing and there'll be no buttons on it either.'

He sipped at the bowl again, coughing between the sips, and said there was powerful strength in the brew and not like the hog-wash they distilled in this part of the country.

'Sure how could they distil good stuff with you people hounding after them day and night.'

'This is Rockcross stuff?'

'It is not.'

'It's made here then? Good luck to them. I never thought they could make stuff like that.'

'What's in your bowl is at half-strength.'

'If it were at full strength I could draw a wagonload of sand or pull a plough. I could even stand up to the housekeeper beyond in the barracks — and that would take some courage.' He drained the bowl and Tom brought him a few cloves that Alice used in baking apple tarts.

The policeman sat on for a while, chewing the cloves, gazing into the fire and rejoicing in the pleasant warmth that filled his whole body. From his pocket he drew out folded examination papers, papers he had sat for in his examination for the post of sergeant, and asked Tom what he thought of them. Tom unfolded each sheet carefully for they were badly frayed in the folds and had been mended on the back by stamp-edging.

Tom whistled with mock surprise as he read aloud different arithmetical problems: problems about approaching trains and diverging cars; problems dealing with distances and areas, problems about cylinders and the heights of towers, and he wondered what in hell's name some of them had got to do with being a sergeant of the police. He read carefully through the geography paper, feeling more at ease as his eye ranged over blank maps with missing towns and rivers to be inserted. One of the essays on the English paper was 'A visit to the Zoo' and on reading it he glanced sideways at the policeman and suddenly burst out laughing. 'Do you know what I'm laughing at?' he hurried to excuse himself. 'I'm laughing at the poor paltry marks I'd score on that snorter of an arithmetic paper. How quickly my knowledge of mathematics has left me.'

'I'm a regular snick at any problem that involves velocities. I shouldn't praise myself too soon, but I think I did well on that paper and it should get me my sergeant's stripes. Excuse me for boasting. I think the stuff you gave me is going to my head.'

'As long as it doesn't go to your feet you needn't worry.'

He drew himself erect with effort and spat the cloves into the fire: 'I'll go off now to the barracks while I'm steady on my props.' He shook Tom's hand strongly and said it was an answer to prayer that sent him as stationmaster to Monabeg.

'You're my friend, Mr Magee, and I'm fond of your daughter and I hope that some day she'll grow fond of me.' He lit his pipe. 'The pipe will do for camouflage in case I meet the boss before I reach my bed. Good night to you. I'm sorry to be leaving you.'

Tom opened the door for him and watched him step off steadily into the night.

FOUR days after Alice's departure her father received a letter:

Dear Father,

   This morning at 6 a.m. Julia had a new baby boy and both are doing extremely well. Richard's in good form over the event and so are Mag and Joe, both of whom are looking forward to their own in two months or so. Aunt Brigid has given Julia and myself great help for she is now free to come and go because Sergeant was killed by a motor car the day before I arrived. She has buried him in a deep hole in her back garden and hopes to plant a rose bush to mark the place; she's so foolish she'd nearly put up a headstone if she got one word of encouragement. I was up seeing the McKenna girls the other day and when I was passing our old house I noticed holes in the hedge and the children making free with the place. I'm afraid the new occupants have no taste for gardening as we well realize from the state of the place in Monabeg. Aloysius McKenna is in Dublin and his sisters tell me he is going off to South Africa again and when he becomes a wealthy man he is coming back to marry me if you please. Oh, I nearly forgot to inquire about Mr O'Brien. I am sure he got a terrific surprise to find me here when by all accounts I should have been going with him to Belfast for the day. I am sure you have explained to him how everything happened so quickly we hadn't time to breathe. I'll send him a postcard in a day or two in case he would think I was rude and didn't appreciate his kindness. Take good care of yourself till I come back. Best of luck with the chess.

Your affectionate daughter,

ALICE

After reading the letter a few times he stepped across the street to the post office and sent a congratulatory wire to Julia and Richard, and in the shop where he always got the morning's paper he told the shopkeeper that he had now three grandchildren and they'd all be coming to visit him some day and he'd bring them along for her to see them. 'Ah, Mr Magee, no one would believe to look at you that you had one grandchild let alone three. You're the youngest looking grandfather about this quarter and that's no lie.'

The shopkeeper's remark and the news about Julia put him in fine form and that day, in his spare time, he made two solid beehives out of the old ones that lay against the hedge, and the next morning, seeing how small a job gave such a tidy appearance to the garden, he began at once to repair the greenhouse and to clear away the dump of tin cans from the back of it.

And now that the eel-fishing had begun in the river and the fish-boxes with ice dripping out of them were conveyed each day to his station he was always out with the hose striving to keep the place free from smells. Sometimes an eel would escape from a box, wriggle across the platform on to the lines, and the porter would pick it up with a pair of pincers and hold it under the pump to wash the grit and dust off it, then prise up the lid of a box and poke it back again amongst its wet and wriggling companions. Then came the cattle morning, one day in every week, and he'd be up early to supervise the cattle being driven by the drovers into the pens at the storage sheds, and once enclosed the drovers would cease their shouting, their dogs their barking, and the morning air be filled with the sweaty mist from the cattle and the milk-smell from their damp hides. The locomotive would back the empty wagons to the pens, and the cattle stumbling and cracking their heads against each other would be driven up shelving platforms into the wagons, and there they would swing and dunt one another till they would find the empty spaces where they could stick out their noses to the fresh morning air or to a sudden fall of rain. Tom hated that day, hated the terrified look in the sad eyes of the cattle and the long strings of saliva that hung like dripping rain from the sides of the wagons. That was his busiest day but on slack days he would get the porter to help him to wheel up barrow-loads of sand to make new flower-beds and build a shelving bank beyond the platform, and when they had the bank made, they printed as a temporary token MONABEG with large whitewashed stones. And after such days' work he brought the porter and the signalman to the pub for a few bottles of stout, and on his return to the station, either found Ben Brady or the policeman, in plain clothes, waiting for him. And the policeman would take from his pocket a few post-cards he had got from Alice and after reading them aloud he would say: 'Alice is a nice thoughtful girl, Mr Magee, and I'm lonesome for her return.'

'I'm lonesome for her myself, I may tell you. When I waken in the long hours of the night I miss her greatly. Even a child stirring in its sleep or giving a little cough is company at such times.'

Alice remained with Julia for nearly three weeks and on her return found the station newly painted, fresh-coloured holiday advertisements on the display boards, the metal hand-bars on the weighing-machine shining with polish, and window-boxes for geraniums erected round the signal-cabin. In the evenings she helped her father to make wire baskets to hang along the platform and in these he hoped to grow dwarf nasturtiums and lobelia. In the summer there would be a bit of brightness about the Monabeg station and people

185

in passing trains would lean out of carriage windows to get a whiff of perfume from the stocks that would be growing in the flower-beds.

On Sunday afternoons after her return Alice and Frank, as they now called him, walked along the river bank, past a little rowing-boat that her father had bought for fishing, and up to the edge of the lough where they stood to watch the March wind lash up the grey-looking waves or blow back the water from the falls in a fine spray that often shone like a rainbow. With his strong arm around her or the wing of his coat to shelter they would sit behind an alder bush, happy in one another's company, while low clouds filled with rain would darken the lough, and the far shore shrink against an oncoming shower. Sometimes if it was late when they came back they could hear in the darkness the tumble of the falls and see the windy signal-light on the railway track that they were approaching, Alice's hair would be tossed by the wind, her cheeks fresh and glowing, and Frank whispering to her in his shy and awkward manner that he was fond of her and hoped she was fond of him.

On St Patrick's Day she prepared a special dinner and after it they walked through the demesne gathering daffodils and resting in the sun on the stone steps of the ruined castle. Young ash trees sprouted behind them in the falling masonry, a blue sky was framed in the vacant doorway and opposite crows were building their nests in the trees, flying to the adjacent firs and after wrenching off the sappy twigs flying back to the branches of the elms.

'They're wise old birds,' Frank said, marvelling at the instinct that made them avoid the rotted twigs on the ground.

'It's surprising how the sticks don't blow down again in that wind,' Alice said. 'I'm afraid we would need some string if we were building them.'

James O'Hara's son passed close to them, a shot-gun under his arm and two rabbits slung across his shoulder. He saw them but pretended not to, and when Alice greeted him he hurried on without speaking and disappeared among the trees.

Presently there was a shot and a pair of crows they were watching fell dead through the branches while others rose noisily from the trees and whirled away like scraps of burnt paper.

'You're cruel, cruel!' Alice shouted, jumping to her feet and running to the tree. 'You'll never have luck!'

'That shot will reduce their population,' he said to her with a sneering smile. 'And tell your fine constable I've my gun licence in my pocket if he cares to have a look at it.' His face was hard, and the grudging look he gave her depressed her. She looked at the two crows lying dead on the grass, one still holding a twig in its grey beak. Hurrying back to Frank she lifted her bunch of daffodils that lay well out of the sun and set off for home scarcely saying a word.

'That O'Hara fellow has vexed you?' Frank kept asking. 'What'd he say?'

'It's not what he said but the way he looked and what he did that hurt me.'

'Don't take it too much to heart. It'd have been worse if he'd shot them when their young ones were in the nest.' And he put his big protecting arm around her and held her close to him.

On reaching home they found a note from her father saying he had gone to Ben Brady's for a while. They had the house to themselves and after she arranged the daffodils in vases and placed one on top of their small piano she took one of his mathematical books from the shelf and asked him to explain logarithms to her.

'The divil with logs,' he said, 'I forget how to do them. Give me anything about velocities and I'm your man' — and he snapped the book closed and suddenly asked her if she'd marry him.

The question startled her, and she thought, at first, he was joking, but he looked firmly at her and repeated his question in a voice that shattered any doubt.

'But I'm only nineteen and my father and Christy and maybe my sisters would be against me marrying so young.'

'But would you be against it? — that's the main question.' And with his strong arms he lifted her on to his knee as easily as if she were a child.

'Would you be against it, Alice?' he asked again as she fingered the lapel of his coat.

'I don't know, Frank. It's all so sudden really.'

He smoothed the back of her head and rested it against his broad shoulder. He could feel her breath warm against his neck and her arm lying almost without weight upon his own.

'There's Father to consider. I'd be leaving him all alone.'

'Time will solve that for us. He's still a young man and he might marry again.'

'He'll not do that. It was mentioned to him once and none of us dare mention it again.'

'He'll not stand in your way.'

'I know he won't. He'd do any mortal thing for us. It's me that would find it hard to leave him.'

'You're fond of me, Alice. Aren't you?'

She nodded but didn't speak, and he raised her head and holding it firmly between his hands he pleaded with her to look straight at him. She smiled and there were tears in her eyes. He kissed her firmly and getting down from his knee she ran laughing down to the scullery. He didn't follow her; he sat on, leaning forward, his hands joined and drooped between his knees. She peeped mischievously out at him but he didn't turn to look at her, and sensing that she had hurt him she slipped back and standing in front of him with her hands behind her back she gazed at his bowed head.

'Why don't you look up at me?' she exclaimed. He sat motionless as if unaware of her presence. She sat on the floor at his feet trying to draw his attention. He closed his eyes avoiding her gaze, but when she smoothed his large hands and pressed her cheek against them he suddenly stood up and lifting her in his arms carried her round the room.

When her father came in Frank told him he wanted to marry Alice. Tom suggested that they wait till they knew one another a bit better. Frank declared that he had fallen in love with her the night he saw her at *Autumn Fire* and every time he had been in her company since then his love for her had increased. Tom wished him every happiness, and after he had left the house he asked Alice what she thought about all this.

'I'm very fond of him, Father. I suppose I love him.'

'It'd be better not to suppose, girl. It'd be better to be sure.'

'I am sure, Father. But what about you? You'd be alone if I got married.'

'Don't think about me. This is a choice you have to make for yourself and no one can make it for you. I'll be always able to fend for myself or get an old housekeeper.'

He advised her not to spread her engagement about the countryside for a while yet, for there were some people, people like the O'Haras, who would resent a daughter of his marrying a policeman.

'Oh, that explains why one of the O'Hara boys was rude to me in the demesne today,' Alice exclaimed and went on to give an account of what had happened.

'You may expect that from some quarters from now on,' her father warned.

And the following Sunday after Mass he himself encountered more of the resentment as he tried to make conversation with James O'Hara outside the chapel gates. O'Hara no longer displayed the same friendliness towards him and as he walked off to collect his bicycle that lay against the graveyard wall O'Hara told him it was well he got rid of the still before the Magees united their strength with the police force.

'Ah, James, if that's a joke I don't like it,' Tom said, hurt.

'It's no joke, I've got rid of it.'

'I hope you didn't do it because of what's between O'Brien and my daughter. I'd rather she was going about with someone of a different cloth, and I'd say the same to O'Brien if the need arose. Love is like the wind, it blows where it likes. We'll shake hands on that,' he went on. 'Ah, James, the secrets shared between us will always remain secrets no matter if my daughter married the head of the whole damned police force in the whole country. No Magee in this townland was ever an informer and no one, please God, will ever be!'

'It was the wife made me get rid of it, Tom. I wish your daughter luck; I do indeed.'

'Thanks, James, I knew you'd be one who'd understand'—and O'Hara shook the hand held out to him and went on his way.

But a few days before Easter the Sergeant of Monabeg along with Constable O'Brien raided the O'Hara farmhouse and discovered the still in full operation for the Easter holidays. Photographs of the seizure appeared in the newspapers along with photographs of the policemen and full details of the ingenious still-house.

On Easter Sunday after Mass as Tom stood as usual on the roadway groups of men turned their backs to him and he could hear the word informer muttered at him from all sides. He sought for James O'Hara and on perceiving him step out from the biggest group of people he joined him and held out his hand in sympathy for his loss. O'Hara ignored him and walked on. Tom followed and held his sleeve but O'Hara shrugged away so vigorously that his coat fell down from one shoulder and he stumbled on the road. For a moment it looked as if he would strike Magee but he walked ahead, fixing his coat while men followed them as far as the graveyard wall.

'Well,' said O'Hara, drawing up suddenly and facing Tom. 'What the hell are you following me for!'

'As God's my judge, James, I knew nothing about it! I hadn't hand or part or whisper in it.'

One of O'Hara's sons stepped from the crowd and raised his fist to him and shouted: 'Why didn't you stay in the town you were in, you dirty informer!'

Tom backed against the wall and stared at them, his mouth hanging loose.

'I told you I'd done away with the still because I didn't trust you,' O'Hara flared at him.

'If my father's gaoled you may clear to hell out of here, you foul informer.'

'No Magee in this townland was ever an informer, nor am I one!'

'Nobody told but you! Your future son-in-law will get promotion for this haul. It'll be a nice wedding present for your daughter.'

All the faces that hemmed him in were ugly with hate and he sought for one that sympathized with him. All the faces were alike and from them all came the word informer. At last he pulled himself together and with his empty hands spread out before him he cried out: 'I'd rather be struck dead than you to think that of me. I never harmed anyone intentionally in my life. I never did. In God's name believe me, believe me when I say I had nothing to do with it!'

'We can't stand here listening to a bloody hypocrite.' The crowd moved closer to him, and a few jostled him and shouldered him against the wall, and as he fell in a slump against it a few sods were torn up from the roadside and flung at him.

'It's a shame and a disgrace for the lot of you,' a few women said, helping him to his feet and dusting the clay from his Sunday suit. 'Nice conduct for an Easter Sunday.'

'I'd nothing to do with the seizure of the still,' he said to the women who were now abusing the men as they retreated in a body along the road.

'And what harm if you had. It's the ruination of this part of the country.'

'I didn't inform, I didn't! Till my dying day I'll shout that out. And you can tell them that. They'll live, please God, to find out the truth.'

As he wheeled away his bicycle he saw that it was flat and the tyres slashed. He arrived home late and Alice had the dinner nearly ready. She asked what kept him, then seeing his haggard face and the clay marks on his clothes she asked if he had fallen off his bicycle.

'No, Alice girl, I didn't.' He shook his head and sat down heavily on the armchair.

'Are you sick, Father?' She put her hand on his forehead and smoothed back the hair that was damp with sweat.

'I'll be all right in a minute. I'm just breathless.'

She brought him a cup of cold water and held it to his lips.

'Don't worry.' He patted her hand. 'Everything will be all right in a short while. Everything will be all right.'

Resting his hands on the arms of the chair he raised himself to his feet and shuffled down to the scullery meaning to take a drink of the poteen, but as he lifted the bottle it slipped from his trembling hands and crashed in smithereens on the floor and he remembered then the night his wife died and how the bottle of whiskey fell in the same way.

'I wish to the good God we'd only stayed in Rockcross! I'd be a happier man this day. I would indeed.'

She helped him up the two steps to the kitchen, loosened his collar, and fetched him a glass of whiskey.

'Alice, I don't want Frank to visit this house again. Things have been said to me this day that no man can bear.' With many pauses and omissions he recounted what happened outside the chapel gates and how his bicycle tyres were slashed.

'But, Father, they can't blame you about O'Hara's still. The priest will be glad and many a mother will be glad too.'

'From this forth the Magees will be called a breed of informers. I'll be an outcast in the townland that bred me.'

'Don't take it so ill, Father. They'll forget all about it in a day or two.'

192

'No nor in a year, nor two years, nor in fifty years will they forget. Where informers are concerned they have long and bitter memories. But I'm not an informer, thank God. Frank O'Brien never heard me mention O'Hara's name nor anyone's name in connection with the stuff.'

'You could write and ask for another change, Father, or retire and live with us when we get married. Or you could go to Mag and Joe in Rockcross. You have plenty of places where you'll be welcome.'

He shook his head disapprovingly: 'To go away would be to admit guilt. I'll stay and finish my years here and God will give me the strength to see our good name cleansed. I'm sorry I brought you here — that was a bad move.'

'Oh, no, it was a great move, Father; I'd never have met Frank if you hadn't.

He nodded weakly, closed his eyes, and dozed over till she called him for dinner.

That evening she was to go to an Easter dance in the hall and he advised her not to go in case someone would insult her. She would not heed him; she said she wasn't afraid of what anyone would say or do; she and Frank would defy them. He watched her dress and go out, admiring her spirit, and he himself sat at the table, the chess-board in front of him, waiting for Ben Brady. But Ben didn't turn up and he surmised that he, too, like O'Hara, had condemned him.

At eleven o'clock he knelt to say the rosary before going to bed, and just as he rose from his knees a stone came crashing through the window adjoining the station. He rushed out quickly and stood in the darkness on the deserted platform; he could hear nothing but the wind in the wires and the rush of it through the trees. In his shirt sleeves and slippers he went up the street, the stone in his hand, and halted beside a group of youths who were standing against the white wall of the pub. He confronted them without fear, and as he stood beside them in angry silence he could see the lights from the dance hall and hear the sound of the music coming through the open door. None of the youths spoke to him. They smoked their cigarettes and blew the smoke towards him.

'Someone is after breaking my window,' he said and threw the stone at their feet.

There was a long pause and then one said with feigned gravity: 'You should go straight to the barracks and inform at once.'

The rest of them burst out laughing and as Tom turned away from them towards the station the stone was flung again and struck him on the shoulder. But he walked on unheedingly and then he heard shouted through the darkness of the street: 'One, two, three, Informer!' and the words sounded as large as letters written upon the sky.

CHAPTER

15

THAT night and the following night he slept but little, and with the Easter holidays in full spate he had to work harder than usual in the booking-office. Christy was to come at the end of the week but wrote at the last moment to say he would spend a week at Rockcross on his way from the college and then go on to Monabeg. He yearned greatly for his coming for he would have someone then to confide in and ask for advice.

During the day he went about his work uncomplainingly, seeking an odd moment's rest where no one would notice him. In the mornings, going up the village street for his newspaper, no one bade him the time of day except the lady in the shop. Ben Brady ceased coming to the house, and the porter and the signalman went about their work with a slowness that exasperated him. The signalman would attend the level-crossing gates with studied slowness, and sometimes Tom, watch in hand, could endure the strain no longer and would hurry forward to open the gates himself two minutes before a train was due, and when he warned the signalman that he would have to report him if he did not carry out his duties with a keener sense of responsibility the signalman shrugged and said:

'Fire ahead for you're really good at the informing.'

'It's not that I want to do it. We have to avoid all risks of accident.'

'There'll be no accident. I've been here twenty years and never a word of complaint was lodged against me from any quarter.'

'All I ask is that you open the gates immediately the signal comes through. It's your duty to do it and it's my duty to see that it's done.'

He loathed these little contentious scenes. It made the blood bolt noisily in his body and at night brought on a spell of dizziness as soon as he laid his head upon the pillow. The room swayed before his eyes like a ship's cabin and when he shut them to avoid it the darkness began to stagger, then to sway like liquid in a bowl, gradually levelling itself out but leaving his heart thumping so noisily that he sat up to dull for a while its terrifying knocking. He crawled out of bed, stood up slowly, and held on to the edge of the dressing table where he had placed his glass of water. He took a drink, opened the window wide and breathed in the night air.

Lifting his rosary beads he got into bed again and prayed for strength to continue his work and prayed that his life be spared till he saw Christy ordained and Alice settled. Holding the crucifix in his fingers he resolved not to give way to fear. He would die when his time came and he would try to be ready for it. He would work; he would pray; he would not go under; Christ would steady him, Christ would stand by him.

He dozed over into a light sleep and the first milk lorries bumping over the level-crossing wakened him and he lay and heard them rattling speedily along the dawn-empty road. The unsunned air cooled the room and he could feel it on his injured shoulder as he lay and watched the darkness fade from the walls, the first birds begin their songs and the crows rise from the trees above the storage sheds.

The sight of his breakfast filled him with nausea but he forced himself to eat because of Alice's anxious inquiries about how he slept and how he was feeling. That morning she herself had received a letter from the dramatic society saying that they would not require her services any longer as she would be leaving Monabeg on the occasion of her marriage. She put the letter in the fire in case her father would come upon it and add to his worries.

She polished his boots, and noticing how breathless he was when he stooped she laced them on his feet and as he lifted his keys and his stationmaster's cap the distraught and drawn look upon his face pained her.

'Father,' she said, 'all this whispering against you can't go on. It must stop or it will destroy your health. I'll ferret out of Frank how they came to know about O'Hara's still.'

'No, girl, you mustn't do that. He couldn't tell you without breaking an oath. In God's good time the truth will out. I'm sure of that as I'm sure of the coming of dawn.'

'It will out when it's too late. Oh, Father, if I broke with Frank would it heal everything?'

'Break with Frank! You can't do that no matter what is said or done to me. To break one pledge to restore another would be wrong. You love him and he loves you. You won't have me all your days and you must look to the future. Don't worry, Alice.' He patted her shoulder, jingled his ring of keys and said firmly: 'In a short while I'll break all this as I'd break a bit of stick across my knee.'

He opened the booking-office and the porter came along and with a solemn face took him by the sleeve and led him to the shelving bank beyond the platform, and there instead of Monabeg printed in white stones he saw the foul word INFORMER.

'This is going too far, Mr Magee, too far entirely. I don't hold with the likes of that,' the porter said and began to rearrange the stones to their original lettering.

'You're a good fella, Jimmy,' Tom said, stooping to help him. 'You don't believe I informed on my best friend.'

'I did, sir, but I don't now. I know you wouldn't do it in spite of what is said. You would not, sir, 'deed by God you wouldn't.'

Back in the booking-office the leaning over the ledgers made him breathless and brought a knot of pressure to the back of his head. He worked on slowly, calmly, and as the

197

day advanced he grew stronger, but at night the dizziness returned and with it the wild flutterings of his heart.

Without telling Alice he walked out the road the following night to the doctor. The doctor examined him, took his blood pressure, gave him tablets and advised him to go for a holiday and get as much rest as he could muster. He had never been to a doctor in his life and on leaving him and walking along the dark country road to the lights in the village he felt that death was near and he momentarily gave way to the fear of never seeing Christy ordained or Alice married. Then suddenly he drew himself up and seeing through the hedges the moon shining on the river he laughed contemptuously at himself. 'If I think like that then where is my faith in prayer and in my own courage?' he said. 'No, I'll not think that way for a man goes the way he thinks. I'll not go that way. In God's name I'll not. Death comes like a thief in the night and how could it come to me and me so conscious of it.' He laughed, laughed at his laughable deductions and breaking a twig from the hedge he felt the tiny freshly opened leaves and walked on, thinking now of Christy's ordination and of Mag who should soon be announcing the birth of her first child. And then suddenly as he threw the twig away from him and saw the light of the police barracks through the trees he thought of James O'Hara's trial that would be held soon and he resolved to go and see him and offer to pay his fine. If James would allow him to do that and shake his hand on it, it would be the first slackening of the rope, the first snapping of the strain.

The next day in the early afternoon he set off on his bicycle for O'Hara's and on reaching the lonin he placed his bicycle against the hedge and walked towards the house, admiring the fine field of newly sown potatoes, the soil fine and dry and taking its fill of the sun. Sheep with thriving lambs were in the fields, the hedges turning green, and the chestnut trees almost in full leaf. Three dogs rushed barking down to him, but sensing he had no fear of them their barks gave way to intermittent growls. Fine healthy hens, their combs geranium red, scratched holes in the empty hay shed and clucked contentedly in the sun-quiet yard. Everything was thriving, thriving as in the old days when his father and brother, God have mercy on their souls, worked and slaved to make the farm what it was. O'Hara certainly fell on his feet when he stepped in and bought it. And no one deserved it better than James O'Hara.

He reached the door of the house but found it closed, and to overcome the fear and timidity that impelled him there and then to flee he knocked politely and waited. No one came. Nothing stirred within the house. He stood with his back to the window, the lower half of which had a cotton-net curtain, and gazed down the cart-rutted lonin to where his bicycle glinted in the sun. He knocked again, coughed, and stared at a neighbour's field, freshly drilled that morning for the soil was still dark, unbleached by the sun.

Once more he knocked, aware that they were all within, holding their breaths, not wishing to see him. He peered over the half-curtain and saw on the table a dish of steaming potatoes, glasses filled with buttermilk, and chairs at the table hastily vacated. They had seen him approach and were now hiding somewhere in his old house. He took a notebook from his pocket, tore out a leaf and wrote: 'Whatever your fine will be, James, I will help you to meet it — Your old friend, Tom Magee.' He pushed it under the weather-board of the door and made off hurriedly.

The dogs, barking, escorted him down the lonin till he lifted his bicycle, and as he pedalled off he looked round once at the house but nothing stirred in the yard except the dogs lying down near the door in the sun. He told Alice what he had done and the reception he had got and she flew into a rage and cried out that the whole breed of the O'Haras weren't worth a snap of his generous fingers.

That evening Christy arrived, a day sooner than he intended, and the excitement and unexpectedness of his arrival increased his father's agitation and his voice grew thick and husky as he told his son of the strange happenings in the little place that reared him. Christy, alarmed for his father's health, inquired from Alice why she hadn't written to him about it all. If he had only known how things were he wouldn't have stayed so selfishly long in Rockcross. Alice told him she hadn't time to write, and besides everything happened so suddenly she thought it would all die down just as quickly. Christy plied her with more questions: had Father been to the doctor, did she know? Had he spoken to the priest about it? And were the police doing anything? To all his questions Alice could give no definite answer and he shook his head hopelessly and said: 'When a young girl falls in love she thinks of nothing only her own affairs. It's a pity that it makes girls so selfish, but there it is, Alice, and I suppose it's a general disease and one can't blame you too much. You do your best.'

At breakfast the father harrowed the same ground again and Christy listened patiently, observing all his nervous gestures, and the word Informer that fell continually from his lips like a malediction.

'You'll have to change your attitude towards it, Father,' he advised him. 'They can't keep up this persecution for long, it will wear thin with time. Your conscience is clear and a man with a clear conscience has everything on his side. Try and rid your mind of it for a while.'

'I wish to the good God I could! I'd gladly do it this instant if I could. Not a one speaks to me after Mass on a Sunday. You'd think I'd leprosy by the way they avoid me. If I go to the pub for a drink the men there turn their backs to me. How can they think for one moment that I would inform on a man that was my friend since we were children. And they think I informed to help my future son-in-law. That, Christy, is hard to bear.'

'The truth will out some day and they'll regret all this. But you must have patience, Father, and endure all.'

'It's hard to have patience when not a day passes but some little thing I value is broken on me. Two nights ago the windows of my little greenhouse were smashed and I'm afraid the frost has got in and killed the young tomato shoots and all my delicate bedding plants.'

'You'll have to complain to the police.'

'I would do that only it would increase their suspicion of me. I know my people too well to do that.'

Christy strove to pluck his mind away from these worries, but whatever subject he raised, whether it was fishing or Mag and Joe or Julia and Richard, his father's interest ebbed and imperceptibly swung back towards O'Hara and the people of Monabeg.

Unknown to him Christy set off to visit the priest and as he came up the gravelled drive that led to the house he saw the old priest outside walking to and fro reading his breviary. He motioned to Christy with a nod that he would be with him in a minute and waved him to a green seat below the parlour window. Christy sat in the sun and looked down at the river valley, its small loughs shining like spilled mercury in the morning sunlight.

'Well,' said the priest, closing his breviary, 'that's a lovely fresh morning, thanks be to God. A few showers of rain would bring everything on with a rush.'

Christy explained who he was and why he had come.

'Yes, I heard about it from a few sources,' the priest said gravely. 'It's too bad that a good man like your father should get so much annoyance. But after O'Hara's trial it will soon die out and they'll leave your father in peace.'

'He's badly shaken over it as it is. Maybe, Father, you'd drop a word or two to O'Hara.'

'Me! If I said one word in your father's defence O'Hara would think I was condoning the loss of his damned still. Indeed you'd never know what twist he'd put on my words.' He toed the pebbles at his feet. 'And to think of him making

201

poteen on Good Friday of all days! The Hand of God was in its capture.'

'The divil's in it now,' said Christy, enumerating some of the things done to his father.

'He should report all to the police. They're paid to protect him.'

'Sure if he did that he'd have to clear out entirely.'

'Tell him from me it was a blessing the still was seized and whoever gave it away did a real good for the parish. The making of that stuff has always been a blot on this parish. Many a Sunday I give off about it from the pulpit but you might as well be talking to bags of cement. And do you know I never suspected O'Hara of making the stuff and me, you might say, his next-door neighbour. I never once got the whiff of it and me out and about the roads so often. You'd hardly credit that but it's true. But they're good people for all that. And when they find out their mistake about your father you'll find they'll be bringing him fresh eggs instead of throwing stones at him.' He patted Christy on the knee and after bringing him inside for a glass of wine he praised the missions and the missioners for their great work and asked Christy to remember him in his prayers on his ordination day and out in Nigeria. 'Sacrifices like yours won't go unrewarded. And I know by the cut of you that you're a real Magee, a hard worker like your father and a hard worker like your uncle that's dead. He was a great loss to the parish. Ah when O'Hara thinks about the Magee sweat and blood that went into the making of his farm he'll be ashamed of himself for all he has done to your poor father.' He patted Christy on the shoulder. 'With your ordination coming in June it will gladden your father and by that time all will have died out.'

'I hope you're right, Father,' Christy said as he walked away from him pondering on the vagaries of old country priests who grow old seeing nothing but good in their people.

Rain fell heavily that afternoon, and in the evening Christy went out fishing with his father in his blue and white rowing-boat which had the name *Rockcross* painted at each side of her bow. As they pushed off into the quiet water, deep with the reflections of cloud, his father said it was too calm, the swallows flying too high, a sure sign they'd have a poor fishing.

'What harm if we catch nothing. It's a glorious evening, thank God, to be out on the water,' Christy said, taking off his jacket and Roman collar before seizing the oars. The boat put a wedge on the water and set the reeds shaking and as they came under the cold shade of the railway bridge water dripped from the girders and a thin wind sneaked over the river, crinkling its surface as fine as a cockleshell. They rowed in the direction of the falls, and edging along-side a bed of reeds his father hooked and landed a young pike and as he rested his foot on its spike to release the hook both of them spoke at the same time of the huge brute that was caught at the lakeside in Rockcross.

'It's strange, Christy, how ugly things stick in our minds and how easily we forget things that are beautiful.'

'It's the old warp in our natures hankering to be made more crooked. We remember them in spite of our better natures. And that struggle will go on till the flesh withers away from us.'

'Our natures are warped and bent as you say — there's no doubt about that.'

Fearing lest his father would descant about the ugliness that surrounded him in Monabeg Christy pulled the boat hard towards the falls, his father imploring him to take it easy or they'd not catch another tail. Candy-coloured water, fine as ice, tumbled over the long hurdle of falls, the noise drumming and drowning their voices and impelling them to silence. The boat edged through the beer-brown froth, and the unseen pin-points of spray wetted their faces and lay like dew on the hairy backs of their hands.

'It's not fish we'll catch but pneumonia, Christy, if you don't hurry out of here.'

He smiled at his father, swung the boat round with its stern to the falls, and as he pulled away the falls narrowed in his wake and he could see above them the wide open lough. High in the May-blue sky white clouds, shoulder to shoulder, stepped slowly across it, and then suddenly the unseen sun let down scaffoldings of rays between the clouds and rested on silver patches of water. Christy gave a long broken sigh, and his father, looking at the light in his son's eyes, turned round to see what his son was staring at.

'My God, Father, but there's no country in the world so fresh and lovely as our own. That light, that scene and that air fairly lifts the heart. I'll hate to leave it and I'll be dying to get back to it. You'll write to me often when I go to Nigeria — won't you?'

'I will indeed — why wouldn't I!' replied his father, suddenly chastened and subdued, realizing the struggle that would go on for ever in his son's heart, the struggle against the heartache of exile.

'Let me take a spell at the oars, Christy, and you take the lines. And if I don't bring you upon a few pike my name's not Magee.'

He spat on his hands, gripped the oars, and as the boat responded smoothly to the friendly pull he praised her as a handy wee boat and boasted that he had got her for a song because her seams were opened from lying out too long in the sun.

Presently both lines tautened simultaneously and he gave an extra spurt to the oars to drive home the hooks, and in a minute or two Christy had landed two nice young pike.

'If I had you with me for a while longer many's a fine evening we'd have together.' Tom turned the boat back along the same course and filled up his pipe and began to smoke.

His son was silent, the corners of his mouth drooped, as

he gazed from shore to shore, from sky to water. His father took the pipe from his lips and put it in his pocket. 'Christy,' he said, his voice hard and strong to cancel the chill at his heart, 'it won't be long, please God, till your great day. A pity your poor mother won't be there for it. But we'll all be there, and I'm sure Mag's confinement will be over before then.'

'My first Mass will be said in Rockcross,' Christy answered, remembering the talk with his mother as she lay on her death-bed. 'And then I'll come on here with you and we'll spend many another evening together.'

'We will that. And I'll rig up a little sail for her and we'll scamper farther afield and maybe if you're here till August I could bring out the old gun and we could have a crack at the duck.'

Going home at dusk he rolled up the lines and baled out the water. They had six fish in all and Christy carried them. They didn't pass through the village but walked along by the silent railway track, stepping over the sleepers that smelt of tar and came on to the road by the level-crossing and into the house, where Alice had supper waiting for them.

And late that night Frank O'Brien made his first call at the house since the seizure of the poteen. Unseen by any of the villagers he made his way through the garden in the darkness and Alice let him in by arrangement. He came to tell Tom that he was leaving Monabeg, that he was being promoted sergeant and sent to north Antrim.

'It's good news for you and Alice but right bad news for me. The people will say that it was the haul of poteen that got you promoted.'

'Promotion would have come if there had been no seizure of poteen. I got it by a written examination. I knew I had done well on the arithmetic paper.'

'This news coming on top of O'Hara's trial will go hard on me.'

'As long as you don't go hard on yourself everything will

turn out all right,' Christy advised. 'In a short while all will fizzle out like a tinker's fire. A group of people can't boycott you for long; they get tired and fall away unless held by something big and heartfelt. Yours will have a short season.'

'All I desire is that my name is cleared from the word Informer. A bad name has a long life in this parish. I know people in it and because their great-great-grandfather was a land-grabber all his descendants are called land-grabbers to this day.'

'But that's different, Father,' Christy tried to explain. They talked for a long time about political informers and of innocent men who were gaoled because of them. And during the discussion Christy endeavoured to convince his father that his case was of entirely different stock and that time, and it would be short, would wither it.

It was two o'clock when Frank stood up to go and they extinguished the light and let him out by the back door, and as he made off in the darkness down through the garden and past the backs of the houses the dogs started barking and a cockerel began to crow, mistaking the movements for the coming of dawn.

'Ah, Father,' said Christy, shuddering from the night air and closing the door, 'you'll have a fine laugh to yourself at this in a year's time. And you'll be telling it all with relish in the pub how the policeman had to sneak away like a thief in the dark and how every bloody mongrel from here to Rockcross began barking.'

'I will, please God,' smiled the father and they sat on talking about Frank and his good nature and how he was a man without guile and unlike the usual run of peelers.

Next morning Frank slipped off to his new post, and the day following Christy departed for his last term, four weeks in all. And on the same day O'Hara stood his trial in the neighbouring town and it was the porter who brought the verdict to Tom as he weeded a flower-bed at the edge of the platform. O'Hara, he told him, was fined in one hundred pounds, refused to pay it, and was going to gaol for a month.

'Sure he should have paid it,' Tom said. 'He's a proud and foolish man.'

'The same boy would have paid it if it were sowing time or hay-cutting time or harvest time. But this is the slack time and his sons is well able for it. He'll come home from gaol a bloody martyr and he a bloody fool! But, Mr Magee, don't let it bite into your mind. I know you're sorry for him and I know the people will know it as soon as the boy comes marching home again.'

In spite of the porter's attitude the news upset Tom and he sat up late that night expecting trouble of some sort or other. Nothing happened until he had gone to bed and the house in darkness. There was a crash of glass as a fusillade of stones was fired at the station. Alice, awakened by the noise, fled in terror to her father's room and he was on the floor and pulling on his trousers as she came in.

'Don't go out, Father,' she implored. 'They'll only strike you.'

'I'm stationmaster and I've no fear of them.' There was another crash of glass.

'Oh, Father, in God's name let us go away from here!'

'Sh-sh, come away from the window.' He switched off the light and came out on the dark and deserted station, his unlaced boots crunching over broken glass.

'I see you all right you parcel of blackguards,' he shouted into the darkness across the track that was the only thing visible. 'I know you all!' he shouted again. 'Some day you'll learn the truth and then you'll be sorry.'

He heard a rush through the hedge and the hurrying of feet on the hard road. He stood for a while, but there was no sound now except the thump of his own heart, the hum of the telephone wires, and in the air the smell of fish from the returned empty boxes that were stacked near where he stood. He tried to detect what damage was done but he could distinguish nothing in the darkness and going back to his room again he found Alice crying at the edge of his bed.

'Leave your door open, Father,' she said, her teeth chattering.

'I will, I will. Get into bed now and have no fear.' And when she was in bed he made the sign of the cross on her forehead and told her that all would pass away as Christy said and that all decent people would condemn it.

He wasn't frightened except for Alice and he decided to encourage her to go to Rockcross for a while and stay with Mag until Mag's confinement was over. Yes, that's what he would do and it would be a plausible excuse to get her away from here till the storm passed. He was settling down to sleep then when it suddenly occurred to him that he would have to report the damage to head office, that he could no longer conceal it from them by repairing it at his own expense. And thinking of it he became wide awake, aware that they would send an inspector down to investigate. Surely, surely, they wouldn't ask him to leave for another station. Surely his good record would stand to him and they would see the improvements he had made here in his short while. No, no, it would break his heart to go changing again at his age, and go away before his good name was cleared, the stain of guilt erased from him and his people.

He rose earlier than usual and discovered that the damage done was less than the crashing in the dark had led him to believe. One window in the booking-office was broken, two in the signal-cabin, and a window-box damaged and the soil spilled out of it. He swept up the glass and the stones and putting on his stationmaster's cap strolled up the village for his morning's paper. Ben Brady was pushing his chair across the road from the shop, holding up the morning's traffic, and didn't see him.

The newsagent was always glad to see him and always had his paper with his name pencilled on it, folded and ready for him at the side of the counter. She was a small woman

208

with white hair and a black blouse clasped tightly about her throat by a gold brooch. She knew him in the old days when he was only an apprenticed clerk at the railway and she always had great respect for him and his family. This morning, she gladly observed that he didn't lean as he usually did with his elbows on the counter and talk to her of the O'Hara affair and how he became involved in it. He stood straight, his hands behind his back like a parade soldier at ease, and smiled out of the window at Ben sitting in the sun on his chair and reading the paper.

'I must get a chair like Ben and read in comfort wherever I happen to be,' he said.

'Do you know, Tom, what I'm going to tell you, that's the first paper he has bought since Larry Duncan's murder trial twenty years ago. He bought it to read about O'Hara and by all accounts he hasn't come upon the paragraph yet. He'll have trouble finding it for it's in a space no bigger than a cigarette card.'

He told her about the breaking of the station windows.

'A lot of senseless blackguards, Tom, that's what they are. And I'm glad you're taking it calmly. If they saw you distressed and could run you out of your lovely little place it'd give them great satisfaction. That's a fine son you have, God bless him,' she added, changing the conversation.

She looked out the window and saw Ben hurrying back across the road again with the paper.

'He hasn't found it and he's coming for his money back,' she said, and opened the till and took out two pennies in readiness. But when Ben reached the open door and saw Tom in the shop he hurried away again without coming in.

'Ben and me used to be great friends,' Tom said, pushing back his cap and resting his elbows on the counter.

'If he'd visit the pub less he could make up his own mind better,' she said, sitting down on her own chair and waiting for 'poor Tom', as she called him in her own mind, to talk about his innocence.

'Ben will come round again, never fear,' she said.

'Maybe it's my own fault. Maybe I've lost the capacity I once had for making friends. I had many here before I left but few new ones when I went away from it.'

'They'll all come round again, Tom, they will indeed. And when your son's an ordained priest they'll be raising their caps to you. They will indeed. That'll be a great day in your life. The very thought of it will drive this O'Hara business to the very divil. I'm glad you're not letting it worry you any longer.'

The sergeant of the police came into the shop and as he did so Tom took out his watch from his waistcoat pocket, straightened his cap and bidding the sergeant good morning he hurried down to the station.

That night a policeman hung around the level-crossing gates. No further damage was done to the station but in the crowded pub a man who had composed a ballad was reciting it aloud:

'One evening in April before the moon brightened
A clutch of police set off well enlightened
They were searching for poteen as well you might see
Being informed true and good by one Thomas Magee.
They made for O'Hara's, well led by O'Brien,
And there in the stable they came on the men;
The still was aworking, the juice running free,
But no one can drink it because of Magee.
He informed on O'Hara and the judge gave this sen-
    tence:
"One hundred pounds down or one month's detention."
"It's gaol for me then," spakes my bold boy O'Hara,
"For I won't pay a pound today nor tomorrow."
And the people did cheer and the rafters did ring
And the judge called for order because of the din.
And off he was sent to the cold prison walls
Far from his fields and the sweet Monabeg falls.

And Magee and O'Brien prepare the next spree
For he courts his daughter and married they'll be.
Promotion he got as all honest men knew
While informer Magee spies out for more brew.
Take heed all ye people who read this old rhyme
Fly far from treason while still there is time
For Judas you know betrayed his Lord for red gold
As Magee sold O'Hara as I have all told.'

The recitation came to an end and the audience thumped the counter and said it was a damned good piece that the schoolmaster couldn't equal, and that a copy should be sent to Magee. He recited it again and again and they learnt lines of it and repeated them in unison.

The signalman was there and in one evening he learnt it off by heart, and the following morning, seeing Jimmy the porter sweeping out the waiting-room and sprinkling the dust with a watering-can, he sauntered along to him and asked him to hold up for a minute or two. As he recited the piece Jimmy leaned on the upright shaft of the brush. Almost inaudible because of his laughter the signalman spluttered to the end of the verse but Jimmy didn't speak.

'Isn't that bloody good, Jimmy?'

'It's bloody insulting, that's what it is — insulting to the best stationmaster in the whole damned country. And what have you got against him I'd like to know, you miserable sponge,' Jimmy shouted angrily. 'Look at all his pints of porter you lowered after a day's toil. What other stationmaster would stand you a drink? Some of them wouldn't give you God's daylight.'

'I haven't taken a pint from him since he turned informer.'

'I don't believe he informed on O'Hara and I won't believe.'

'The facts are clear,' said the signalman, holding up his fingers. 'Number one: O'Brien courts his daughter. Number two: seizure of O'Hara's still. Number three: Magee knows the whereabouts of the same still. Number four: O'Brien gets promotion and skips off. Ipso facto: Magee informed. It's as plain as the ribs in my corduroy trousers.'

'Number five: I'll cleave the miserable head off you with this brush if you don't climb up to your perch in quick time.'

'Oho, so you'd fight, would you. You keep in with him and maybe some day you'll get promotion too.'

The porter raised his brush, the signalman caught it by the handle, and the noise of their scuffling on the platform brought Tom out from the booking-office.

'Is there not enough venom outside without bringing it in here,' he said to the two of them.

'Any that's here,' said the signalman, 'it was you that brought it.' He didn't wait to explain further but ascended the steep wooden steps to his signal-cabin and banged the door behind him.

'What's it all about, Jimmy?'

'Nothing, sir, nothing. He's just in a bad temper. Don't heed him, sir, we'll get on with our work as if nothing had happened. And if you don't mind, sir, I'd be glad if you'd take me out with you for an evening or two's fishing.'

'I'll be glad of your company since the son went off.'

'I've a few bait an Englishman left behind him and never claimed and I'd like to try them. There's nothing like an evening's fishing to take the bite out of a man's mind.'

'There's something in that, Jimmy. When you go on the water you somehow leave your worries behind you on the land.'

'I'm your man. Any evening you just say the word and I'll be there.'

CHAPTER
16

DURING the next three days Alice scarcely left the house except to go into the garden to bring clothes off the line or fetch a few vegetables for the dinner. All her conversation was taken up with Frank or with entreating her father to leave Monabeg should another place be offered to him on account of the stone-throwing and the broken window-panes in the station. She told him he would never have peace here and he in turn told her he would never have peace out of it until his good name was cleared and O'Hara once again friendly with him. 'It will never be said that the Magees of Monabeg were informers,' he repeated to her with firmness.

On Friday of that week a letter came from Joe to tell of the arrival of Mag's baby, a baby girl; and with his letter came one from Frank inviting Alice to visit him at the week-end. Her father urged her to go either to Rockcross or to Frank. But how could she go and leave him alone, not only to fend for himself but maybe to endure another night of stone-throwing on his own? For himself he had no fear and he begged her to have no fear for him and to go wherever her heart lay. He understood and would not find fault with her if she went away for a day or two.

'But am I not being selfish, Father?'

'No Alice, you're not. I want you to go, to get away from here for a while. Deep in your heart you'll feel this pull towards me and towards the family but your time has come now to slacken it but never, please God, to break from it completely. I don't believe any of us could do that no matter what happened. It's like warmth in the blood; we can't get rid of it even if we wanted to.'

She left on Saturday morning to visit Frank, and in the evening Tom and Jimmy the porter had the oars and the fishing-gear ready to set off as soon as the evening train had passed through. And it was Jimmy who hurried forward to open the level-crossing gates when he heard the bells ring in the signal-cabin, and on coming back to the platform he stood with Tom, their hands behind their backs, gazing impatiently down the empty lines and hearing the train whistle in the distance. Tom looked at his pocket watch, held it in the palm of his hand, tapped his foot and complained she was three minutes late. And then presently round the bend jaunted the little evening train, waving her grey cudgel of smoke. Her carriage windows reflected the sloping sun, and in the fields alongside ran the train's shadow, black and wobbly as a child's drawing. She slid into the station and there leaning out of one window was Julia, waving to her father. The train stopped and he ran forward to open the carriage door as he used to do in the old days in Rockcross for her mother.

Little Dick and Marie were with her and the new baby wrapped in a white shawl.

'This is a great surprise,' he said kissing Julia and lifting Marie in his arms. And while her pram and case were taken from the guard's van he held little Dick firmly by one hand and they stood like that till the train whistled and rumbled away over the bridge like distant thunder. Jimmy wheeled in the pram to the house and carried in the case and after Tom had introduced him to Julia he told him to take the oars and the rowlocks and try his luck on his own bat.

Tom stirred the fire under the kettle on the range, pulled forward an armchair for Julia, and unbuttoned Dick's coat and hung it on the back of a chair.

'Such peace and quiet there is here, Father,' she said in a tired voice. 'And the little place is shining.'

'Alice works hard and I sent her off for a day or two this morning to see her beloved Frank.'

As he spoke he noticed the blue shadows under her eyes, the pained droop at the corners of her mouth, and realized that the last birth did not go easy with her. She met his tender gaze, but he winced away from the sorrow he saw in her own eyes and turning quickly to Marie and little Dick he remarked how big they had grown in such a short time. She unwrapped the shawl from around the baby and he touched his cheek with his forefinger and clicked his tongue at him. She wouldn't bath the baby this evening she decided; she'd just sponge him with warm water and hurry him to bed as he hadn't slept much since they left Rockcross.

He poured some hot water for her into a basin and after testing it with her finger she rummaged in her bag and drew out a towel wrapped around the baby's bottle. The bottle was half full and some of the milk had curdled and clung to the sides like bread crumbs. She placed it on top of the range to warm but he told her he had lashings of milk and it would be wiser to make up a fresh bottle.

'So you're not able to feed him yourself, Julia?'

'A little, Father, that's all. He doesn't get enough and I have to supplement.' She turned the baby on her lap and held her hands out to the heat to warm them before undressing him. 'It's cold, Father, for the month of May.' And she gave a nervous shudder.

'It is,' he agreed, though he was aware that the coldness was in her own famished body.

He went down to the scullery and came back with milk and a hot water bottle that he'd put in a little cot he had stored away for an occasion like this. He would rig it up in a jiffy if little Dick would help him. Dick clattered after him up the small stairway and Marie followed, negotiating the six steps one by one and clinging to the banisters at the same time. The children smiled and laughed at their accomplishment, delighted with the drumming sounds of the steps under their feet.

'Hush, children,' Julia would admonish them as they

stamped across the floor to her and back to the stairs again. 'Hush, children, or Granda will send us all home again.' She fed the baby, hiding her breast with the corner of her shawl because little Dick had once asked her why she let the baby chew her stomach.

She was giving him his bottle when her father came down to the kitchen again after making up the beds and the cot. The baby drank greedily and when he had the bottle drained she held him upright against her shoulder and patted his back every time he hiccuped. Her father inquired about Rockcross, but she knitted her brows, unable to hear what he was saying because of the din that Marie and Dick made on the bedroom floor above their heads.

'Let them be,' the father said, 'they'll sleep all the sounder when they get into bed.'

Taking safety pins from her blouse she tidied up the baby for the night and carried him upstairs, leaving behind her a cool smell of talcum powder and a bundle of clothes on the floor.

She gave Dick and Marie hot milk and biscuits and having tucked them into their beds she came down to have a long talk with her father. He wouldn't let her put a hand to the making of their supper but made her sit in the armchair and rest herself, and all the time she kept inquiring about how he was faring now with the neighbours.

A few were thawing out, he told her. But he expected things to worsen when O'Hara was out of gaol and when Alice married her policeman. He was going to tell her about the stone-throwing but not wishing to worry her he desisted and went on to make light of his trouble, telling her that he had never much capacity for making friends anyway.

'You've been through a lot, Father, you have indeed; you have been through more than what you told in your letters,' she said, for she had been studying his face as he spoke and it struck her how old he had grown since she last saw him. Then suddenly her self-control gave way and she burst into tears.

'Ah, Julia girl, don't take it too badly. It will pass in God's good time. I'm not afraid of them.'

'But the tears are for myself,' she said brokenly. 'It's Richard. I've left him.'

He let her reel out her worries knowing that it would loosen the sorrow that burdened her. She couldn't live with Richard any more. Of late he had worsened and at the christening of Mag's baby he used it as an excuse to come home disgracefully drunk. He was gambling heavily; he was in debt again and was gradually losing his clients and the old stalwarts that always gave him their sale of hay and grazing land. She was tired of him; time and again she had saved him from disgrace but this time she'd leave him to his boozing friends to extricate.

'You're tired out, Julia,' he said, not wishing to give her advice till sleep had smoothed the rough edges of her mind. 'We'll have a good heart-to-heart talk about all this to-morrow.'

She dried her eyes and sighed: 'I'm sorry, Father, about this outburst for I feel you have more than your own share of trouble. But I had to tell someone.'

'And why wouldn't you tell your own father.' And he pulled a chair to the table for her to eat the supper he had prepared.

There was a drumming of little feet above their heads from time to time and at last he rose from the table and upstairs discovered Dick and Marie at the window peering down at the railway lines that caught the last of the sun. Swallows creaked like new leather as they swayed and tilted over the track and sped up to their nests under the scalloped eaves of the storage sheds.

'Where's the trains, Granda? Are they sleeping in the big house?'

'They are, Dick. They're all in bed fast asleep. You'll see them in the morning.'

After supper he brought Julia outside to the garden. The

217

sun had set, the four apple trees crouched in silence, their faded blossom strewing the grass. Washing lay on tops of the hedges behind the grey houses, and in the still air sounded the noise of the falls and the sizz of the mosquitoes that dandled above the water barrel at the side of the house. Julia breathed deeply, rejoicing in the silence that soothed like a relief from pain. And when she was in bed and the baby asleep in the cot beside her he tiptoed into her room and in the light from the window he saw her smile.

'Oh, Father, I'll sleep. I'll sleep long and deep. You're very good. Oh, God, if Richard were only half like you I'd be satisfied.'

'Don't say things like that. He'll pull himself together all right. This little break from him won't do either of you any harm. You must get back the old spirit you once had. But we'll not talk like that now. If you want anything during the night just knock the wall and I'll be in in a jiffy.'

'Tomorrow's Sunday and I'd like to go to Mass if that's possible.'

He strove to dissuade her from that decision, explaining that with young children to mind she would be fully excused. She seemed determined to go and not wishing to cross her he told her quietly to leave the final decision till the morning.

Next morning he himself rose early and going out quietly from the house he cycled to an early Mass in a little church five miles away and when he returned he was surprised to see washing on the line, the baby in his pram in the garden, and breakfast on the table.

'You're a determined woman,' he said as she asked him to get Alice's bicycle ready and allow her to get to Mass. He was to keep an eye on the children till she returned, and since there were no bees yet in his hives he let the two of them into the garden and tied the gate with string so that they could not wander on to the village street.

Dick in his Sunday clothes played at the rain-barrel at the side of the house. It was three-quarters full, and standing on the concrete platform that raised it from the ground he leaned over the rim and sniffed the dark mouldy smell. On seeing the reflection of his face in the water he shouted at it and it answered him in a voice deeper than his own. Tired of that he fetched a stake from the flower-bed and began to nose off the red fungus like lentils that clung to the inside of the barrel, and when he had them all prised off he tried to sink the cane but the more he shoved it deep down into the water the quicker it popped back to the surface, bringing with it three or four tiny bubbles which he blew at till they burst. Bracelets of sooty marks ringed his wrist and he rolled up his sleeves and lifting two flat stones from the garden he placed them on top of the platform and heaved himself up on to the slimy rim. He saw a glittering tin-top at the bottom of the barrel and he leaned over and tried to touch it with his stick. His face was red and there was a pain in his chest from the constriction of his breathing but he persisted in his efforts to touch the shiny coin of tin that tantalized him. He raised himself higher and once more leaned over; he touched the tin and then suddenly he overbalanced and his legs disappeared over the edge of the barrel. Marie's screams brought her granda rushing from the house, and with one heave he pushed the barrel from the platform and out of it flowed black slimy water and little Dick, his white blouse and trousers the colour of the barrel. The water he had swallowed choked back his sobs and flowed out from the corners of his mouth. His granda turned him over on his front on the path, placed the wet head gently to the side and leaning over him pressed at the base of his lungs and called out encouragingly: 'Throw it up, Dick,' as the stagnant water vomited from the child's mouth.

'Sick, Granda,' he cried, and his granda, relieved, sat him upright on the path and took the stick from Marie, who was scraping it in the fallen water and plastering it on her frock. He carried them into the house away from the sickening smell of the water and by the time Julia had got back from

Mass he had Dick washed and in bed, the soiled clothes steeped in a bath, the shoes drying on top of the range, and himself wheeling the pram with the crying child up and down the garden.

'Ah, Julia, that seemed to me the longest Mass you were ever at' — and he calmly recounted what had happened, adding a touch of humour to ease her concern.

She took over from him and in a short while had things in hand: Marie's frock changed, and little Dick with a towel round his neck and a basin on top of the bedclothes in case he would be sick. By the time she had dinner ready her father lay sound asleep on the sofa, his mouth hanging open, one hand touching the ground. She gazed at the pale face and he suddenly seemed to her an old man. The children were too much for him, and she shouldn't have gone to Mass when she was not expected to go and he had advised her not to. And then the journey he had put upon himself in order to please her: cycling ten miles on a fasting stomach and he only half the man she once knew. 'God forgive me, I shouldn't have done it,' she said to herself, and going about the house quietly she kept the dinner warm on the rack till he awakened.

In the afternoon Alice returned, and in the evening the two sisters sat in the garden in the last of the sun. Dick's clothes were drying on the line, and a wind was blowing across the flat fields carrying the scent of hawthorn that lay like snow on the hedges. Alice spoke of all that Father had come through: the stone-throwing at night, the cutting silence of many of the neighbours, and how poorly he was sleeping of late.

'And to think that he didn't tell me one-quarter of it and you didn't tell much of it in your letters,' Julia said, and picked a speck of dried cream from her skirt. 'Not a quarter of it did he tell me. And who would have thought that a few months could bring such a change on him.' She paused and bit her lip. Tears came in spite of herself and one dropped on her lap. 'How good he is and I'm afraid we've all been too selfish with him. I intended to leave Richard but now I'm going to go back to him. What are my troubles compared to Father's? In a short while he'll have lost Christy, and in a short while he'll have lost you in the same way as he has lost me and Mag.'

'No, Julia, that will never be. Frank loves him and he'll take Christy's place.'

'Ah, Alice child, marriage will pull you away and that pull is stronger, stronger by far, than your attachment to Father or to me. But strong as it is it is not stronger than Father's love for us.'

They sat on, their minds struggling with some mystery in life that they both felt but could not put a name to. The sunlight left the garden and a cold evening breeze fidgeted in the grass and in the apple trees. Julia sighed and rising stiffly to her feet she unpegged the clothes from the line. They were stiff and white and as she bundled them together in her arms they smelt sweetly of the good clean air. That night she wrote to Richard but before she had time to send it by the morning's post Richard himself and Aunt Brigid arrived in his car, having set out from Rockcross at six in the morning.

It was Aunt Brigid who came in first, in by the garden door, and met Julia and Alice washing the breakfast dishes. Their father had gone off to the booking-office and she ordered them not to disturb him as she'd see him later. They were surprised at her visit and on inquiring how she had come she drew Julia to the side and whispered to her that Richard was outside in the car and that he only wanted one thing: that she and the children would come back to him. She scolded Julia mildly for leaving him at such a time — and Christy on the threshold of his ordination. Of course, all the Rockcross neighbours thought that she had gone on a holiday and they must never be enlightened as to the truth. Julia must promise her that. And as for the debts they were all cleared up and she mustn't ask any questions about them.

'And lastly, Julia,' she said, and clasped Julia's two hands, 'he has promised me he'll do his best. He'll turn over a new leaf.'

'He has turned over so many new leaves I'm afraid he needs a new ledger,' Julia tried to say harshly, but a smile broke across her face and she threw her arms around her aunt.

Aunt Brigid went out to the car, and Richard walked with her to the house, his hat in his hand like a man at a funeral. Ordering him inside to Julia she beckoned Alice to the garden that was now covered by the shadow from the house, and as they sauntered along the path Alice prepared her for the great change she would notice in her father. 'He's not the same man at all since he left Rockcross, Aunt Brigid,' she said sadly.

'And Rockcross is not the same tidy station since he left. Maybe we could manage to get him back again, back to his own job when Wilson retires. I could start a little whispering campaign to that effect when I get back. And incidentally, you know I'm arranging a little reception in the hotel after Christy's first Mass and we could bring the full force of the Magee connection down on him on that occasion.' She stooped and broke off a sprig of wallflower, sniffed it, and pinned it to her breast. 'And Mag's baby you know is called after me. Mag is a sweet girl though I don't care much for the man she married. And by the way,' she said, holding her head sideways, 'you haven't been sleeping on your feet since you came here. It'll not be long I suppose till your big day, and then of course the pram will follow.'

Julia came to the door and called to them and, as they approached, out came Richard holding little Dick and Marie in his arms. 'We haven't told Father you're here so slip round, Aunt Brigid, and give him a pleasant surprise.'

Aunt Brigid went into the house, and after freshening her face with a little rouge she walked smartly to the booking-office window and changing her voice she asked for a single ticket to Rockcross. At first he didn't know her, and then he smiled and as he came out to meet her she kissed him on the side of the cheek.

'Where on earth did you drop from, Brigid?'

'I walked all the way like a tramp to see you,' she said, and now that he was out of the gloom of the booking-office and in the full light of the airy platform she saw that he had failed greatly, and unable to conceal her horror she cried out: 'Oh Tom, dear, you look ill! What have you been doing with yourself?'

'Enjoying myself every evening at the fishing,' he said, wincing away from her comprehensive stare.

'Oh, you must take more care of yourself,' she said, wagging her head and telling him of people in Rockcross, healthy people who took no care of themselves and gradually withered away like snow off a ditch, and died one after another.

'And poor Sergeant's dead too,' he said, edging her towards the house and directing her conversation on another route.

'Dead and buried in my patch of garden,' she answered, and then after a long pause she launched into an account of his last hours after the bus had struck him. 'And do you know what the vet said that attended him: never in all his dealings with canines did he ever record on his thermometer as high a temperature as that of poor Sergeant's.'

'Well, that's something to be proud of,' he said, not thinking.

'Oh, Tom, how can you be so cruel!'

He tried then to take back his words, saying that he didn't mean it in the way she construed; and she in turn aware that he was giving her his full attention held fast to her accusation. At last he had manœuvred her into the house and in the presence of Richard and the children he was able to escape her continual buzz.

In the early afternoon with the hot sun twisting shadows

of heat from the road Richard, with Tom's and the porter's help, prepared for the road. The pram would not fit into the boot of the car and they had to rope it to the roof. But when they had everything stored and their coats put on again they gathered the women and children on to the road and after much wrangling as to who should sit with whom they all finally abdicated and left it to Richard. Quietly he told Aunt Brigid to sit in the stern seat with the two children and allow the captain's wife and her baby to sit on the port side of the wheel. When they were all seated on the port and starboard side he got in and taking the wheel he gave a few toots on the horn and backed out from the station. Aunt Brigid kissed her hand and called through the window: 'Till the fifteenth of June, Tom, take care of yourself for Christy's sake.' Julia waved the baby's hand and smiled sadly at her father, who waved his stationmaster's cap in reply.

And after the car had gone off he walked slowly back to the house with Alice and asked her to get Jimmy to fetch a half dozen bottles of stout from the pub. 'It'll be a relief to get a drink of stout after listening to your Aunt Brigid. She's kind but she talks too much. It's well she didn't get married. She'd have lost more than poor Sergeant I'm thinking.'

That evening he sauntered out to the tailor's to get measured for a new suit for Christy's ordination day. He came back within an hour and as he shuffled across the kitchen tiles and sat heavily in an armchair scarcely speaking to her she knew there was something on his mind. She asked him if he had met anyone at the tailor's or on his way back but he didn't seem to hear her. She continued her work at the light from the window, carefully sewing leather patches on the elbows of his working jacket. She glanced at him as he leaned forward in the chair and combed his hair with his fingers. She sat quite still and she distinctly heard him mutter to himself: 'I'll not go. I'll not go.'

She lifted another needle and threaded it by holding it against the light of the window. Then her thimble fell from her lap and her father yawned, and rising to his feet took down his chess-board and arranged the pieces upon it.

'You'll have to teach me how to play chess,' she said.

'I will, Alice, but not this evening. I'm just not in the best of form.' He took from the shelf a book of chess games and began to play one of them, moving each piece after prolonged thought.

Without disturbing him Alice stuck her needle in the unfinished patch and folding up the jacket and tidying away her work-box she slipped quietly from the house. She hurried beyond the village street and coming to a lonin almost overgrown with briars she made her way along it looking at the holes in the clay made by Ben Brady's chair. Swarms of flies gathered around her face and clothes and she was glad to reach the open space in front of Ben's house. The door was open and Ben was sitting in the gloom of the turf fire, the light shining on his face like varnished wood. She rapped the open door and called out to him, and without rising from his chair he pulled another one by the rungs with the crook of his stick and after wiping the seat of it with the lining of his cap he asked her to sit down. A mug and a teapot sat on a stool beside him.

'I'd ask you to take a sup of tea with me only my crockery's not too clean,' he said.

'Thanks, Ben, but I'm just after tea before leaving the house,' she said, sitting with her handbag on her lap and gazing at the red turf in the grate. 'I wonder would you do one thing for me? Would you ever visit my father again?'

Ben spat into the fire and the spit alighted like a black beetle on the red-hot turf.

'Ah, do, Ben,' she pleaded, putting a hand on his sleeve. 'My father had nothing to do with O'Hara's still.'

He stretched out and lifted the mug. He drank noisily and wiped his mouth with his sleeve.

225

'It's hard to believe, girl, he had nothing to do with it. Everything points to him as the informer. I tried not to believe it but in the end I had to give in.'

'I could swear before God he had nothing to do with it.'

'I don't want a young girl to swear. I do not. I'll believe you. I'll try to believe in your father and I'll sail down one of these evenings as if nothing had happened.'

'Don't say I called to see you.'

'Would it vex him to know that?'

'I don't know, Ben. But I do know that it's you he misses.'

She stood up, and Ben leaning on two sticks shuffled to the door with her. Swallows streeled around the house and the sound of the falls drummed across the open fields.

'It's quiet here, Ben.'

'It is and it's lonely. I'm just dying for a game of chess and dying for somebody to play with.'

'For my sake let him win a game or two and put him in good form.'

He laughed, showing a few old teeth. 'I will. I'll do it because a sweet girl asked me.'

She suddenly kissed him on the cheek and disappeared among the arching briars of his lonin.

'A damned fine wee girl,' he said to himself. 'A pity she's marrying a damned peeler — a peeler who seized the best distillery in the bloody country. Poor O'Hara! Whoever informed on you I do not know, but I'm beginning to believe it wasn't Tom Magee.'

The following evening though the rain was falling and rolling like glass beads off his greasy cap he set out for Tom's, pushing his chair in front of him and calling into the pub on his way. He sat at the window of the pub gazing down the road that led to the river. He sipped his pint slowly, and after Tom had passed along the deserted street carrying three fish on a string he got up and followed him. It was Alice who let him into the house and it was she who made him change into an old jacket of her father's till his own

226

was dried at the fire. She tried to get the wet cap from him but he refused to give it to her and sat as he always sat with the cap on his head.

'I'm dying for a game,' were the first words he said to Tom; and the chess-board was produced and the pieces placed on it as if continuing a game that had been interrupted. And an hour later as Alice brought them supper on a tray it was Tom who had won the game and it was he who was demonstrating the key-move that led to his success.

'And you'll have more success in the middle of June,' Ben said. 'Your son will be ordained and it'll be as great a day for you as the day you got married.'

'I'll not be at it, Ben. I'll not be there.'

Ben stared at him uncomprehendingly and waited.

'The tailor was telling me that O'Hara will be released on June 15th, the same day as my son's ordination. The Monabeg Pipe Band is to be at this station to welcome O'Hara.' He paused, stretched out his hand to the chess-board, and lifted a piece and placed it down again. 'And I'll be here too. If I was away from the station on that day the people would say I was afraid to face them. But I'm not afraid, Ben. I'm not afraid because I didn't inform.'

'And you tell me you're not going to your son's ordination?'

'No, Ben,' and Tom shook his head. 'But I'll leave after O'Hara's train comes in and I'll be at my son's first Mass in Rockcross on the following morning. That's my plan and, please God, I'll carry it out.'

'Do you know, do you know ... ' spluttered Ben, unable to arrange the words that stumbled at the back of his befuddled mind. 'Do you know what I'm going to say? You didn't inform on O'Hara! And may God forgive me for thinking that you did. You didn't! You didn't!' shouted Ben, and the spits flew from his mouth. 'Indeed, by the good God, you didn't.' And he raised his cap reverently and put it on again. He struck the table with his fist and the chess-men bounced on the board. 'The first man that says you did I'll open his skull with the back of my chair.' He spat on his hand and held it out to Tom. 'Lay it there and say you forgive me. I turned my back on you the other day in the shop. I shouldn't have done that.'

'There's nothing to forgive, Ben. Nothing.'

'Do you know, Tom, what I'm going to say?' He shook his head solemnly. 'It's a bad day for anyone in this county to get mixed up with the police. I've nothing against your wee girl and I hope she'll be happy with her man. And I like him but I don't like his uniform. You understand?'

'I do, I do.'

It was dark when he was leaving and as he pushed his chair along the village street he saw a knot of youths against the white wall of the pub. Deliberately he slowed up as he was passing them and shouted in a loud and challenging tone: 'The Magees of Monabeg were never informers and never will be!'

In silence they peered after him as he disappeared in the darkness but nobody laughed for fear of him and after the scrape of his chair could no longer be heard they began to talk about O'Hara's homecoming, and later as they broke up for the night some of them marched past the station singing loudly:

'One evening in April before the moon brightened
A clutch of police set off well enlightened
They were searching for poteen as well you might see,
Being informed true and good by one Thomas Magee....'

WHEN June 15th came round Tom rose with the sun
and altered the white stones on the shelving bank to read
WELCOME instead of MONABEG, and at intervals along the
platform he hung wire baskets with yellow and red nasturtiums and some with blue forget-me-nots. When Jimmy, the
porter, arrived he got him to shine up the brass handles on
all the doors and give the glass on the lamp-heads an extra
wipe with the duster. Tufts of grass were pulled out from the
stones among the railway sleepers, flower-beds were freshly
raked, and every speck of straw and dust swept from the
platform.

The train was due at midday and half an hour before that
time the sun shone strongly, and through the open window
of the cool booking-office Tom heard the sound of the bagpipes as the band approached the village. People appeared
at the windows and doors of their houses, and dogs barked
and fought each other in the middle of the sunny street.
Presently the music ceased and when Tom looked out again
he saw the Monabeg Pipe Band troop through the village,
the big drum tapping faintly to the beat of the marching
feet. They wore red tartan kilts and green tunics; their white
gaiters were freshly pipeclayed, their shoes polished, and
the metal fastenings on their sash-belts glinted in the sun.
Ahead of them, stiff as a mechanical toy, marched the drum
major, his tasselled pole held horizontally in front of him as
they wheeled four deep into the parking space behind the
station. Behind came a freshly varnished pony-trap, its shafts
pulled by six men each of whom wore white gloves, and

behind the trap came women and children. Within the gloom of the booking-office Tom could see without being seen. In some way he was proud of them and he only wished he was one of them. The bandsmen took off their Glengarry caps, wiped their brows, and adjusted straps and belts, and then at a signal from their leader they filed into the station, leaving the pony-trap outside, its shafts in the air and the white pulling-ropes twined round them to keep from trailing on the dusty ground. Women and children moved in from the street and at the open door of the newsagent's stood herself and the sergeant of the police smiling and talking to her and laughing at Ben Brady who was heading for the station, pushing his chair furiously along the middle of the road.

Out of breath Ben reached the platform and pushed his way through the lined-up bandsmen and planted his chair in front of them. The band-leader implored him, for the love of God, to go to the back and not spoil the appearance of the assembly but Ben folded his arms, sat on as if he hadn't heard him, and spat across the lines with good-natured contempt. The band-leader, holding his silver-knobbed pole like a beadle, ordered his men to move three paces to the right, and as they did so Ben, realizing he was left coldly at the edge of the group, got up and again planted his chair in the centre.

'You're a crooked, carnaptious oul bugger,' the leader said to him, and at that moment the bell rang in the signal-cabin and the signalman descended the wooden stairway to open the level-crossing gates. The bandsmen blew up their pipes and stood waiting for the leader's sign, and then out from the booking-office slipped Tom and took up his position at the waiting-room door. No one noticed him as he stood well back, his black boots shining and the braid on his stationmaster's cap freshened up for the occasion. A light wind blew a smell of tar from the railway sleepers and stirred the ribbons on the bagpipes.

The train came in, the people cheered, and as O'Hara appeared at a carriage window the band struck up 'The Minstrel Boy', and at the end of the first verse the engine-driver gave his whistle three short blasts and one prolonged one to announce his impatience to be on his way. Passengers cheered from the windows, not knowing what they were cheering, and then as the six gloved men strode forward and carried O'Hara shoulder high from the carriage the train pulled out, stirring a fresh current of air behind it.

'Welcome home!' the people shouted, holding up their hands to shake O'Hara's.

Ben Brady raised his chair aloft and called three cheers for the man that was gaoled. They cheered loudly, and then Ben, pointing his chair to Tom, whose cap he could just make out, yelled: 'And now, friends, we'll give three cheers for the man we've wronged.'

'No! Never!' some shouted and others booed, and as they rushed and stumbled from the platform some of them knocked Tom against the waiting-room door and as his cap fell off it was kicked and trampled among their feet and sent spinning off the platform on to the railway track. The porter retrieved it and brushed the dust off it with his sleeve and when he climbed back to the platform there was no one on it but Tom and Ben Brady, and outside the band playing 'O'Donnel Abu' as they hoisted O'Hara into the pony-trap and pulled him through the village.

'Go on the pair of you and don't miss the fun,' Tom said to Ben and the porter as they leant against the white railings looking out on to the crowded street.

'Maybe I should go a few perches with them,' Ben said, listening to the cheering and thinking he might miss a free bottle of stout on an occasion like this. 'And whisper, Tom, don't heed their insults. A day will come when they'll rue it.'

'I'll be off to Rockcross this evening and you can give me all the news when I get back.'

'You'll get that son of yours to say a prayer for me.

I'm an oul heathen and I'd need somebody to pray for me.'

'You can ask him yourself for he'll be coming back with me for a bit of fishing before he sets out for Nigeria.'

There were more cheers from the street outside and a loud voice reading an address of welcome to O'Hara.

'I'll go, friends, to hear the orations,' and Tom watched Ben set off, the porter helping him through the swing-gate and passing his chair to him over the white wooden fence. The porter came back to Tom, and as he was recommended to take charge in Tom's absence he once more asked for last instructions.

'I've a list made out and I'll go over it with you after you get your dinner,' Tom said.

'That'll do fine.' And the porter set off leaving Tom alone on the deserted, sunny station.

Tom locked up the booking-office, picked up some litter from the platform, and went out to the garden. He tried to relax, but as he held the lighted match above the bowl of his pipe his hand trembled. He tightened his grip on the match and stared at his shaking hand as if it belonged to somebody else. He dragged strongly at the pipe and after it was well lighted he crossed his legs and listened to the band moving along the three-mile stretch that led to O'Hara's.

Though he could not see the band because of the thickness of the hedges he could follow it in his mind's eye along the road he knew so well, and when the sound of the bagpipes rose in volume he knew they were crossing a bridge over a stream where the land lay wide open to the bogs, and when the sound dulled away to a faint hum like a bee's he knew they had reached the first milestone and were passing under the tunnel of trees at the demesne where the road was always wet and smelt like a rain-barrel. Gradually the sound wedged forth again and they were ascending the hill that led to the church. The parish priest with his binoculars on the approaching crowd would be enjoying the spectacle from his garden, ready to disappear into the haven of his house before

232

they passed his gate with their poteen-maker enthroned on a borrowed trap.

Tom smiled and as the sound dwindled to a faint speck he thought of Christy and the fine day he had got for his ordination. He looked at his watch. The ceremony would be over by this time and they were probably strolling round the college grounds and discussing his own absence. Christy would probably be rereading his last letter in which he had explained why he couldn't go. Poor Christy would forgive him, and tonight when he'd meet him in Rockcross he'd surely not refer to his absence but would on the contrary ask all about O'Hara's reception. But he wasn't at all sure what the girls would say to him. Yesterday, before Alice set off in the train, she quarrelled with him and her words, proud with spirit, he'd never forget: 'Father,' she said, 'I don't want to come back here again if you don't come with me to your son's ordination. I mean that! And I don't want you to come to my wedding if you don't pack your bag and come to a far greater ceremony. There isn't another man in Ireland would do what you're doing. You're eating your heart out because of some sense of honour that is to me nonsensical. They'll think all the less of you for doing it, less of you as a man and less of you as a father.' That was Alice for all the world. Poor Mag would never say that to him no matter what he did. She'd always stand up for him. Please God, he'd see her tonight and see her baby.

He yawned, a yawn that was half a sigh, knocked out his pipe on the side of his boot and watched the wind scatter the ash upon the grass. He looked at his note-book and ticked off all the items he had enumerated for Jimmy to attend to. His eye halted at one entry: leave out oars, row-locks and fishing tackle. He struck his pencil through it, got up, gathered the things together and stowed them in a sheltered place at the side of the rain-barrel. He would have a read of the newspaper before packing his bag, then he would have a nice meal of salad and cooked ham and he'd be ready

233

then for the road. But when he searched in the house for the paper he couldn't find it and he suddenly remembered that in the morning's excitement he had forgotten to call for it. He smiled and wondered what the newsagent would say to him for this unusual lapse of memory.

He strolled round to her. She was knitting at the back of the counter and stood up as he came in and reached for his newspaper.

'No wonder you forgot it this morning and the whole country-side astray in the head. Never did I see such a display of foolery as this morning's. I don't mind the band coming out to welcome home a football team, but to welcome home a poteen-maker is flying in the face of Providence. The priest condemns the making of it and they turn around as if he was talking to milestones and enthrone a maker of the stuff.'

'I could do with a noggin of the stuff this very moment for I feel as tired as an old horse.'

'Do you know, Tom, but a month in gaol would put you on your feet. O'Hara's so well mended he could cut the hay himself by the looks of him.' She paused as Tom leaned forward on the counter. 'No word was said to you, I hope?'

'Not a word.'

She thought then of discussing his absence from his son's ordination but noticing the harassed look on his face she diverted her conversation to the lovely hay-weather that had set in. Tom sat down on a bench at the side of the counter and not wishing to hurry away he asked for some tobacco, and as she was weighing it a little boy came carrying a glass jam-jar of spricks and a yellow rod with a net like a candle-snuff attached to the end of it.

'You'd good luck today,' Tom said, holding the wet jar and looking at the three fish with their goggle eyes and tiny transparent fins. 'You like fishing?'

'I do, Mr Magee,' the boy said, and turning to the shop-keeper asked for a pennyworth of broken biscuits to feed his fish. He sniffed, wiped his nose on his sleeve, and picked a thread of moss from his crumpled fish-net.

'Come you round some evening and I'll bring you out to fish in my boat.'

'You've no boat, Mr Magee. I seen her at the bank and she's all bust up.'

Tom whirled out of the shop, crossed the railway track and came to the river bank where a tramp lay asleep in the sun. He reached the canal-cut where he always moored his boat and there tied to the stake was only the bow-half of his boat, her name *Rockcross* blotted out and 'Informer' printed with tar below it. The boat had been sawn in half and on the grass was a line of shavings fine as meal. He lifted a handful of them; they were no longer white, were turning brown and he knew then the work had been done in the darkness of the night. He threw the shavings into the still water and they lay like fallen seed.

'There are some things hard to bear,' he said to himself, looking away to the falls whose shoulders caught the sun. 'O'Hara wouldn't side with villainy of this sort. He would not. Indeed he wouldn't.' Taking out his knife he cut the mooring rope and with his toe pushed the half boat into the water. It spun round like a tub, turned over, and like a beehive lay on top of the water. 'You're free to join the other half wherever hell it is. You're like the two halves of my own life.'

He climbed back to the path, and nearing the tramp he saw him sitting up eating thick slices of bread, held with both hands like a mouth-organ.

'Wash it down with a bottle of stout,' Tom said, handing him a shilling on recognizing him as the tramp he had allowed once to sleep in the waiting-room. 'You weren't born in this part of the country.'

'No, sir, I wasn't.'

'They're bad people around here?'

'No, sir, they're not. I'm never hungry while I'm here. You're one of them yourself, sir, and you're a decent man.'

'I was one of them but I'm going away.'

'Wherever you go, sir, you'll have luck.'

'There are some things that are worse than hunger and you know nothing about them,' Tom added, and with his head down went back to the newsagent's where his paper lay folded on the counter. The sergeant was there, leaning sideways, one elbow on the counter.

'I hope the lad was telling lies?' the newsagent asked as Tom entered.

'There's some things in this life hard to stand,' he answered and gazed at the sunny street framed in the doorway.

'So your old enemy is released,' the sergeant said in a bantering voice. 'He got a few days clipped off for good behaviour.'

'He was never an enemy of mine, Sergeant,' Tom said, his eyes on the doorway and a dog lying down in the sun. 'O'Hara would condemn the things done to me, I'm sure of that.'

'Are they bothering you again?'

'I had a little bit of a boat for fishing. My son was to … ' The words caught in his throat and he stepped towards the doorway. His head was dizzy and he rested his hands on the jambs of the doorway. His head cleared and without turning round he said: 'I never informed on O'Hara and you know that well, Sergeant.'

He straightened himself and passed into the street, but the road came up to meet him, and as he fell flat his cheek struck the ground and his stationmaster's cap tumbled from his head.

They rushed out to him from the shop. 'Don't touch him. It's his heart,' the sergeant said, watching the ears turn purple, the hands turn wax. The newsagent knelt on the road and whispered an act of contrition in his ear. The sergeant felt the pulse at the wrist; there was one beat and then, perhaps, another. A few people had gathered from the other shops and they helped to turn him over gently. A patch of blood gritted with dust was on his cheek, the eyes were half open and the newsagent gently closed the warm lids.

'He had nothing to do with O'Hara's still,' the sergeant said. 'He'll never know now that you all know it.'

They carried him into the shop and laid him on a bench and the newsagent pulled down the blind on her window and left the door partly open. The sergeant, hurrying up to the barracks, slapped the dust from the knees of his trousers and immediately rang up the priest in Monabeg and the police in Rockcross.

It was near midnight when the first of his relations arrived by car: Christy, Richard, Joe and Aunt Brigid. They had been travelling all day: first to Christy's ordination, and then back to Rockcross in the evening where Mag, who couldn't go to the ceremony, awaited them and broke the news. They were tired, but the station house, which they expected to be in darkness, had lights in many of the windows, and inside neighbours had gathered and had already coffined the body. O'Hara and his sons were there, the newsagent and neighbour women, Jimmy the porter and Ben Brady. They all stood up as Christy entered, shook hands with him, and expressed their sorrow.

'Thank you, friends, for what you have done,' he said, going into the room where they had laid out his father. Richard, Joe and Aunt Brigid followed him, and on coming from the room again they sat awkwardly among the people, hearing the newsagent outline in detail the last moments of Tom Magee's life, and out of respect for the O'Haras, who were listening to her, she did not repeat Tom's or the sergeant's last reference to them. And while she told her story with sadness and without rancour other women were quietly preparing a meal at the table.

Some of the men stayed on till dawn and the women folk waited till the first train arrived bringing Alice, Mag with her baby and Julia with hers.

'If you want any help you have only to say the word,'

the newsagent spoke for all, 'for in Tom Magee the Monabeg people have lost the best stationmaster we ever had.'

Left alone his children consulted with one another where their father was to be buried, here or in Rockcross. They were too heartsick, too stunned, for disagreement, and Christy after long reflection said quietly: 'We'll bury him here among his own people. This, I feel, would be his own choice.' Alice stared at him, the warm tears stinging her eyes, for she suddenly remembered her father scraping frost from the headstone at the grave and saying that no other name would go on it. She broke down completely, locked the words deep in her heart, feeling that Christy knew her father and his wishes better than she did herself.

The following morning it was Christy who said the Requiem Mass in the church where his father had served Mass as an altar boy. The church was crowded and even Ben Brady, who was only seen there at Easter, the first of November and Christmas, had pushed his chair the two and a half miles and was now sitting on it near the door and was cupping a hand to his ear when the parish priest came to the altar rails and stood before the coffin.

'It is hard for me,' said the old priest, 'to speak to you this morning. We are all struck with sorrow. You all know what has happened and what was the cause of it. It is Saint James, the apostle who lashed out at the sins of the tongue, that should be addressing you this morning. But God knows I'm no Saint James either in words or in anything else. He tells us that man can tame every kind of beast and bird but has failed to tame the tongue, a restless pest that is full of poison. We use it to bless God, our Father; and we use it to curse our fellow men. Blessing and cursing rush from the same mouth. There isn't much reason in that, is there. The man whose remains lie before you this morning has been the victim of too much talk, talk of the wrong kind. He loved you and you insulted him. He was one of you and you wouldn't have him. He lowered himself by returning here as stationmaster when larger places were within his reach. And within a short time he made that little box of a place beyond a thing of real beauty. He loved this country where he was reared as a child, and he left his own family to come back to it. The Magees have been in this townland before I came to it, before my predecessors came to it, and the oldest of our parishioners can say that a kinder and more faithful people never lived. This man that we pray for this morning is the last of his generation. He loved you too much and that was his undoing. He had respect for what you thought of him and his family, and out of that respect and in order to clear his good name he did not go to his son's ordination. He has cleared his name. But the cost, my dear people, was very high.'

Sobs broke from some women in the congregation and men lowered their heads.

The old priest stopped and joined his hands: 'I'll say no more. This peace-loving man who loved his work and never forgot the place that reared him I commend to your prayers and the prayers of your children. May his soul and all the souls of the faithful departed rest in peace, Amen.'

The O'Haras helped to carry the coffin to the grave and it was they a few days later who had engraved upon the headstone below his name, the date of his death, and his age, the words: STATIONMASTER, FRIEND OF THE PEOPLE.

And to this day in that countryside a small cluster of houses lying among the fields is called Mageestown.